CHRYSALIS CHRONICLES

THE EYES OF THE DESERT SAND

CHRYSALIS CHRONICLES

THE EYES OF THE DESERT SAND

BY

EDWIN WOLFE

Fox Hunt Publishing Group

Aauvi House Publishing Group

Library of Congress Control Number: 2011937392

Wolfe, Edwin

Chrysalis Chronicles – The Eyes of the Desert Sand / by Edwin Wolfe

Summary: No recollection of anything prior to his eighth birthday, a young boy is
mysteriously drawn to a young girl, and together they are keys to solving the
story's biggest puzzle and unlock the door to the four portals.

ISBN 978-1-884573-25-5 (Hardcover)

[1. Fantasy – Fiction. 2. Children's – Fiction. 3. Manhattan – Fiction.
4. Worlds – Fiction. 5. Evolution – Fiction.] I. Title.

10 9 8 7 6 5 4 3 2 1

Printed in the United States of America

THIS BOOK IS DEDICATED TO MY WIFE, LORI. WITHOUT HER COAXING AND INSPIRATION IT WOULD NEVER HAVE MADE IT PAST A COUPLE OF WACKY DREAMS AND AN OLD HIGH SCHOOL POEM. SHE HAS BEEN MY WIFE, CONFIDANT, AND CHEERLEADER — SHE IS MY TALETADDLER.

THANK YOU SWEETHEART.

CONTENTS

The Eyes of the Desert Sand

On an old abandoned airstrip in a desert far away, lands an unknown flying saucer in the revealing light of day. There are no creatures there to see it in this tortured barren land, no plant life there to feel it just The Eyes of the Desert Sand. As the saucer doors swing open in a misty fog they see, a man from within the saucer from where could he possibly be? Emerging from the saucer he steps down to the ground, pausing for a moment as he stops to look around. He carries a flag of colors with shades from black to white, as he plants the flag into the ground it becomes a beautiful sight. Returning to his saucer as quickly as he came, the doors swing shut behind him like a picture in a frame. The saucer leaves undetected by the entire world at hand, unknown to all existence but The Eyes of the Desert Sand.

Eric Moeszinger, *A Moment in Eternity*

CHRYSALIS CHRONICLES

THE EYES OF THE DESERT SAND

INTO THE RABBIT HOLE

The Foxes were an ordinary middle-class family thrust into a lavish existence by the overwhelming success of George's first video game, *Lords and Dragons of the Dark Realm*. Living in a penthouse on the Upper East Side of Manhattan was a little like being a fish out of water for the Fox men. City life didn't exactly suit George or his son, Ethan; but George's wife, Betsy loved it — after all, living in the fashion capital of the world did have its perks.

A loving mother and devoted wife; as far as her two men were concerned, Betsy was the yardstick by which all women should be measured. She was a petite, brown haired, brown eyed woman with classic girl next door features. Her bubbly demeanor and girly-girl attitude made her the perfect uptown girl — Betsy was built for city life.

George Fox was a tall gentle giant of a man. His dark slicked-back hair gave him something of a nineteen fifties look. But what people noticed most was the mischievous smile permanently plastered on his face. He was either the world's happiest person or he'd just written the punch line to the world's funniest joke; very fitting given his sarcastic nature, he was always joking about something and was quite the prankster to boot.

Apart from his reddish brown hair, brown eyes, and freckled complexion, Ethan Fox was not your average thirteen year old boy — especially not by today's standards. While most kids his age liked nothing better than to be glued to the boob-tube playing video games, he'd much rather be outdoors; "the real adventure is out there in the real world" was his motto. He just didn't get how all his friends were so hooked on video games — an ironic point-of-view given his father's success.

The Fox men didn't take to city life like Betsy, their favorite times were those spent out in the boonies; the secret location of the Foxes country cabin as George would explain it. Out in the country, Ethan could explore, he loved playing at the creek the most; catching frogs and lizards was always challenging, they didn't exactly walk up and ask to be held. However, it was snakes that freaked Betsy out the most, "*Ethan — it could be poisonous!*" she'd shriek. But he knew which ones to avoid — he was an avid book reader and watched the Discovery channel regularly.

One particular snake incident, almost gave poor Betsy three heart attacks; the first, when he came running to the cabin holding a five-foot gopher snake dangling at his feet. It took a while, but he *finally* talked her into letting him keep it in the empty lizard cage George had built him, just until his dad got home to see his catch. That's when the second heart attack almost happened, when he *calmly* informed her that the snake had somehow escaped and was on the loose inside the cabin. Three days later, Betsy finally talked herself into believing that the snake had somehow made it outside. And that's when the third heart attack almost happened, when she got the *surprise* of her life while folding laundry. Needless to say, Ethan would never be allowed to bring a wild animal within a hundred feet of the cabin ever again.

City life wasn't all that bad though, Ethan loved spending time with his parents. Any chance to see his dad in public was sure to be good for a few laughs. It wasn't *if* George was going to do something to embarrass Betsy, it was *when* and *how*, it never failed.

Ethan would never forget what happened on one infamous night, a couple of weeks earlier, while dining at the family's favorite Chinese restaurant. It started with Betsy excusing herself to go to the ladies room. That's when George decided it was time to play a game, the "crack Ethan up game." He started with a few funny faces and squeaking noises, but Ethan hung tough holding in his laughter. George would have to think of something much better to win this one.

As George pondered his next move, the waiter arrived with three glasses of water, each with a slice of cucumber floating in it. A wide grin suddenly swept over his face as he plucked the cucumber slices from the glasses, grabbed his chopsticks, and ducked his head under the table. Moments later, a loud wallowing noise began to rumble out from beneath the table, and then in an even louder voice, "I am *Charlie — the Walrus man of Wiltor* — I am here to speak with Ethan Fox!" he growled as he emerged from beneath the table.

When Ethan saw George's face, he could hold it no longer. George had chopsticks protruding from his nostrils like tusks and cucumber slices in his eye sockets like large disc-shaped eyes, George was *Charlie the Walrus man of Wiltor.* Ethan was exploding with laughter. George had won this round, but his victory dance would have to wait, because at that moment Betsy was returning from the ladies room.

Walking up behind her husband, Betsy could not see his face. She was completely unaware of his silly masquerade. "What's all this laughing I hear, did I miss something?" she asked, looking at Ethan who was facing her. "Is your father being silly again?" she continued, turning to face her husband. Startled by his custom *Charlie* mask, she let out a loud high-pitched shriek. This got the attention of any patron not already watching the spectacle as the restaurant erupted with laughter. But not Betsy, she was so red from embarrassment, the natural color would not return to her face for several hours. Not surprisingly, it was a quiet drive home that night.

But that was two weeks ago, today the Foxes were on the first leg of a much needed family vacation. Given the strange events of the previous week, Ethan was more than happy to be anywhere but home. Lately, you could cut the tension with a knife at the Fox family home, but he had to take most of the blame. After all, how many parents would believe a boy who told them a sandman had sent two vampires and a hooded stranger to abduct him? Strange thing though, he was convinced that his parents *did* believe him. Sure they tried to sound convincing in their disdain for his story, but he knew they were hiding something. Was it somehow connected to his loss of memory five years earlier? Or was it the strange poem he had mysteriously written in his sleep? He wasn't sure, but one thing was certain, he would not rest until he got to the bottom of it.

Little did he know how soon his chance would come.

Getting away from it all was the order of the day for the Foxes. And today, that meant spending the day at the Santa Cruz Beach Boardwalk in sunny California.

"Nothing like junk food and roller coasters to cleanse the soul!" George announced as they arrived at the park.

Ethan loved rides of almost any kind, but roller coasters were his favorite; the faster the better as far as he was concerned. But for now, the rides would have to wait, Betsy had run off to browse the shops along the boardwalk; however, before she left, she made *darn sure* her husband was occupied. Anything to make sure he would not do something embarrassing. She could just imagine coming back to the scene of George teaching children along the boardwalk about the joys of a "whoopee cushion." So for now, George was in line at the snack bar getting lunch; it was all part of her plan, she knew he'd never turn down junk food.

"Waiting in line is a mere bump in the road to caloric bliss," George explained to Ethan as Betsy set out to shop.

CHAPTER ONE

Ethan was standing by a railing at the edge of the boardwalk, staring at the horizon while he waited for his dad. It was a beautiful bright sunny morning, but what he liked most was the fresh smell of the ocean breeze. One thing about the ocean, it always put Ethan into a trance; he could watch it for hours gazing into the distance taking it all in. Mesmerized by the waves, his mind would race as he imagined what sort of giant ocean creature might be about to burst up from the murky depths. Sometimes he'd even spot the odd whale or dolphin jumping, but so far today, nothing out of the ordinary.

His trance was interrupted by the pitter-patter of little feet running down the boardwalk behind him. He turned around to watch as a small boy ran by, holding a giant hotdog oozing with mustard and ketchup and globs of green pickle relish. The boy's run quickly slowed to a crawl as he quietly snuck up behind another unsuspecting boy wearing white puffy shorts with giant pockets.

Ethan watched in amazement as the boy sprang into action. It was like a rattlesnake strike; he quickly crammed the hotdog into the other boy's front pocket. Then as if not yet satisfied by his mischievous accomplishment, the boy wasted no time, he quickly began smooshing the pocketed hotdog around from outside the boy's shorts. Ethan could not help but to laugh, it reminded him of something George might have done as a child.

"Ethan — *Ethan Fox!*" shouted George from the snack bar counter, "get over here and give me a hand!"

As usual, George had bought more junk food than he could carry. When Ethan got to the snack bar, he could not believe his eyes: three jumbo hotdogs, four corn dogs, a large pepperoni pizza, two candied popcorn balls, three bags of cotton candy, and three bucket sized sodas. Even for George, this was quite the bounty; an octopus would have a hard time carrying all that food.

By the time they carried all that grub to a nearby picnic table, Betsy was back from her little shopping detour. If one thing was for certain, it was that she loved to shop as much as George loved the snack bar. So for the next hour, as they sat to eat lunch, she proudly showed her men each and every item from her shopping bags — four bags full of stuff she just had to have.

After their lunch break, it was time for what was sure to be Ethan and George's favorite part of the day, the rides. Ethan had done his homework, looking up the rides on the Internet and mapping out a plan of action. Their first stop would be the Haunted Castle, followed by the Pirate Ship, Double Shot, Wipeout, and last but not least, the world famous Giant Dipper.

Betsy didn't like most rides, but she'd tag along just the same. She just loved watching her two men having the time of their lives on the "terror rides" as she called them. In her world, there was only one ride, the Carousel. Ever since she was a little girl, she had always been fascinated by the Carousel. There was nothing like the calm serenity she felt when she rode it. But for now, her turn would have to wait until her two men were tired out, and that might be sooner rather than later at the rate they were going.

"That should challenge our full tummies," George said, pointing up at the Giant Dipper with a grin.

Ethan was amazed by its enormity as they approached the giant roller coaster; the closer they got, the bigger it got — it was huge!

"Ethan — you can skip this one if you want," said Betsy, mistaking the look of excitement on his face for that of terror.

"Are you kidding?" he quickly corrected his mother. "Can we ride it twice?"

"I should have known better — you two are going to throw up for sure," she smiled. "When you are done, it's my turn on the Carousel."

Two vomitless rides later, Ethan and George were ready for a break.

"That was *awesome!*" shouted Ethan to his mother as he stepped down off the platform. "When you get up there — to the top — you can see out over the ocean *for miles!*"

"Yeah, and that first dip is a real doosey, too — I almost lost my lunch the second time."

"Have you two finally had enough?"

"Why, yes indeed — after you, my dear — to the Carousel," George replied, motioning for Betsy to lead the way.

Along the way, Ethan began to get a strange feeling, like he was being watched. Stopping to turn around instinctively, he immediately noticed a young girl about his age. It was hard to tell, because he was looking into the sun, but she looked sad, like she was lost and disoriented.

The sun's rays glistening off her yellowish-blonde hair made it look as if a shimmering golden halo was resting upon her head. She was wearing a white sundress with yellow flowers almost perfectly matching the color of her hair. Although he could not see her well enough to know for sure, he got the distinct impression that she was looking back at him — as if she somehow recognized him.

Then, she began to smile.

Not exactly the ladies man, Ethan had never had a girlfriend; not even a passing fancy for any of the girls at school. But right now — for some reason — he was strangely drawn to this girl and that made him blush.

"Ethan! What are you looking at?" George called out from a distance. "Are you coming?"

"*Nothing* — be right there dad!" he shouted, turning for just a second to see where his parents were.

But when he turned back around to look at the girl, she was gone; and that gave him a strong sense of disappointment.

On the way to the Carousel, George insisted that they stop at the snack bar for ice cream, so he and Ethan would have something to munch on while Betsy had her fun.

"How in the world could you be hungry already, after the lunch you ate?" Betsy asked rhetorically.

The line for the Carousel was not nearly as long as the one for the snack bar that George had waited in earlier. Once on the Carousel platform, Betsy walked from horse to horse, studying each one as if they were somehow talking to her. She finally decided on a beautiful white horse with a blue saddle, its head cocked in a majestic pose. She had such a bright smile on her face, she looked like she was a little girl again as she climbed up onto the saddle.

Slowly the Carousel began to spin, picking up speed as Betsy disappeared from George and Ethan's view to the right. Looking to the left to watch for her to reappear, Ethan was surprised at what he saw. Riding on a white horse, exactly like the one Betsy had picked, it was her! The sun drenched girl he had seen moments before! And this time, he could see her beautiful bluish-green eyes clearly, and they were looking right at him!

She no longer looked sad; in fact, Ethan noticed she was wearing the same smile that appeared on Betsy's face the instant she stepped onto the Carousel platform. The ride continued for what seemed like an eternity. Each time the girl passed within his view, smiles were exchanged. The flirtation became so obvious that even George noticed in between licks from his second ice cream cone.

"Hey Tiger — looks like you've got a live one there," George elbowed Ethan with a gentle jab to the ribs, causing him to blush an even deeper shade of red.

The Carousel began to slow just as the girl disappeared again from Ethan's view. It stopped in the same position as it had started, with the girl on the other side.

"Hey there buddy — go talk to her. I'll wait here for your mother."

Ethan wasted no time jumping to his feet. His father's encouragement only seemed to enforce what he was already feeling — he should go talk to her. Not one to normally take chances, he wasn't sure *what* he was going to say or from *where* he was getting the nerve. He was about to walk up to a total stranger and start up a conversation. But something about this girl seemed to draw him in, and one thing was clear, he had to try.

His jog around the Carousel couldn't have taken more than a few seconds. Keeping his eyes on the platform as the riders stepped off; he scanned the crowd looking for her. Having had no luck finding the girl in the crowd, he scanned the Carousel. He finally spotted the white horse she had been riding just seconds before, but she was not there. Joy quickly turned to disappointment as he realized, the girl was gone.

Tired from a full afternoon of rides, games, and shopping, the Foxes were ready for some leisure time. And of course, cheeseburgers as George would insist. After their third trip to the snack bar — in less than four hours — the Foxes headed to the beach for a makeshift picnic. It was quite a long hike along the beach before Betsy finally found a flat patch of sand, devoid of any driftwood or annoying sea kelp.

"Perfect!" she announced, pulling a giant yellow beach blanket from one of her shopping bags.

As she finished spreading the blanket out over the sand, George wasted no time plopping down onto it with his bag full of cheeseburgers.

"Cheeseburgers anyone?" George muttered, reaching into his bag of goodies. "I got enough for everybody."

"I'm sure you did," whispered Betsy as she sat down on the blanket next to her husband.

Still full from lunch, Betsy and Ethan decided to share a cheeseburger leaving the remaining four for George. The Foxes spent the next thirty minutes, on their private little stretch of beach, nibbling away on cheeseburgers and listening to the sound of the surf. So far, they had successfully accomplished their order of the day; it was a great family vacation.

But for Ethan, it was about to get a whole lot better.

"What's next?" George asked, washing down the last bite of his fourth cheeseburger with a gulp of soda.

"How about we play in the water and get our feet wet . . . like we used to . . . ." suggested Betsy with a girlish grin.

"No way!" Ethan warned. "I'm not going in there! Don't you remember *Jaws*? According to the Discovery channel there are great whites all over the place in these waters. . . . I'll just hang out here and rest."

George already had both shoes and one sock off.

"Suit yourself, but you're gonna miss out on all the fun . . . I bet you didn't know your mother was a mermaid."

George struggled to lift his huge frame up from the blanket. Minutes later, he and Betsy were skipping off towards the waves — hand in hand — like mischievous childhood sweethearts.

"There they go — the *Beauty and the Beast*!"

George's sarcasm was really starting to rub off on Ethan.

Ethan watched as his parents splashed around in the surf like playful sea otters. But his attention was soon interrupted by thoughts of the mysterious girl on the Carousel. "Who was she? What was her name — ?"

"Hi, my name is Haley —" a soft feminine voice spoke up from behind him, "I saw you watching me on the Carousel."

Startled, Ethan jumped to his feet flopping around in the process. When he finally regained his balance, he was pleasantly surprised by who he saw. It was her! The girl from the Carousel! And her name was Haley!

"I-I-I wasn't watching you — you — you were watching me — weren't you?"

"Yes, I guess I was."

"Why?"

Ethan blushed at the realization that he wasn't just imagining their attraction.

"I don't know . . . I don't remember much before I saw you," she began to sob. "I was just suddenly here. I don't remember where I came from . . . or how I got here. I-I was just here. . . ."

"Don't worry, everything is going to be okay, you'll see."

"At first I was terrified in the middle of that crowd of strangers, but then I saw you and somehow my fear just went away. I feel like we've met somewhere before, but I don't know where. . . . I don't even know your name . . ."

"My name is Ethan."

"Are those funny people your parents?" she asked, pointing at George and Betsy as they continued to splash around in the waves.

"Yeah — but sometimes I feel like I'm the parent."

"I see what you mean."

They both broke out in laughter. Her laugh was infectious, like a baby giggling and it made Ethan laugh even harder. They continued talking for several minutes exchanging more laughs than he could ever remember having.

"Strange — I don't know where I came from or how I even got here, but somehow being with you makes me feel safe — like everything is going to be all right."

Haley reached down to hold Ethan's hand. Suddenly, he felt like a butterfly was about to fly up from his stomach and out of his mouth. He nervously swiped his feet through the sand as he stood talking with her.

He was drawing something with his foot.

"What does that symbol mean?"

"Nothing, really — just some dumb symbol I made up — it's like a secret ID. I put it in the corner of all my school work."

That's when Ethan noticed the unique ring on Haley's finger. It was unlike any ring he had ever seen. Made from polished black metal of some sort, the ring was shaped like an infinity sign — ∞ — bent so that her finger could pass through both loops.

"*Wow* — that's some infinity ring you've got there! I'm sure they don't just sell those anywhere. Maybe we can use it to help track down where you came from?"

"That's so sweet that you want to help me, but I don't want to think about any of that right now —"

Haley reached down to grab hold of Ethan's other hand as she faced him.

"— come on, let's go for a walk on the beach and find some seashells," she finished.

Haley was gently tugging at Ethan's arms as they started down the beach holding hands. He felt as if he was walking on clouds. He did not want this day to end. It was all happening so fast. But the strange connection they felt was not the result of some chance encounter — there was something much more powerful behind it.

The stretch of beach they were on had a slight bend to it and soon they were out of sight from George and Betsy. Ethan stopped abruptly.

"We shouldn't go much farther — I forgot to tell my parents where I was going."

"We have walked pretty far," she agreed. "I guess we should start heading back —"

"Oh look — a sand dollar!" he interrupted excitedly, running over to pick up the seashell he had just spotted.

Ethan handed the seashell over to Haley who was now blushing a little herself.

"Here — they're supposed to bring you luck," he smiled.

"It's beautiful!" she gushed.

Haley dusted the sand off the small disc shaped shell, exposing the unique flower like pattern on the sand dollar.

Suddenly, Ethan had that strange feeling again, like they were being watched. Then, out of the corner of his eye, he saw a bright blue flash streak by. Turning away from Haley, looking inland to see what it was, he could not believe what he was looking at. Standing at the edge of the beach, was a three-foot tall blue bunny rabbit with yellow polka dots. It looked like somebody's crazy idea of an Easter bunny with pastel pink shorts and red suspenders. Wiping his eyes in disbelief, he did a double take, but this time the bunny was waving at them.

Haley tapped Ethan on the back to get his attention.

"What's wrong?" she asked.

"Don't you see that — ?"

Ethan pointed at the strange creature.

"See what?" she asked, looking around struggling to see what he was pointing at. "I don't see anything."

"You don't see a blue bunny rabbit waving at us?"

He blurted out his question before he could realize how crazy it sounded.

"No," Haley laughed, turning back towards him.

"*I'm serious*! It's right there in plain sight!" he scolded, stopping her in mid-laugh.

"Well — just because I don't see it, doesn't mean it's not there."

Haley's response put Ethan at ease.

"I'm going to take a closer look," he said as he began walking towards the creature.

"Wait for me! I've got to see this!"

Haley followed along.

As they neared the creature, Ethan not only could see it better, but he could hear it as well. Standing in front of them — still waving — it was laughing like a mischievous child.

"Where is it? Is it still there?"

"It's right in front of us!" he insisted.

Then — the bunny stopped waving.

"Happy day Ethan Fox!" the bunny spoke. "Are we having fun yet?"

It was giggling as if it had just told a joke.

"Who are you?" Ethan asked.

"I'm Jasper and it's time for me to go — The Residence awaits!" he said, spinning around and scurrying towards a large cluster of rocks.

Ethan watched in disbelief. Then —

The creature stopped, turned back towards them and said, "Zo-Zo!" before waving a final goodbye and disappearing behind the rocks.

"*What did it say?*" Haley demanded.

"Its name is Jasper! And it said, 'Zo-Zo'!" Ethan shouted, following in hot pursuit.

"Wait for me!" Haley cried, following Ethan as he approached the cluster of rocks.

"Shhhhhhh — he went behind these rocks," whispered Ethan.

As they rounded the cluster of rocks, quietly following Jasper's trail, they were both surprised by what they saw.

"Do you see that — ?" Ethan asked.

"Yes — but what is it?"

"I don't know . . . but I'm going to find out," Ethan replied bravely.

Ethan and Haley were standing at the top of a perfectly carved staircase descending into the dark wet sand of the beach. It looked like someone had built a sandcastle staircase into the beach.

"I wonder where it leads . . ." Haley pondered as she struggled to look down the dark corridor tunneling down into the beach.

"I don't know, but Jasper must — I'm going to go check it out, you wait here!" he ordered as he cautiously approached the mysterious staircase.

"Be careful!" she cautioned.

As Ethan slowly navigated down the first couple of stairs, it got darker with each step. Then in an instant, just before losing consciousness, his mind flashed with visions of tiny purple and green speckles of light — like sparks from a Fourth of July fireworks celebration. And then, everything suddenly went black.

NOWHERE, ANYWHERE, AND EVERYWHERE

Ethan's head was still fuzzy when he finally came to. He was sure he had heard muffled voices and rustling in the room as he was lying on the ground, but now it was completely silent. As he stood up, he could see he was now in a large room. It looked like the Study of an old rustic mansion with antique couches, chairs, and tables that decorated the interior — the basic layout for a Study of its size.

At one end of the room was a huge fireplace, so big Ethan could walk into it standing upright. To the right of the fireplace was a pedestal upon which a large thick golden book sat encased in a glass enclosure. To the left, stood an odd looking candelabrum with four white candles attached to the inside of a standing circle. Each candle was pointing inwards towards the center of the circle where a spherical replica of Earth hovered as if held up by invisible strings.

Ethan felt a strange sense of déjà vu as he stared at the candles, each burning a flame of a different color: red, green, blue, and yellow. Yet unlike a normal candle, these seemed to defy the laws of physics. Each flame burned towards the center of the circle as if somehow holding the tiny Earth replica in place.

Turning around to explore his new surroundings, he slowly began to make his way towards the other side of the room. He was astonished by the tall floor to ceiling bookcases going all the way down both sides of the room; there were thousands of books on the shelves. On the far side of the room, there were two doors, one to each side of a tall full length painting that hung at the center of the wall. The painting was of a beautiful angelic woman wearing a white gown bathed in ice crystals that looked like diamonds. She was hovering in mid-air against the backdrop of a frosty ice wonderland.

"Wow — she's *beautiful*," a voice spoke up, startling Ethan.

"Haley! How did you get here?"

"Where — are — we?" she asked, looking around the room in amazement.

"I don't know . . . but how did you end up here, too?"

The concern in Ethan's voice was evident.

"Well — I was watching you go down those stairs in the beach and then you disappeared. So I went in for a closer look and somebody pushed me in from behind. Then everything just went black."

"Everything just went black," a high pitched voice mocked from somewhere in the room.

"Wow — she's *beautiful*," a different voice shouted from another direction.

"Who said that?" Ethan quickly scanned the room looking for the source of the voices.

"Who said that?" yelled a third voice from yet a different direction.

"This isn't funny!" Haley cried, spinning around on her feet.

"*You do the hokey-pokey and you turn yourself around, that's what it's all about,*" the voices sang out in unison.

"Stop it!" Haley pleaded. "PLEASE, STOP IT!"

"It's okay," Ethan reassured, putting his arms around her to comfort her. "They don't sound dangerous to me — more like a band of *smart asses!*"

"*Smart asses!*" one of the voices cried out, causing the others to giggle loudly.

"I'm an idiotic dork," Ethan bated the menacing voices.

"I'm an idiotic dork," one of the voices mimicked, as the other two erupted in laughter.

"Newton is an idiotic dork — Newton is an idiotic dork," two of the voices chanted, teasing the third.

"I AM NOT!" an angry voice shouted back.

A book suddenly flew off one of the bookcases, startling Ethan and Haley.

"They sound like young children," Ethan whispered to Haley.

"Children?" one of the voices lectured in a suddenly serious tone. "Did you say *children*? My dear human child, your age is but a mere fleck of existence compared to the likes of us."

"That sounded like a grumpy old man," Haley winked.

She had caught on to Ethan's game.

"Linus is a grumpy old man — Linus is a grumpy old man," two of the voices sang out, mocking the third.

"So we know about Newton and Linus, but we don't yet know the name of the third dummy," Ethan said, winking back at Haley.

"Albert is a dummy — Albert is a dummy," Newton and Linus teased.

"Albert, Linus, and Newton — they're all scientists," Ethan blurted out, remembering those names from a Discovery channel show he had watched.

Feeling confident, Ethan spoke in a stern voice, "We're tired of these games, show yourselves now!"

But the room was silent.

"Albert! Come here this *minute*!" Haley commanded loudly.

Suddenly out of nowhere a small red ball appeared on the table in front of them, it was about the size of an apple.

"Where did that come from?" Ethan looked puzzled.

"Newton, come here *now*!" Haley demanded.

A blue ball appeared on the table next to the red one.

"Linus — it's your turn!" Ethan shouted, catching on to Haley's ploy.

But nothing happened.

"Linus — did you hear Ethan? Come here this *instant*!"

A green ball appeared next to the other two.

"Now what — ?" she asked as they stood staring at the three balls on the table.

"I don't know . . ."

The room fell into a still silence.

"So — were we frightened by three colored talking balls?" she asked. "Hey dummies! Where did you all go?"

Haley's taunting didn't seem to work as the room remained silent.

"I know —" Ethan spoke up, "have I shown you the cool juggling tricks my dad taught me?"

A huge grin appeared on Ethan's face as he picked up the three colored balls and began juggling. He could barely hear the three muffled little voices. They were laughing and screaming at the same time — like kids on a roller coaster. The voices grew louder as the balls began to grow; they were beginning to unravel.

Shocked by their sudden metamorphosis, Ethan quickly threw the balls up into the air jumping back in surprise. A loud popping noise echoed through the room, followed by colored flashes of light that blinded them at first. But neither Ethan nor Haley could imagine what would land on the table in front of them.

The three colored balls had been transformed, replaced by three small creatures, each the color of their respective ball. The creatures were no more than two feet tall, with tiny slits for noses, and large yellow catlike eyes. They had small devilish horns, punctuated by rows of spikes that flowed down to the end of their forked tails.

Ethan was amazed as he studied the creatures.

They had long arms with folds of skin underneath that attached to their bodies like flying squirrels; the smooth skin on their bellies was surrounded by colorful gold speckled feathers that covered the rest of their bodies.

"I'm Linus," the green one said, holding his hand out politely.

"I'm Newton," the blue one followed, extending his hand.

"So I guess you are Albert," Ethan said, shaking each of their tiny hands. "My name is Ethan and this is Haley."

Ethan nodded towards Haley.

"*Ethan Fox* — are you Ethan Fox?" Linus sounded astonished.

"How did you know my name?"

"Well — it's not every day a human shows up here," Newton chimed in, "especially one named Ethan Fox. Ethan Fox is quite the celebrity around here. . . ."

"Celebrity? How could I be a celebrity? I don't even know where here . . . is."

"Yeah — where are we?" Haley asked.

"Well, you are nowhere really," Linus answered.

"And anywhere," Newton replied.

"And everywhere," Albert added.

"That makes no sense at all," Ethan complained.

"It makes perfect sense," Linus corrected. "Yet more than a human child can understand."

"So you've met RGB," a strong deep voice spoke up from across the room.

Startled, Ethan and Haley both spun around to see where the new voice was coming from.

A tall man was entering the room through the door on the left. He wore a long half-black half-white hooded robe split down the middle. On the black side was an emblem that vaguely resembled the candelabra near the fireplace. Four colored circles: red, green, blue, and yellow, surrounded a fifth, planet Earth. All five were loosely encircled by a web-like encasing as if enclosed in a Chrysalis.

Ethan got a creepy uneasy feeling as the stranger entered the room; it felt as if an invisible hand was lightly stroking the back of his neck.

The hooded stranger looked towards the floor as he made his way across the room. Raising his head as he neared, the stranger slowly lowered his hood revealing his face. And it nearly sent Ethan into *shock*! He knew this face! It was that face! It was him, the man who had tried to kidnap him that night — nearly a week ago!

"Ethan!" Haley yelled, rushing over to catch him as he fell back against the couch. "What's wrong?"

"I-I feel a little faint . . ."

Ethan's mind was racing back to the events that began two weeks earlier.

ENTER SANDMAN

It was a quiet night in the Fox household. They had just gotten home from a disastrous night at a downtown Chinese restaurant. And Betsy was not happy with her husband at all.

"I'm going to bed," Betsy announced before walking upstairs to her bedroom.

"It's okay . . . she'll be fine tomorrow." George winked. "Hey, how'd you like to check out my new game idea?"

"Sure dad," Ethan fibbed, knowing his real response would break George's heart.

"So here's the idea —"

George pulled an oversized sketch book from his briefcase.

"— if a tree falls in the forest and there is nobody there to hear it, is there a sound? Of course there is!" George finished, quickly answering his own question before Ethan even had a chance to.

"I'm thinking of calling it, The Ears on the Forest Trees!" George roared.

"The Ears on the Forest Trees —" Ethan repeated.

The Ears on the Forest Trees sounded strangely familiar to Ethan as his mind began to race.

"So how are you going to explain a bunch of funny looking trees with ears?" Ethan laughed.

He was looking at the drawings in George's sketch book.

"Well —" George paused for a moment, "I was hoping you would help me out with that."

"I don't know dad, this one is way out there . . . maybe I don't have your imagination. . . ." Ethan smirked.

"Oh, really — well I think you'll do just fine."

Later that night, as Ethan was lying in bed, his mind began to race again. It was as if there was something he desperately needed to remember; but what was it? It felt like a distant memory was hidden deep in his mind trying desperately to get out. He could not concentrate on anything else, but he could not remember either. He was finally able to fall asleep, only to wake up the next morning with strange visions flashing in his head. It was as if he'd had a dream he could only vaguely remember.

Over the next several nights, the same pattern persisted. Ethan would lay in bed unable to sleep; concentrating on something he could not quite remember. Each night it got harder and harder to fall asleep and it was taking its toll on him. Yet each morning, when he woke up, he had the distinct feeling that he was getting closer. Finally, on the fifth night, he was so tired he felt as if nothing could keep him awake. The exhaustion from getting almost no sleep the previous four nights had made him very irritable — and everybody in the Fox household felt it.

"I've got to get some sleep tonight," Ethan said as he laid there counting sheep in his head.

But counting sheep never worked for him and tonight was no different.

"Why can't I remember?" he wondered, picking up the notepad and pencil he had left on his nightstand, just in case.

Suddenly — all at once — he got the strange feeling that someone or something was in his room with him. And then, he was out like a light.

The next morning, he woke up with the notepad and pencil still in his hands. As he glanced down at the paper, he was surprised by what he saw. There was writing on the notepad. And he had definitely written it, as it bared his secret symbol, the one he always drew on the corner of a page.

"I don't remember writing anything," he whispered to the empty room as he began reading the words:

The Eyes of the Desert Sand

On an old abandoned airstrip in a desert far away, lands an unknown flying saucer in the revealing light of day.

There are no creatures there to see it in this tortured barren land, no plant life there to feel it just The Eyes of the Desert Sand.

As the saucer doors swing open in a misty fog they see, a man from within the saucer from where could he possibly be?

Emerging from the saucer he steps down to the ground, pausing for a moment as he stops to look around.

He carries a flag of colors with shades from black to white, as he plants the flag into the ground it becomes a beautiful sight.

Returning to his saucer as quickly as he came, the doors swing shut behind him like a picture in a frame.

The saucer leaves undetected by the entire world at hand, unknown to all existence but The Eyes of the Desert Sand.

"Is this what I've been trying to remember?" Ethan wondered in disbelief. "How could I have written a poem I don't know and not remember doing it? I know — I'll show it to George! He always comes up with this kind of stuff."

Feeling confident, he was sure his dad would have something to say about it.

* * *

Later that afternoon, Ethan headed downstairs to George's office study with notebook in hand. He knew George would be there hard at work on some crazy idea. But not as crazy as what he was about to show him.

"Come in!" George hollered from within his study.

"Hey dad —" he said, entering just in time to see George sink a trash can basket with a wadded up piece of paper.

"Three pointer!" George proclaimed, grinning. "What can I do for you kiddo?"

Ethan took the seat across the desk from his dad.

"Well — you know how you've been asking me to help come up with weird stuff for your new video game?"

"Yeah, did you come up with something?" George chuckled.

"Kind of, but it's creepy how I did it," Ethan answered, handing the notepad to George.

As George sat reading, the smile slowly drained from his face. It was not the response Ethan was expecting.

"Where did you get this?" George asked in a concerned tone.

"I don't know . . . I think I wrote it in my sleep."

"Oh — okay — well um — this is good — but not exactly what I was looking for," George said in a dismissive tone.

Ethan left the room disappointed, but he was sure of one thing, his dad was hiding something.

Later that night, as Ethan was lying on the couch watching television, he could hear his parents upstairs arguing. But his parents never argued. Curiosity quickly got the best of him as he quietly began creeping up the stairs to eavesdrop. He finally got close enough to hear the end of their muffled conversation.

"I *knew* you would jog something in his memory!" Betsy yelled quietly, "always asking him to help with your fantasyland stories!"

"You're probably right," George agreed, "I just wanted him to live a normal childhood."

It turned silent and Ethan quickly retreated down the stairs.

Needless to say, the next few days were quiet around the Fox household. Ethan's parents were both on edge, and he knew it had something to do with his past.

"What are they keeping from me — ?" he wondered.

Ethan had no memory of anything before his eighth birthday. It was something that had always bothered him, but no matter how hard he tried, he couldn't remember anything. His parents had always told him it was due to a trauma he suffered in a car crash. Now, he was beginning to have his doubts: first the crazy poem, followed by George's strange reaction, and then the argument he had overheard — it just didn't add up.

"They are definitely keeping something from me and I have to get to the bottom of it!" he decided.

"Ethan!" Betsy yelled from upstairs, "are you ready?"

"Yeah mom — ready and waiting!"

"Tell your father it's almost time to go — he still needs to get ready."

"Sure mom —"

Ethan headed to his father's study. When he got there, he noticed that the door was slightly ajar. Slowing to a tiptoe, he quietly crept up on the door and peeked through the crack.

He watched as George climbed his bookshelf ladder. He was holding something in his left hand but it was obstructed from Ethan's view. When he reached the top, George pulled three books from a shelf revealing a small trapdoor behind the bookcase. As he slid open the trapdoor, Ethan could now see what his dad was holding, a withered old brown book with shiny golden writing on the cover. He continued watching as George put the book away in the cubby hole and closed the trapdoor. Then, he replaced the books hiding his secret stash and climbed down from the ladder.

Ethan quietly tiptoed back down the hallway before announcing his presence.

"Hey dad!" Ethan said loudly, re-approaching the study door, "mom wants you upstairs — time to get ready!"

Tonight's Fox family event was the third annual *Gothic Comic Book Convention* or *GothCon* as the gothies had proudly dubbed it. Unlike other conventions of the genre, *GothCon* was the only one held at night. It was much creepier than the average run of the mill comic book event.

George's *Dark Realm* video game series had been such a success that it spun off a comic book series; and those, too, had become hugely successful. As a result, George always felt obligated to make a special appearance for his loyal fans. But this year was different, George had been selected as the keynote speaker, and that meant this year it would be a family event!

"I'm ready!" George announced, slowly making his way down the staircase.

Upon seeing George's costume, Ethan's eyes met Betsy's as she let out a quiet giggle.

"You didn't tell us it was a costume party," Betsy joked as she eyed the spectacle that was George's attire.

"Don't worry — you two are fine — you'll be sitting on the sidelines, but I'm the keynote speaker. I've got a roll to play!" George explained as he reached the bottom of the staircase.

George's getup was something only a diehard gothie would appreciate. A character from the *Dark Realm* series: *Rubio the Evil Minion of Krator.*

Rubio's face was a tattered mass of flesh, pieced together like a jigsaw puzzle over his exposed skull. He had no nose, only a hole where one should be. Beneath his chin a large spider emerged from a hole in his neck. His shredded black jacket oozed with blood dripping down to where rusty chains wrapped around his waist; holsters for his blood soaked hatchets. A spike was driven through his right hand while his left held a hook; an impaled rat squirmed at the end. His pants were tattered, eaten away by black insects clinging to them like creepy crawlers.

"Wow! You went all out!" Ethan complimented George's costume as they were leaving.

"Fitting attire for a creep fest," Betsy added as they emerged from their building into the light of a full moon.

"Tonight — we ride in style," George boasted, taking Betsy's hand as the limo pulled to the curb.

The ride to the venue was uneventful as Ethan sat in silence wondering, "What are they hiding? Has it got something to do with that old book my dad is hiding behind his bookcase?"

One way or another, he was going to find out.

The limo pulled up in front of a dreary hotel. It was definitely off the beaten path from the normal Manhattan social scene. The dimly lit street made it easier to see the red carpet leading to the hotel entrance. It was lined with black lights making the red look black under the darkness of night. As they exited the limo, a huge applause erupted from the crowd now gathering outside the hotel.

"Look! He came as *Rubio*!" someone shouted as the crowd began cheering.

"This place sure fits the bill," Ethan whispered, looking at the gothic building.

He looked up to see two stone gargoyles perched at each corner of the hotel's rooftop. Glancing back and forth — from one to the other — he thought his eyes were playing tricks on him. He could have sworn he saw a piercing red glow coming from their eyes as he looked from one to the other. He had the eerie feeling that whichever one he was not looking at was looking at him.

"Ridiculous," he thought to himself, "this place must be creeping me out."

Ethan continued to reassure himself as he walked the black carpet with his parents. Once inside the hotel, things got even darker and creepier. The floor exhibits consisted of all sorts of sick and twisted themes.

"This makes *Rubio* look like a girl scout," Ethan joked to his dad as they looked around the exhibit room.

"I don't get it — ?" Betsy whispered to Ethan. "This is so creepy. How can they all be having so much fun?"

"There are some sick puppies here — that's for sure," Ethan quietly whispered back. "Like a roomful of demented children playing with dead things."

The place was definitely having an effect on Ethan. Even he was thinking creepy things. As he scanned the crowd his gaze stopped at a particularly disturbing exhibit, a large burning sign read:

GATES OF HELL: THE TALES OF ICHARUS GATES

But it wasn't *Icharus Gates* that caught his eye. It was the strange creature standing off to the side. A sandman, continuously reforming as sand spilled to the floor from its body only to merge back into the pile at its feet. It had vaguely defined facial features and two small pits where eyes should be.

"Quite a sandman costume — huh!" George hollered from several feet away.

"It looks so *real!*" Ethan hollered, walking back towards his parents.

Ethan glanced back, just in time to see two tall dark figures arrive. Two very *real* looking vampires were now talking with the sandman. He continued watching as the sandman looked over and pointed in his direction. Suddenly, his heart began to race as he realized, the sandman was not pointing towards him! The sandman was pointing at him! And the vampires looked interested!

"Time to head backstage so I can prepare for my speech," George announced just in the nick of time.

"Ah — ah — all right — I'm with you," Ethan muttered as if the words were frozen in his throat.

Ethan decided on the way backstage, he was officially freaked out.

"Get a grip," he told himself in his head. "You're letting your imagination get the best of you. It's all fake . . ." he continued his pep talk.

After an hour backstage, Ethan had finally talked himself down from freak-out mode. It was time for the moment they had all been waiting for, George's keynote address.

"LADIES AND GENTLEMEN!" a voice boomed over the intercom, "IT IS WITH GREAT PLEASURE THAT I INTRODUCE TO YOU! THE CREATOR OF THE DARK REALM! THE ONE! THE ONLY — GEORGE FOX!"

Applause erupted from every corner of the convention.

"Break a leg," Betsy smiled, standing up on her tippy toes to give George a kiss.

"Knock 'em dead dad!" Ethan shouted as George took the stage in his ghoulish costume.

Like his mother, Ethan didn't get all the hoopla or fanfare. But as he watched his dad take the podium, he was sure of one thing, he was proud of his dad.

About a half hour into George's speech, Ethan began to feel natures call, he had to pee.

"Mom — I've gotta go to the bathroom — I'll be right back," he said before trotting down a backstage corridor.

He remembered seeing a restroom sign down one of the backstage hallways. Then halfway down the long corridor, he noticed how quiet it had gotten. A sudden chill crept through his body as he began to realize, this was a bad idea.

He turned around and before he knew it, two dark figures descended upon him. The two vampires quickly wrestled him to the ground and put a bag over his head. Though he could see nothing, he felt a strange gliding sensation, as if he were floating down the hallway. Grabbing an arm of one of his attackers, he tried to pry himself free, but it was useless; he was helpless against their strength. He could feel the cold sandpaper texture of their skin against his own. Then, it dawned on him! These vampires were *real*! And they were taking him somewhere!

"Stay calm —" a soothing voice whispered inside his head.

"Now I'm hearing things," he thought as a strange calmness overcame the terror he was feeling just seconds ago.

Suddenly, he felt a thunderous jolt as he slipped from his kidnappers grasp, thudding to the ground. Quickly removing the bag from his head, he looked down the corridor in front of him, it was empty. Spinning around on his hands and knees, he was surprised to see not two but three tall figures standing before him. As the two vampires made a hasty exit through a door at the end of the hall, the third figure was standing over him, looking down at him as if ready to attack.

Ethan looked up at his attacker, he could see that this was not a vampire, this was a man. He wore a long half-black half-white robe. He had a bluish white complexion and long black stringy hair. His long pointy nose stretched from his narrow brows to below his thin upper lip. Ethan began to tremble as he stared into the stranger's devilish eyes, each one a different color; his left eye was deep green, but his right one was bluish grey with a crescent moon-shaped pupil.

"What do you want with me?" Ethan asked, trembling in silence as he and the stranger exchanged stares.

"Everything will be all right, Ethan Fox," the soothing voice spoke up from within his head.

Ethan did not know where the voice was coming from but it made him stop trembling.

"Ethan — where are you? Are you all right?" Betsy's voice called out from the end of the corridor behind him.

He turned towards his mother and yelled at the top of his lungs, "I'M RIGHT HERE MOM — BUT I'M NOT ALL RIGHT — GET HELP!"

But when he turned back to face his attacker, there was nobody there. He was all alone near the end of the corridor standing in front of a sign that read:

Men's Restroom

OUT THROUGH THE IN-DOOR

"Ethan! Ethan — wake up!" Haley's voice cried out as everything slowly came into focus. "Are you okay? You fainted!"

"I-I thought I saw him," Ethan mumbled, struggling to pick himself up off the floor.

"Saw *who*?" Haley asked, looking across the room at the stranger who was now obstructed from Ethan's view.

"The man who tried to kidnap me. . . ."

"*Kidnap you*?" Haley cried, staring daggers at the robed stranger.

"I can assure you, Ethan Fox — it is not I who has been trying to abduct you," the stranger spoke in a low gravelly voice. "We've been keeping an eye on you. Very unfortunate mistakes led to a lapse in your safety. But you can rest assured; we are not here to harm you —"

"I saw *you* with the two others!" Ethan interrupted, turning to face the stranger.

"Did you get a good look at your attacker?" the stranger asked, approaching Ethan.

"*Yes* — I saw you as plain as day!"

"Then I would imagine you might see some differences," the stranger said, bending down to give him a closer look.

"Your eyes — your eyes are blue — his were different and creepy."

"It appears my dear brother has joined them," the stranger said, talking to himself. "I had no evidence before . . . but this offers proof . . . mother will have to believe me now —"

"*Who are you?*" Haley interrupted in a demanding tone. "And *what* would your brother want with Ethan? And *where* are we? And *what* are these little creatures? And *why* are we here — ?"

"All of your questions will be answered in due time," the stranger replied, walking towards the enormous fireplace. "First — let's get comfortable — please, take a seat while I refresh the fire."

Ethan and Haley hesitated before sitting down on a large couch in front of the fireplace.

They watched as the stranger reached into a bowl full of small red marbles with orange and yellow splotches. Plucking one from the bowl, he threw it down hard at the base of the fireplace.

The marble erupted into a small inferno, burning for a few seconds before the flames began to change shape; the flames slowly rose up from the floor morphing into the form of a small fire creature.

Ethan and Haley watched in stunned silence as the foot tall fire creature walked over to a neatly stacked pile of logs.

Carefully jumping onto the pile, the creature knelt down and began to listen to the logs as if somehow communicating with them. A few minutes went by before the creature unexpectedly jumped to its feet with a log in its arms. Making its way back to the fireplace, the creature stood hugging its log — like a mother cuddling her child.

Seconds later, a faint whistle could be heard coming from the fire creature. The whistle grew louder and louder until suddenly the creature leaped into the fireplace with the log in its arms. The whistling stopped with a loud popping noise followed by a red puff of smoke. The fire creature and log had landed perfectly into place on the newly burning fire. Then — as if getting into bed — the creature eased itself down onto the log and slowly melted away into the burning fire.

"What was that?" Ethan and Haley asked in unison.

"That was a firelyte — much simpler than matches, don't you think?" the stranger replied. "When the log is finished burning it will transform into a black firelyte diamond."

As the stranger explained, Ethan noticed a small pile of shiny black diamonds beneath the burning log.

"I've never understood the human fascination with a natural fire . . . the aftermath is so messy —"

"Humans —" Haley interrupted, "you said, 'humans'?"

"I know . . . you must be brimming with questions, but first we'll start with the introductions. I know who Ethan Fox is, but who might you be?"

"My name is Haley, Haley Hunt — I think. . . . I don't remember much before I met Ethan, but how do you know Ethan?"

"Even your answers are veiled in questions," the stranger smirked. "I am Daavic Ravenwood — my brother, Damien is the one who tried to abduct Ethan. I know this may sound farfetched — but please bear with me. I think you would both agree based on what you've already seen, there are many things not understood in the human world —"

"There —" Haley interrupted, "you said it again, the 'human' world. Are you an *alien* or something?"

"Roughly, one human week ago —" Daavic continued, ignoring Haley's question, "a sandman answered the call of a very tired human child. The sandman went about his business sprinkling Z's on the child to help him sleep. But instead of falling asleep, the child proceeded to write the words to an ancient poem not known to the human world —"

"— The Eyes of the Desert Sand!" Ethan interrupted, finishing Daavic's sentence.

"Precisely," Daavic continued. "Normally a sandman is a quiet nomadic creature, putting people to sleep is usually an uneventful task. However, when something out of the ordinary happens — as it did on this occasion — they are very excitable. After witnessing Ethan Fox write the words to the ancient poem, the sandman went mad. He worked himself into a gossiping frenzy. He nearly traveled the world, telling anyone who would listen, the story of the human child — the child who knew something that he should not. Word spread quickly as speculation ran rampant. Would this child be the one to finally bring meaning to one of the universe's greatest mysteries — ?"

"Bring meaning to it?" Ethan interrupted, "I don't even remember writing it!"

"That explains why everyone seems to know Ethan," Haley continued stubbornly, "but you still haven't told us — where we are or how we got here?"

"The answer to the first part of your question will have to wait," Daavic replied, "but I am as curious as you as to how you got here. So let us delve into that, shall we? What happened to the two of you just before you arrived?"

"We were on the beach, looking for seashells," Haley began. "Then Ethan saw a blue bunny creature waving at us. I couldn't see it, but Ethan could, so we followed it. Then we found a creepy staircase in the sand, and when Ethan went down the staircase, he disappeared —"

"That explains how Ethan got here," Daavic interrupted, "but how did you arrive?"

"As I moved in for a closer look, someone pushed me down the stairs, behind Ethan," Haley finished as she gasped for breath.

"This creature that only Ethan could see, what did it look like?" Daavic inquired seriously.

"Well, Ethan said it was a blue bunny with —"

"Haley! I'm right here! I can answer for myself," Ethan scolded, immediately feeling bad for doing so.

"I'm sorry — I got excited — you should tell this part."

"It looked like a blue Easter bunny — about this tall," Ethan continued, holding his hand a few feet above the ground, "with yellow spots. It spoke to me, it said its name was 'Jasper' and then it said 'Zo-Zo' and ran away."

"*Jasper!* Jasper the blue taletaddler — !"

The sound of shock in Daavic's voice was evident; he seemed to be talking to himself again.

"Ethan, was this the first time you've seen Jasper?" Daavic asked.

"Of course, I'm not in the habit of imagining things."

"The creature you saw was a taletaddler and it said, 'XO-XO' not 'Zo-Zo'," Daavic explained, spelling out the letters. "That is how a taletaddler says goodbye, it means hugs and kisses."

Ethan had to chuckle at Daavic's explanation.

"What is a taletaddler?" Haley asked.

"Taletaddlers are harmless creatures known in the human world as a child's imaginary friend. To adults they are invisible, but they are quite *real* I assure you. They normally choose a human child, age twelve or younger, befriending them and making themselves visible to only that child. Taletaddlers are the world's greatest storytellers, often telling wonderful tales to the child they've chosen. Many of the human world's greatest authors have gotten their material from the stories of taletaddlers —"

"That's ridiculous," Haley interrupted.

"Really —" Daavic challenged. "Could you possibly believe stories as inspiring as the *Harry Potter* novels were written solely by a human? No human could create such a masterpiece without the seeds of a taletaddler."

"What would a taletaddler want with us?" Haley asked, changing the subject.

"And why would it choose me?" Ethan asked. "I'm thirteen."

"You're thirteen —" Daavic repeated, pulling a small device from his pocket. "Then you should not be able to see a taletaddler."

"Is that an *iPhone*?" Ethan asked as Daavic tapped away at the colorful screen.

"Heavens no!" Daavic explained, "It is an Elemental Modulator. We call it an ELMO for short. A human — a Mr. Jobs, I believe the name was — did get a quick look at one once, and a short time later the *iPhone* was born."

"What does it do?" Ethan asked.

"This will tell me how old you are."

Daavic got up from the couch and walked over to Ethan. He gave the screen one final tap before holding the device up to Ethan's eyes.

"Look at the dot in the center of the screen and tell me when your taletaddler appears."

"There!" Ethan snapped as Jasper's image appeared on the screen.

"This is very unexpected. . . ."

Daavic stared down at the device as if trying to conceal his surprise.

"It appears you are thirteen — but that should not be possible, no human child past twelve has ever seen a taletaddler."

Daavic returned the device to his pocket.

"Are you insinuating Ethan is not human?" Haley had a puzzled look on her face.

"No — not at all — his DNA is human," Daavic replied. "I was merely pointing out that we seem to have more questions than answers at the moment."

There was a silent pause in the room.

"They are *mine*! I saw the humans first!" Albert yelled from across the room, breaking the uncomfortable silence.

"No you didn't — *I did*!" Newton countered.

"Irrelevant!" Linus shouted. "I was the first to introduce myself so I own the humans!"

"RGB! You will treat our guests with respect! They belong to no one!" Daavic commanded, breaking up the quarrel.

"Which brings me to my next question," Haley announced, "what are they and why do you call them RGB?"

"Those three little troublemakers are pyrodevlins — Albert in Red, Linus in Green, and Newton in Blue — collectively we refer to them as RGB, for short, since they normally get into trouble as a unit. Sadly, there was a fourth one that kept them in line. But the yellow one, Kepler, was taken by the Grim . . . the same group trying to abduct Ethan Fox."

"Where are the pyrodevlins from? And where are we? And why is an evil group trying to abduct Ethan?"

Haley questioned relentlessly.

"I'm sorry — I've already said more than I should," Daavic replied. "Your questions will have to wait until you meet my dear mother, headmistress Ravenwood. She will answer all of your questions."

Daavic was motioning towards the doors at the far end of the room, "Come — I will have Irvin show you to your rooms —"

"Rooms —" Ethan interrupted, "but I can't stay — I need to get back to my parents, they're probably worried by now."

"I'm sorry but that won't be possible. There are too many questions, and until we get to the bottom of things, the headmistress has decided that you must stay with us. Don't worry about your parents, they are safe. We will see to it that they are not worried in the meantime."

Daavic motioned to the exit once again.

When they reached the other side of the room, Ethan instinctively headed for the door he had seen Daavic enter through, the one to the left of the painting; but as he reached for the door knob it vanished.

"You can't go out through the in-door," Daavic said as he opened the door on the right.

"The in-door — ?" Ethan wondered, following Daavic and Haley.

They were now standing in what appeared to be the Front Room of the house.

"Oh! Wait! I forgot something in the library," Haley cried.

"We call it the Study," Daavic corrected. "Go ahead, run along and fetch it."

"What did you forget?" Ethan asked.

"The sand dollar you gave me on the beach — I set it down on the table."

"It's just a stupid old seashell."

"Ethan, that stupid old seashell is supposed to bring you luck. I think we could use a little luck right now — don't you? I'm getting my seashell!"

"Okay — I'll go with you."

As they reentered the Study they were stunned to notice that they had entered through the door to the left of the picture.

"How is that possible — ?" Ethan wondered, turning back towards the door to reach for the knob, but again it vanished.

"Ethan, you can't go out the in-door," Haley teased. "I think I'm beginning to understand this place."

While Haley skipped off to retrieve her seashell, Ethan was still studying the door when loud shouting suddenly erupted from the table. Startled, he spun around to see what was going on. Haley was frantically running around the table shouting as Albert, Newton, and Linus enjoyed a game of keep away.

"Ethan! They won't give it back to me — please help!" Haley cried as Newton threw the seashell across the table to the waiting hands of Albert.

"I've got an idea!" Ethan shouted.

Running to the fireplace, Ethan quickly grabbed a handful of firelyte marbles from the bowl on the mantle. Rushing back to the table, he came to Haley's rescue.

"Albert! Here — catch!" Ethan yelled, tossing one of the marbles at Albert who instinctively caught it.

"Newton! Linus! Catch!" he shouted, throwing a marble to each of them.

Newton, who was now holding the seashell, suddenly panicked. He threw the seashell up in the air as he reached to catch the red marble.

"I've got it!" Haley cried victoriously.

"Great! Let's get out of here," Ethan said, motioning towards the out-door.

"*No! Not a firelyte capsule!*" RGB screamed in unison. "We're *allergic* to firelytes!"

"Uh — oh . . ." Ethan said, spinning around just in time to see RGB throw the capsules to the ground.

The firelyte capsules erupted into three small infernos engulfing the floor.

Ethan stood watching — expressionless — as three firelytes began to emerge from the flames.

"It's okay — they'll just go pick out a log and jump into the fireplace," Haley chuckled.

"I don't think so . . ." Ethan said, pointing at the fire creatures.

Ethan and Haley watched in disbelief as the firelytes each grabbed a leg of a small wooden end table. Hoisting it up, they began whistling in unison as they marched towards the fireplace.

"Let's get out of here!" Ethan hollered, turning to Haley.

"Good idea!" Haley agreed as they started for the out-door.

THE GRUMPLING
OF THE HOUSE

After stepping back into the Front Room, Ethan and Haley began to look around. They were in a dimly lit room with a huge front door; it was large enough to accommodate a small giant. A narrow black carpet stretched from the front door to the opposite side of the room, where a huge black slab stood firmly against the wall. To each side of the carpet, assorted furniture decorated the beautiful hardwood floors that encompassed the room.

"There's no ceiling —" Ethan announced, gazing up into the night's sky.

"It was there earlier," Daavic interrupted, as if it was no big deal that a large portion of the ceiling was missing.

As Ethan continued scanning the room, he noticed what looked like a large soap bubble, floating in the middle of the room above a coffee table.

"What's that — ?" he asked, pointing at the baseball sized bubble.

"Its purpose has yet to be determined," Daavic replied.

"A bubble only has one purpose —" Haley smiled as she approached the floating sphere, "to be popped!"

She poked at it with her finger but it did not pop. Her finger went through it as if it were not even there; then, she blew at it but the bubble still did not move.

"Must be a ghost bubble," Ethan joked.

Having lost interest in the phantom bubble, Ethan continued exploring. At first glance, the rest of the room looked normal, until he walked to the other side and looked up the staircase. The stairs seemed to keep going up as far as the eye could see — into eternity — like a stairway to heaven.

"How many floors does this house have?" Ethan asked, turning to Daavic.

"As many as it needs —"

"Where does this lead?" Haley interrupted, pointing to a door under the staircase.

"Never go in that door! The basement is strictly off limits!" Daavic scolded, ignoring her question.

"Why would we go into a creepy basement anyway," Haley countered, surprised at Daavic's response.

Opposite the staircase, stood the wall with the Study door they had just entered through, it stretched the length of the room: to the left of the front door, another door stood on that wall, followed by a black chest of drawers standing at the wall's center; above the chest, a colorful abstract painting hung on the wall — the strange artwork looked as if it were moving; to the right of the chest was a small bench; and to the left of it, sat a giant mirror with a black frame engraved around the edges with a string of cryptic symbols.

"Wow! I bet that weighs a ton," Haley said to Ethan as he studied the giant mirror.

Farther down, past the Study door, a tall end table stood against the wall; a small lime green box sat on it. Beyond the table, the room ended with a small patch of ceiling overhead creating a cave like enclave. Inside the enclave was another door with a sign above it that read:

•THE HALL OF DOORWAYS •

"What is The Hall of Doorways?" Ethan asked, pointing up at the sign.

"It is what it is. . . . I'm going to find what's keeping Irvin — you two stay here," Daavic said, walking towards The Hall of Doorways and exiting the room.

"I wonder who this Irvin character is . . ." Haley pondered, looking at Ethan.

"Must be the butler or something —"

Suddenly, out of the corner of his eye, Ethan spotted something green streaking down the staircase. He turned, just in time to see what looked like a large green moth fluttering through the air. It came to a stop, landing on the wall at the base of the staircase.

Moving in for a closer look, he saw a green blob with eyes glaring back at him. About the size of a child's fist, it was slowly blending into the wall it had landed on. By the time he got to where it had landed, it was gone.

"Did you see that?" Ethan asked excitedly.

"See what?"

"A big green moth or something — it just flew down from upstairs! It landed on this wall and then just disappeared!"

Ethan was pointing at the empty wall.

"Are you seeing things again?" Haley joked. "Wait a minute — look. . . ." she said, pointing at the phantom bubble that was now moving.

They both watched, as the bubble slowly drifted towards them as if attracted by an unseen force. It sped up ever so slightly as it moved closer; finally coming to rest, nestled against the wall where the moth had disappeared. Then, suddenly, the green blob reappeared, popping off the wall and fluttering over their heads.

"I saw it that time!" Haley yelled — chasing the moth-like creature as it fluttered towards the back of the room.

"It's heading for The Hall of Doorways!" Ethan shouted, following behind.

"*No*! I think it wants inside that little green box on the table," Haley said as the creature landed on the table.

"Then we'll have it cornered!" Ethan yelled.

Next, the tiny creature tapped three times on the side of the box. Instantly, the lid swung open, and the creature hopped inside closing the lid tightly behind it.

"We have it cornered — but how do we open this box?" Ethan asked, prying at the lid with his fingernails.

"I saw it tap on the box like this . . ." Haley said, tapping three times causing the lid to swing open. "It's empty!"

"It disappeared on the wall — I think it can blend into things —"

"Ethan, look!" Haley interrupted, pointing at the bubble that was again drifting towards them.

"Blasted tag along!" a faint muffled voice grunted, as the fuzzy green blob suddenly reappeared, popping up out of the box, and unraveling in mid-air.

A tiny green creature landed on the table in front of them.

"Gruggins McGhee, grumpling of the house, at your service," the creature said, bowing down before offering a handshake.

Gruggins was about four inches tall with a mouse-like body and stubby little arms and legs. His face was that of an old man with a fat bulbous nose — like *Mr. Magoo*. Aside from smooth skin on his face and belly, short fuzzy hair covered the rest of his head and body. He was brilliantly colored; bluish-green with a purple and yellow eye pattern prominently centered on each of his long moth-like wings — they resembled the eye on a peacock feather.

"Since the day it arrived that dreaded bubble has been following me around," Gruggins complained, flopping back a tuft of his hair.

The hair at the top of his head formed a tall pointy peak that bent forward under its own weight — like the top of a soft serve ice cream. But the thing that really caught ones attention about Gruggins was the stunning gold jewelry he wore from head-to-toe: bracelets on his hands and feet, necklaces of varying sizes, and a long chain that wrapped around his waist several times.

Gruggins was blinged out!

"Hello Gruggins — my name is Haley and this is Ethan," Haley said, shaking his tiny hand with her fingers.

"Quite a grip you've got there!"

Gruggins flirted with Haley.

"I heard that we had some unexpected guests," he said, turning to Ethan who was staring down at him with a blank look on his face.

Gruggins spoke in a soft slowly measured tone, the slight rasp in his voice, fittingly sounded as if the words were coming from a wise but grumpy old man.

"So you're Ethan Fox," Gruggins said, looking up at Ethan. "You don't look so special to me — and judging by that dumb look on your face, I'd bet you've never seen a grumpling before."

"U-m-m — no — I haven't," Ethan managed.

"I suppose that shouldn't surprise me, but I've never seen a human before either — and you don't see a dumb look on my face, do you?"

It was obvious Gruggins did not like Ethan.

"It appears you've met our resident grumpling," Daavic interrupted the unpleasant exchange.

"Are you being courteous to our guests?" Daavic asked, directing his gaze at Gruggins.

"Of course, master Daavic — always courteous," Gruggins scowled.

"Irvin will be along shortly to take you to the headmistress and then to your rooms," Daavic said, looking at Ethan and Haley.

"*Please master Daavic*, not Irvin, not that mush mouthed morph-dork," Gruggins complained. "I cannot be subjected to his constant drivel and showboating theatrics. May I be excused?"

"You may," Daavic replied nodding.

"Thank you sir," Gruggins said gratefully.

"And to you — I bid a fond farewell," Gruggins added, bowing to Ethan and Haley before hopping back into his box and shutting the lid behind him.

"Grumplings have a very low tolerance for certain things," Daavic explained, "and Irvin seems to push all the wrong buttons. But they are both valuable members of our staff and need to put an end to their little feud."

"That was an odd little creature," Haley muttered.

"Indeed, grumplings are the most curious species you will ever encounter," Daavic added. "They have the unique ability to de-cloak a leprechaun's gold —"

"Leprechauns — ?" Haley interrupted. "You expect us to believe in leprechauns?"

"As I stated earlier, given the things you have already seen, I would not think it quite the stretch. But I forget you are new to our world . . . so please, let me explain. Yes — leprechauns do exist and they are particularly nasty little creatures, I must say. But unlike the tales from human lore, real leprechauns do not keep their gold in a pot at the end of a rainbow. Quite the opposite in fact, they scatter it about everywhere, hidden in plain sight. Leprechauns have magical abilities, one of which is the ability to cloak their prized stash of gold."

"You mean they can make it invisible?" Ethan asked.

"A leprechaun's cloak is much stronger than mere invisibility; a leprechaun's cloak renders the object invisible and untouchable, as if cloaked from existence — and that is where grumplings fit in. You see — when a grumpling comes within a giraffe's neck of leprechaun gold, the cloaking magic is destroyed. Grumplings are the only known creature with such an ability; it makes them a mortal enemy in the leprechauns' eyes. The situation was so bad that the leprechauns almost hunted grumplings to extinction."

"That sounds *horrible!*" Haley protested.

"It started long ago at the Greenfield Massacre," Daavic continued. "Until that point, leprechauns and grumplings led a peaceful and friendly co-existence. But then one day, for reasons unknown, an army of leprechauns descended upon the grumpling village at Greenfield. They massacred half of Earth's small grumpling population that day. Many escaped and went into hiding; but after that day, leprechauns continued to hunt grumplings, using their favorite food as bait — four leaf clovers."

"Why doesn't somebody stop the leprechauns?" Haley asked.

"Nobody wants to go to war with the leprechauns — did I not mention that they are particularly nasty little creatures? But we did the next best thing, rounding up the remaining grumplings, and moving them to one of the only places on

Earth a leprechaun will not venture. Except for Gruggins, the entire grumpling population is safely tucked away there."

"Why is Gruggins here and not with his people?" Ethan asked.

"Gruggins has taken the grumpling oath — he has pledged his life to the Ravenwood family. My mother stumbled across his lifeless body — one morning — while out on patrol. He was nearly dead, but she spent months nursing him back to health. When he finally came to, he had no memories of his past other than a bitter hatred of leprechauns — his memory has never returned. He was grateful to my mother for all she had done, so he pledged his life to her and her family, and joined us as the grumpling of the house."

"But if he couldn't remember anything — where did the name Gruggins come from?" Ethan asked.

"It's funny that you ask, it's a cute story actually," Daavic smiled. "When my baby sister first saw the grumpling, she was only just learning to speak. Trying to pronounce the word 'grumpling' was quite difficult for her — Gruggins was all she could manage. But the grumpling was drawn to her and soon began answering her calls for Gruggins, so he adopted the name. He later added McGhee as a bit of irony to annoy the leprechauns."

"Why does Gruggins wear all that gold?" Haley asked. "Doesn't that put him in danger with the leprechauns?"

"Unlike other grumplings, Gruggins is a very volatile character. He's made it his life's mission to wage a one grumpling war on the leprechauns. The jewelry he wears is a sign of defiance, it is meant to anger them — souvenirs from all the leprechaun gold he has de-cloaked over the years. We've tried to warn him of the dangers, but there's no getting through to a stubborn grumpling. At least we can keep him safe here."

Daavic turned towards the noise of footsteps, coming from The Hall of Doorways.

"Gruggins McGhee is a goon faced flobbyknocker and his father wears leprechaun slippers!" a goofy cackling voice cried out as the door burst open.

"*Irvin* — do not antagonize Gruggins!" Daavic scolded.

"So this is what humans look like — much uglier in person," Irvin added, ignoring Daavic's order.

"Irvin! They are not stupid — they can hear and understand you!"

"Duh — if you say so," he continued. "Well if you're not stupid, then I guess I'll introduce myself. Irvin McGillicutty at your service, here to see to your every need, answer to your every whim, and wait on you silly little creatures hand and foot, as my master has ordered."

Irvin was an odd looking being, nearly six feet tall, with pale white skin that looked as if he had been molded from white candle wax. His face was smooth with little definition — like that on a department store dummy. He wore a black tuxedo with a bow tie and a rose corsage that appeared to grow out from his body as if a part of it.

"But first, how about a little fun — I've been practicing this one to try out on a human," Irvin said, suddenly leaping into the air.

Ethan and Haley watched in disbelief.

Irvin morphed into a large egg, with small arms and legs, and facial features that looked like *Mr. Potato Head*. Landing next to Gruggins' green box, he sat perched at the edge of the table, rocking back and forth slowly.

"*Humpty Dumpty sat on a wall — Humpty Dumpty* was a big fat klutz!" a goofy voice chanted, as the egg began to slide off of the table.

Landing splat on the hardwood floor, the egg cracked open, and transformed into a giant fully cooked egg sunny side up.

"How do you like your eggs?" Irvin asked as facial features suddenly appeared on the yolk.

"Scrambled!" Haley cried out, laughing hysterically.

"However the lady likes it," the voice answered, as the egg on the floor quickly transformed into scrambled.

"That was *awesome*! How did he do that?" Ethan asked, watching as the pile of eggs slowly morphed back into Irvin McGillicutty.

"Irvin is a mimic, a member of the shape-shifter family," Daavic explained. "But unlike other shape-shifters — a mimic can only morph for a short time."

"Did you know that shnickyrooners and shnackleboxes and things like that," Irvin began to ramble, "they really only happen to old ice cream cones when giant tree turtles eat watery diapers in a blue elevator of leaf monkeys making the leftover apple trees take the school bus!"

"Why is he talking like that?" Ethan asked. "He's not making any sense!"

"No one knows for sure, maybe to amuse himself, maybe to irritate Gruggins, or maybe it actually means something to him," Daavic speculated. "But it's a fairly common occurrence so you should learn to ignore it if you can."

"Well — I suppose it's time for me to present you to headmistress Ravenwood," Irvin said, snapping out of the unintelligible rant. "But before we go — I've brought you each a surprise, a gift from your humble servant."

Irvin fumbled around in his pants pocket.

"Oh, there it is," he announced, pulling a balled up fist from his pocket.

Holding his arm out in front of Ethan, Irvin opened up his hand to show Ethan his surprise.

"What is it?" Ethan asked, looking down at a tiny brown pouch resting at the center of Irvin's palm.

"It's a pocket tote! And this one is for Ethan Fox!" Irvin eagerly explained, turning the tiny pouch around to expose the letters, "E. F." monogrammed on its side.

"What is a pocket tote?" Haley asked.

"Duh — only the must have item for any adventurer!" Irvin replied. "And Ethan Fox must be an adventurer — he ended up here, didn't he?"

"What does it do?" Ethan asked.

"First lesson is free, check this out!" Irvin winked, tugging lightly at a draw string on the side of the pouch.

Ethan and Haley watched in silence.

Suddenly the pouch began to grow in Irvin's hand. The more he tugged at the string, the larger it grew, until finally reaching the size of a small shopping bag.

"Your gift is inside," Irvin said, smiling at Haley as he reached into the bag.

After rummaging around for a second or two, he proceeded to pull a small metallic statuette from the bag, it was a cat.

"Oh! I just love kitty cats! Thank you!" Haley cried, smiling as she took the small trinket from Irvin.

"But that's not just an ordinary kitty cat," Irvin explained. "That is a copycat and when you hold it for the first time — as the new owner — you must name it so it knows who to mind."

"Who to mind? It's a statue!" Ethan sighed.

"Go ahead — you will see," Irvin urged Haley.

"Tabby — her name is Tabby!"

"Tabby it is, now for your free lesson. Pick an object — any object in the room — and as you look at it, stroke the copycat and repeat this phrase: *Tabby cat, Tabby cat, make me a copy.*"

"Tabby cat, Tabby cat, make me a copy —" Haley repeated, "now what?"

"Now Tabby will do the rest, put her down on the floor."

As Haley set the statuette on the floor, Tabby suddenly sprang to life, mcowing a few times before walking over to Haley and gently rubbing up against her feet. After getting acquainted with her new owner, Tabby walked back to where Haley had set her down. She circled the spot three times and then proceeded to lie down on the floor where she slowly morphed into a small green box — a perfect copy of the one Gruggins was resting in.

"That's it! That's what I was looking at when I said the phrase!" Haley explained. "But how do I get my kitty back?"

"That's the best part — a copycat always returns to its owner, *watch this*!"

Irvin picked up the green box from the floor and ran up the stairs. "All you have to do is say her name!" he yelled down from the next floor.

"TABBY CAT!" Haley shouted.

Suddenly, Irvin appeared out of thin air. He was standing a few feet in front of Haley holding the box in his hands. The box morphed back into a small metallic cat. Tabby jumped down onto the floor, walked over to Haley's feet, and froze in place — Tabby was a statuette again.

"Thank you Irvin! This is the coolest present ever!"

"Yeah — thank you Irvin, but what am I supposed to do with this bag?" Ethan asked.

"Oh, how careless of me, I got sidetracked — your lesson isn't over yet! *Watch this*!"

Irvin returned to the pocket tote where he again began tugging on the draw string. It continued to grow. He stopped as it reached the size of a large trash bag.

"Okay — here's the fun part! I need something rather large to demonstrate."

Irvin picked up a big heavy lamp off a table. After shoving the lamp into the now enormous pouch, he began tugging at a different draw string on its other side. But this time, instead of growing, the pouch began to shrink. Irvin continued pulling at the string until the pouch finally shrank back down to the size of a walnut.

"There you go! Pocket sized for the on-the-go adventurer!" Irvin said, handing it to Ethan.

"Cool! But where did the lamp go?"

"It's still in there, go ahead and see for yourself."

"But it's so small and way too light for that giant lamp to still be in there," he argued.

Ethan pulled at the string to make it grow again.

"It's getting heavier!" he announced, setting the pouch down while continuing to tug at the string.

Ethan proceeded to open the pouch, pulling the lamp from it, before shrinking it back down to pocket size.

"Just be careful when shrinking it back down," Irvin cautioned. "If you pull too hard on that string it can shrink too fast and disappear. I shrunk one so small once, I never could find it —"

"Well — now that gift time is over," Daavic interrupted, "you should take our guests to meet my dear mother. And when she is done with them show them to their rooms."

Daavic turned his gaze towards Ethan and Haley as he went on. "I will see you both, again, bright and early tomorrow morning. I've got something very special to show you."

"Follow me — !" Irvin directed.

On their way, Irvin stopped at Gruggins' table, picked up his box, shook it vigorously, and yelled, "The leprechauns are coming for you, you little green flying rat!"

"IRVIN! You two have got to put a stop to this idiotic feud! I will have no more of this!" Daavic commanded.

"Come with me — !" Irvin said, motioning towards The Hall of Doorways, ignoring Daavic's rant.

"*I'll show you a flobbyknocker*, you rubber faced, mush mouthed, morph-dork!" Gruggins exploded, erupting from his box.

Gruggins was holding a long tube that he quickly raised to his lips as he drew in a deep breath. He blew hard into the end of the blowgun as a dart zipped out the other end. It found its intended target, hitting Irvin square in the butt!

"AHHHHHHOOOOOOOWWWWW, *master Daavic*, the grumpy wart-moth shot me again!" Irvin screamed, grabbing his butt where he had been hit. "He did something to me! I am changing and I can't control it!"

As the screaming got louder they could see that Irvin was beginning to morph again, but this time it was not under his control. When the transformation was complete, he looked like a purple goose, with a round bulldog face, and two long clumsy antennas — Irvin was a Flobbyknocker!

"Gruggins! What have you done?" Haley cried.

"He's okay — he'll change back in a couple of minutes," Gruggins chuckled with a satisfied grin.

"He does look funny," Ethan said, watching as the two balls at the end of his antennas clanked together.

A few minutes later, it was over; Irvin had morphed back into himself.

"W-w-where was I? Oh, yes — taking you two to headmistress Ravenwood," he said, motioning to them.

It was like nothing had ever happened.

The Hall of Doorways was wider and taller than any normal hallway Ethan had ever seen; it was obviously built to accommodate something very large. On each wall, huge doors lined the hallway with no space in between; where one door ended another began. It was eerie, black wall to wall carpeting with a mirrored ceiling making it look black as well.

The lighting was even stranger; there were no lights in this hallway, only a giant beetle like creature that clung to the ceiling, emitting a bright purplish light from its belly. The beetle was somehow reacting with the mirrors on the ceiling; light rained down about twenty-five feet in each direction abruptly ending in pure darkness — like an invisible wall painted pitch black.

As they walked down the hallway, the creature followed along from above and the light did too. New doors emerged from the darkness in front of them as doors they passed disappeared into the blackness behind.

"Are we almost there?" Haley asked. "This place is creeping me out."

"This is it! The thirteenth door on the right!" Irvin announced. "So why are you going to see the headmistress? What are you in trouble for?"

"We're not in trouble," Haley replied.

"Oh, s-s-sure — that's what they all say! I sure would like to be a fly on the wall when she hands out your punishment," Irvin added as he quickly morphed into a giant fly landing on the door.

"It's going to be curtains for the two of you!" Irvin continued as the fly transformed into a set of curtains covering the door.

"Give it up McGillicutty," Ethan said, pushing the curtains aside to open the door behind.

THE

RESIDENCE

Upon entering the next room, it took several seconds for their eyes to adjust to the darkness they were now standing in. It was a huge round room, lit by dim floor lights that ran along the exterior edges of the room.

"A dome room . . ." Ethan whispered.

The walls of the room curved inwards, towards the ceiling, ending at a thick blanket of fog that hung in the air above. At the center of the room, a small circle of light brightly pointed out where they were apparently supposed to go. As they approached the lit area, the base of a black marble staircase came into view, disappearing up into the layer of fog above.

"Welcome Ethan Fox," a soft feminine voice whispered from the darkness.

"Did you hear that?" Haley asked.

"Yeah — she said, 'welcome Ethan Fox' but who said it?"

"That's funny . . . I heard my name," Haley said.

"I've been looking forward to meeting you Ethan, I'm sure you have many questions," the calm motherly voice continued.

"There it was again! And she definitely said 'Haley'!" Haley insisted.

"I am speaking to both of you," the voice clarified, "please follow the stairs so we can get acquainted."

As they neared the base of the stairs, Ethan turned his attention towards the lit floor, freezing in mid-stride.

"Strike that — a sphere room!" he said, looking down at his feet where he could see that the floor was missing.

The walls of this room, curved down as well, forming a perfect sphere. And they were walking in mid-air at its cross section.

"It's like we are walking on invisible glass," Haley said, suddenly noticing why Ethan stopped.

"This place keeps getting creepier and creepier," Ethan said, continuing towards the mysterious stairway.

As they ascended the stairs, through the thick fog layer, the upper half of the room came into view. Upon reaching the top of the stairs, they found themselves at the outer edge of a circular platform — an observation perch. It was like a crow's nest sitting dead center of the spherical room. The floor of the platform seemed to appear out of thin air as their feet touched the top step. Turning towards the center of the room, they were immediately greeted by their host.

"By the heart of Wormfreid!" the woman gasped, looking at Haley as she approached. "You look just like her. . . ."

She was a middle-aged woman of medium build. Her beautiful facial features and calm smile immediately put them at ease. She had long black hair with small silver pinstripes that looked as if an artist had painted them on. She was wearing the same black and white robe that Daavic wore, but this one was decorated with a black and white butterfly with four colored spots: one red, one green, one blue, and one yellow. But *this* butterfly was alive, fluttering around like a cartoon on the surface of the fabric as if trying to escape.

"I see you're interested in my little guest," the woman said in a soothing tone. "A 'flutterby' as we call them, but they don't always flutter-by, sometimes they get stuck. I bet you've never seen one before. . . . Well — have you ever heard the human saying about a butterfly flapping its wings?"

"The Butterfly Effect — I remember from science class," Ethan replied. "When a butterfly flaps its wings in one part of the world, it can cause a hurricane in another part of the world."

"Very good, and this little guy could almost do such a thing," she continued. "It can literally exist in two places at once, and for now, it appears that this one has taken a liking to my robe —"

"That's impossible," Ethan interrupted. "Nothing can exist in two places at once."

"Sure it can, it merely needs to exhibit sub-atomic behavior," the woman explained. "Nothing is impossible my dear, you can just take my word for that. . . ."

"Oh — no — where are my manners? My name is Jordanna Ravenwood. I already know who you are, Ethan

Fox — you've caused quite a stir in our world. Unfortunately, I believe that is why you are here —"

"You said I look just like her," Haley interrupted, "who are you talking about?"

"And you must be Haley," Jordanna said, gently shaking her hand. "My daughter — she was taken from us over a hundred years ago. You are far too young, but I do not believe that your resemblance to my daughter is a coincidence. Not to mention the fact that you've showed up here with Ethan — neither is a coincidence in my opinion."

"Where exactly is here?" Ethan asked.

"We call it The Residence — it is our headquarters here on Earth. It doesn't really exist anywhere in the human sense. Think of it as a doorway to everywhere and anywhere, if you will."

"Headquarters on Earth — are you aliens or something?" Haley asked.

"We are the Caretakers," Jordanna replied, "and no, we are not aliens — distant cousins would be a better way of putting it. I've always disliked the term alien. It has such a negative connotation, don't you think?"

"Caretakers — Caretakers of what?" Ethan asked with a puzzled look on his face.

"Caretakers of Earth — we watch over all species native to Earth and police against outside influences on the human world. The Caretakers have been here as long as humans. We are made up of a coalition of intelligent species, relocated here, to nurture the evolution of the human race."

"That sounds like quite a task, how do you do all that?" Haley asked.

"You are quite right — it's not easy — but we get by with a combination of technology and what you might call, special powers."

"You have superpowers?" Ethan asked.

"We are not like *Superman* if that's what you are asking, but we do have many special abilities that might be deemed as super to the human world."

"What kinds of abilities?" Haley asked.

"Caretakers possess the ability to influence the evolution of any life forms on Earth. However, our rules prohibit us from using these abilities on humans. Our purpose is to ensure that the human species evolves strictly on its own."

"You can influence evolution — so you could turn a goldfish into a shark?" Ethan asked.

"Well that is an extreme example," Jordanna laughed. "But in a word, yes — a Caretaker could make a goldfish evolve into a shark. There is normally a good reason for changing the evolutionary direction of a species. A species that might be evolving down the wrong path might require our help. A better example, would be giving a duck a bill instead of a mouth with teeth. It requires us to keep a tight watch on all species native to Earth. Unfortunately, there have been the occasional abuses of these abilities, now only a very select group of Caretakers are tasked with evolutionary duties."

"How were the powers abused?" Ethan asked.

"Well — it was quite harmless really," Jordanna began to explain. "Many, many years ago, my sons, Damien and Daavic were going through evolutioner training. They were each assigned a handful of animals on the continent of Africa. Their task was simple; watch over and monitor these animals and give them an evolutionary nudge if necessary."

Jordanna took a deep breath, waiting to see if the children had questions, but they didn't, so she went on. "One of the animals assigned to Damien was a white horse species he was very fond of. As brothers often do, the boys would sometimes get mad at each other and feud. One day after a particularly bad argument, Daavic decided to play a prank on his brother by rapidly evolving his prized horse species. When Damien checked on his species, he was *shocked* by the change in appearance of his favorite animal: it was smaller, its ears had been changed, and it now had black stripes. Daavic had evolved it into what is today known as a zebra."

"For months Damien blamed himself for what had happened," she continued, "but then one day he somehow found out his brother was responsible. Instead of getting mad and fighting about it, Damien kept it to himself — he was planning his revenge. A week later, when Daavic went to check on his species, he was *surprised* by what he saw. His favorite animal species, a small desert llama, had been dramatically changed: it had been enlarged, its legs had been lengthened, its neck stretched very long, and large dark brown splotches now covered its previously beautiful golden layer of hair. Damien had evolved it into a giraffe."

"Wow! That's quite a story —" Haley said.

"Yeah —" Ethan interrupted, "but I'd rather find out more about why we are here in the first place."

"Yes, of course — please, come sit with me," Jordanna said, motioning them towards a large captain's chair in the middle of the room.

"But there's nowhere for us to sit," Haley said, looking at the lone chair.

"Sure there is," Jordanna smiled, tapping the screen of the ELMO device she had produced from her robe.

Suddenly, two smaller versions of the chair appeared out of thin air, one to each side of the large chair.

"First — let me show you something," she said, walking over and sitting down in the larger chair. "Come, sit —"

As they walked towards the center of the room, the outside edges of the crow's nest began to disappear as if the floor was disintegrating. Sitting down in their chairs, Ethan and Haley were both surprised to see that the floor was almost completely gone, except for the small area below their feet and chairs.

"— now grip the arms of your chair and recline back like this . . ." Jordanna instructed as she did the same.

Following along, Ethan and Haley both reclined back, causing the rest of the floor to disappear along with their chairs. They were now seemingly floating in mid-air at the center of the spherical room.

"No need to be alarmed — this room has a very special purpose."

"This is cool!" Ethan said, looking at Haley.

"Not many humans have seen what you are about to see," Jordanna said, touching the screen of her ELMO device.

Suddenly, the inside walls of the room transformed into a detailed map of the world — they were hovering inside of a gigantic globe.

"O-o-okay — so you have a very cool map of the world," Haley said.

"What are all the colored dots?" Ethan asked.

"Living creatures — the green ones represent the human race, the blue ones are plants and animals native to Earth, and the yellow ones are species not native to Earth."

"What are the red X's?" he asked.

"They mark certain irregular events or trouble areas that may need or have needed Caretaker intervention —"

"Let me guess!" Ethan interrupted, "the white ones are Caretakers and the black ones are the bad guys!"

"Very good, but we call them Grimleavers —"

"Grimleavers," Haley barked, "are they the ones trying to kidnap Ethan?"

"Yes — and they will continue to do so until we find out why, which is why you must stay here with us for the time being."

"But they looked like vampires," Ethan said.

"Yes, you did see vampires, but let me explain. Vampires are one of the Grimleavers deadliest creations — their loyalist of servants. You see, Grimleavers were once Caretakers, some of our most powerful and influential members, in fact. At first, they existed only in secret, spreading their evil from within the Caretaker organization. As members of stature, they could get away with virtually anything, they were beyond suspicion. For hundreds of years, we were at a loss, to explain the unusual events that seemed to occur out of nowhere. Some even believed that Earth was cursed beyond our control."

"Then a terrible thing happened," Jordanna continued. "Our leader, Odin Ravenwood was killed; betrayed by his best friend, Victor Qruefeldt, the leader of the Grimleavers. If any good came out of that day it was the fact that they were now exposed. No longer could they secretly wreak havoc and thwart the Caretakers efforts. The secret was out and the three of them went into hiding — Victor and his two accomplices, Drake Evans and Jason Crowley, the three Grimleaver founders."

"Was Odin your husband?" Haley asked.

"No — my husband was Ryvias Ravenwood, Odin was his father," Jordanna replied in a somber tone. "Not the luckiest name, Ravenwood. In our entire history on Earth, only two Caretakers have ever been killed, and both were members of the Ravenwood family. Odin was killed by his best friend and then Ryvias by his own son."

Jordanna wept.

"Damien killed his father?" Ethan asked.

"Sadly — yes — and then he abducted his sister, Danielle, and went into hiding with the Grimleavers. We still have no idea what became of my dear Danielle. We searched the world over but found no trace of her."

"If the Grimleavers were once Caretakers, then they must have the same powers," Haley muttered.

"Unfortunately — they've evolved more powerful abilities, they no longer resemble the beings they once were. When they broke away from us, they began to use their powers in forbidden ways, abducting species and evolving them into horrendous monsters to use against us. Not only is such a thing forbidden, there are consequences for doing so. A physical transformation takes place as well as a mental one; the result is a hideous demonic appearance and the mentality to go along with it."

"If you know where they are, why don't you do something about it?" Ethan asked, pointing at the black dots on the globe.

"We don't know where they all are. Most of those black dots represent small pockets of some of the weaker species they have managed to conjure up. In other cases, they represent monsters that we have captured or corralled in some manner. But even if we did know where they all were, we would not want them to know that."

"But what do the Grimleavers want with Ethan?" Haley asked.

"The answer to that question, we do not know. But if I were to speculate — I would say that it has something to do with The Eyes of the Desert Sand; a special poem of unknown origin, it has been known to our world for thousands of years. But never has a human uttered the words — until now. When Ethan wrote down those words, it made him a target for some reason, and that is what we need to find out."

"Anyway — I think you have heard enough for one day," Jordanna said, tapping on the screen of her ELMO device.

Leaning forward, to get up from her chair, the crow's nest floor instantly reappeared as her feet touched the ground.

"Irvin will show you to your rooms," she said as Irvin emerged from the staircase. "Tomorrow at breakfast, Daavic will introduce you to more Caretakers. Then he'll show you around The Residence a little. After that, we can discuss what to do next."

"Shnickyrooners and things like that," Irvin began to rant. "Did you know that blue lizard faced ice puppets are usually the only reason why light bulbs go out for lunch. And if it wasn't for the singing lips of frozen beetle arms then we never would know how the red trumpet bounces!"

"Well, I never thought of it like that Irvin, but now that you mention it, it makes perfect sense!" Ethan replied, winking and smiling at Haley.

"Shhh — don't tell anyone why the little blobs of stinky white sock bubbles are still in the hall pantry next to the elephant poop," he whispered, smiling at Ethan as if he had just found his new best friend.

"Come — I will show you to your rooms," he said, snapping out of his chant.

"Here we are!" Irvin announced as they arrived at doors "5L" and "6L" in The Hall of Doorways. "The sixth door on the left is for Ethan Fox, and the fifth door on the left is for Haley Hunt," he said in a professional tone.

"I will be back to gather you in the morning. And then I will do my best *Bobby Flay* and cook you a meal fit for a king!"

Irvin's face instantly morphed into *Bobby Flay* with a crown on top of his head.

"I already know how the lady likes her eggs, but what would Ethan Fox like for breakfast, any special requests?"

"I'm sure whatever you are serving will be fine," he replied.

"Okay, sleep tight — I've arranged for very special accommodations, I am sure you will feel right at home," Irvin said waving.

When Ethan entered his room, he was surprised to see that it was an exact replica of his room at home.

"Wow! Irvin's thought of everything . . ." he whispered to himself, looking around to see everything in its place. "I just wish I could speak with Haley."

Suddenly, he saw one of the small ELMO devices on the dresser, next to the door. Picking up the device, he noticed a single button icon on the touch screen. It read: "Intercom App" at the top and "Speak with Haley" at the bottom. With a single tap of the button, he could hear her voice as if she were in his room; she was humming an eerie sounding tune.

"Haley is that you?"

"Yes — but where are you?"

"In my room — they left us a way to talk, I guess."

"It sounds like you are standing right next to me," she said. "Have you sat on your bed yet? It's the most comfortable thing I've ever lied down on."

As Ethan approached his bed, he was surprised to see it change form as he neared. It transformed into a soft pillowy cloud hovering a foot off the ground.

"Boy you weren't kidding!" he said as he eased himself down onto the puffy cotton like material. "I bet these beds are sandman approved!"

Haley laughed.

"Haley — what was that strange tune you were humming?"

"I'm not sure . . . I made it up, I think," she replied. "I've had it in my head ever since I saw you on the boardwalk."

"Huh, it sounds very familiar," he said.

"Well — I don't really know where I might have heard it. I don't remember anything before seeing you, remember?"

"By the heart of Wormfreid . . ." Ethan said softly, thinking aloud.

"What? I couldn't hear you."

"By the heart of Wormfreid — don't you remember, she said that right before saying you looked just like her daughter."

"Yes, but what's it mean?" Haley asked.

"I don't know . . . but somehow it sounded familiar to me, too; like I've heard it before."

"Now that you mention it I —"

"Haley!" he interrupted in a serious tone, "You remember when Jordanna said she does not believe it is a coincidence that you are here with me?"

"Yeah — ?"

"We have other things in common that I haven't told you about. I have no memory of anything before my eighth birthday. My parents gave me some story about a car crash and having a head injury. And up until a week ago, I'd always believed them."

"But you don't anymore?" she asked.

"No — after I remembered that poem, I went to my dad and showed it to him. He was freaked out about it. And then I overheard him and my mom arguing. My mom seemed scared that I might be remembering things. After that, they acted very strange — I know they are hiding something."

"Do you think the same thing happened to both of us?" Haley asked.

"I don't know . . ." Ethan replied, "but I do agree with Mrs. Ravenwood about one thing, your being here with me is not a coincidence!"

A BREAKFAST TO
REMEMBER

The next morning, Irvin arrived bright and early as promised.

"Shnickyrooners and things like that . . ."

Ethan could hear Irvin's ranting outside his door as he gently knocked.

"Have you ever seen a chocolate pig play ping pong underneath the fat noodle legs of a purple water rat?"

"No Irvin — I haven't, but I bet it's not something I'd want to miss," Ethan replied giggling as he opened his door.

"Indeed!" Irvin continued, smiling at Ethan's friendly response. "It's quite like the hair at the tip of a hockey puck's peach whiskers — but not quite as lonely!"

"Why do you waste your time with that double talk?" Haley asked, emerging from her room.

"I almost think I'm beginning to understand it," Ethan joked, making Haley laugh out loud.

"They are in the Breakfast Room, awaiting your arrival — just a few doors down, the eighth door on the left," Irvin said, motioning down the hallway.

Ethan and Haley followed along.

"A word of warning," Irvin said in a hushed tone, "about The Hall of Doorways — you've already been through the zeroth door on the left, that was the Front Room — but never go through the zeroth door on the right, which is the Doorway to Nothingness, as we call it. Anything going through that door ceases to exist."

"What are the doors past the zeroth doorways?" Haley asked.

"Those are the negative doors," Irvin replied. "Stay away from those too, they lead to the past, and what's done is done, I always say."

As they arrived at the eighth door on the left, Irvin opened it, motioning them into the Breakfast Room.

They entered a large square room with dark hardwood floors like those in the Front Room; the room was part kitchen, part dining room. The kitchen side of the room had a fully loaded chef's station — like something you'd see on a *Food Network television show*. The other side of the room looked like the dining area of a quaint bed and breakfast: to one side of the dining area, Daavic and the others were sitting at a large round table with ten chairs; on the other side, was an antique piano with a matching bench; and in the corner, sat a gigantic oversized chair, large enough for a giant — it was so big, the legs were almost as tall as Ethan.

CHAPTER SEVEN

"Don't be shy — pull up a seat and join everyone," Irvin said, motioning towards the round table. "Chef Irvin will be just across the room, slaving away in the kitchen."

Instantly, the top of his head morphed into a tall chef's hat.

"Please — come sit with us," Daavic called out from the table. "Let me introduce you to more valuable members of the Caretaker staff."

As Ethan and Haley approached, everyone at the table politely stood to greet them.

"This is Brianna Tanglewood," Daavic said, motioning to a woman with blue snakelike skin.

The brilliant blue color of her skin was punctuated by unique black swirling patterns scattered over her body. Her upper body was that of a very slim human woman, tapering off at the torso, and merging into the body of an enormous coiled snake at the floor.

"Hello —" Ethan said, reaching out to shake her leathery hand.

She had pleasant facial features and long green hair that moved around, shimmering in the light as if made from satin. In fact, her hair was alive; each strand was a small tube like worm — as thick as a piece of spaghetti — with tiny eyes and smiling faces peeking out at the ends.

"Pleased to meet you —" Haley politely held out her hand.

"Likewise, my dear, and what a pretty ring you've got there . . . I don't think I've seen one quite like that. . . ."

Brianna was fixated on Haley's black infinity ring.

"And this is Nicholas Knight," Daavic continued, gesturing towards the tall man standing next to Brianna.

Nicholas was a muscular man with a tanned golden complexion. He was wearing a long white robe with gold trim on the shoulders and collar. He had pale blue eyes with piercing black pupils. Long white hair fell well past his shoulders, behind his back where large angel like wings protruded from outside his robe.

"Hi —" Ethan began, stopping in mid-sentence.

Ethan was startled by the vampire teeth peeking out as Nicholas smiled.

"Hello Nicholas, it is a pleasure to meet you," Haley interrupted.

Haley seemed to feel right at home among the odd cast of characters.

"And Bella Wentworth," Daavic continued, gesturing past Nicholas at a middle-aged woman of medium build.

Except for her four arms, Bella almost looked human. She had red hair that stood up on top of her head in a beehive hairdo. Other than that, she had average looking human features.

"Hello —" Ethan said, apparently puzzled over which of her four hands to shake.

"Oh — this is so exciting — I've been so looking forward to meeting both of you — we have so much to discuss — so much to talk about —" Bella jabbered. "We don't get many humans here, you know, so I —"

"Next to Bella is Alexander Sturgis," Daavic interrupted her in mid-sentence.

Though a bit older than the others, Alexander was the first completely human looking Caretaker they had met, so far.

Simply put, he was tall, dark, and handsome. His dark brown hair and eyes perfectly accented his tan complexion. He wore the same style white and black robe as Daavic and Jordanna.

"Nice to meet you," Ethan said, shaking his hand.

Alexander's stern handshake, immediately gave Ethan the impression that this was a man of confidence.

"Hello Ethan —" Alexander said with a comforting smile, "have you enjoyed your stay, so far?"

"Everyone has been more than kind," he replied.

There was something strangely familiar about this man.

As they finished with the introductions, Ethan and Haley took their seats beside Daavic; Ethan to the left and Haley to the right.

"We are still awaiting the arrival of one additional guest—" Daavic explained. "— oh, there he comes now," he finished, as the loud thundering sound of giant footsteps approached from The Hall of Doorways.

When the door opened, Ethan's gaze immediately went up. Entering the room was a giant of a man, at least twelve feet tall. As if in a state of shock, he and Haley were quietly staring at the giant stranger.

"And last — but not least — I would like you to meet Azron," Daavic interrupted the silence as he stood to introduce the giant.

"Now I understand why the doors are so big!" Haley announced, standing to greet the new arrival.

Azron was enormous; he had scraggly black hair and thick whisker stubble that looked like burnt rice covering most of his face. But what stood out the most about Azron's appearance, was not his size, it was the single oversized eye bulging from the center of his forehead. Yet at the same time, it was obvious that he was a gentle giant, in the way he calmly greeted Ethan and Haley with a friendly smile.

"Hello, Ethan Fox —" Azron said in a deep soothing voice, "I hear you stumbled across The Residence following a mischievous taletaddler?"

Azron slid the giant chair from the corner of the room over to the table.

"From what we've been told," Ethan replied.

"Yeah — but we still don't know who pushed me down the stairs," Haley added as she shook Azron's pinky finger with both of her hands.

"Yes — and that's only the beginning of the mystery —"

"Which brings me to why we are all here," Daavic interrupted. "It appears the Grimleavers are obsessed with abducting young Ethan Fox as we expected they might. So the headmistress thought it necessary that he meet the heads of the Caretaker Anti-Grimleaver Enforcement — CAGE, as we normally call it."

"Everyone at this table has had a loved one abducted by the Grimleavers," Alexander spoke. "So when headmistress Jordanna decided to form this task force, to actively pursue the Grimleavers and fight against them, we were the most logical candidates — CAGE was born."

"Why did the Grimleavers abduct your loved ones?" Ethan asked.

"Maybe we should all share our stories," Daavic suggested. "I know my mother has already told you of the Ravenwood family misfortune —"

"In order to defeat the Caretakers," Nicholas interrupted, answering Ethan's question. "The three original Grimleavers were not powerful enough to defeat us on their own. So they formed a plan to abduct species with unique abilities and use their Caretaker abilities to evolve them into dangerous and powerful monsters. Each species' abilities are different, which makes for unique possibilities when crafting monsters. My wife, Nicole was taken by the Grimleavers; she was devolved into Earth's first vampire. Since then, vampires have flourished — they are natural killing machines and multiply with ease. They have become a loyal army of Grimleaver soldiers —"

"I noticed your teeth, aren't you a vampire? Haley blurted out with a puzzled look on her face.

"Not a vampire, but a blood sucker just the same," Nicholas smirked. "I am a vampril, which is quite different. Early humans often mistook us for angels, on those rare occasions where one of us was spotted. We are a strong but peaceful species, much more evolved than vampires. We do drink blood, but not that of humans, these teeth are made for piercing the tough skin of a blood turnip."

Nicholas smiled exposing his sharp fangs.

"A *blood turnip* — what's that?" Haley asked with a yucky look on her face.

"It is a parasitic fruit that grows on the back of a burrowing stone grub," Nicholas replied.

"Vamprils used to be one of the most numerous species among Caretakers," Daavic added, "but after Nicole's abduction, the vampril men were worried that their spouses, too, might be abducted. They were losing faith in the Caretakers and did not believe in our ability to protect the well being of their loved ones — so they went into seclusion. Only Nicholas stayed, remaining behind to help the Caretakers continue their fight against the Grimleavers. To this day, not even Nicholas knows of the whereabouts of his vampril brethren."

"So — you are telling us that vampires are *real* and they are after me?" Ethan sounded frightened.

"I am afraid so Ethan Fox — this is not just a bad dream you are having," Brianna replied, "and it doesn't end there. Many creatures that humans believe are *not real* actually do exist on Earth. The Caretakers have merely done a masterful job in hiding them from the human world: vampires, werewolves, zombies, cyclops, and even Medusa herself — they are all *real* — and some of them are even represented here at this table."

"Azron and his twin brother, Gaball, are members of the soleyed dwarfgiant species," Daavic began to explain. "Gaball was taken by the Grimleavers; he was devolved into a flesh eating giant — a monster — a cyclops. He is now twice Azron's size and has a horn; he's undergone a grotesque transformation."

"He even became too much for the Grimleavers to handle," Azron added with a hint of pride in his voice. "He escaped and began wreaking havoc on the human world; he devoured everything in his path. He even ate a few humans before discovering his favorite food, leprechauns —"

"We were finally able to lure him to a secluded valley where we trapped him," Daavic interrupted. "The Valley of the Shadow of Death — the leprechauns call it. Brianna's sister has a similar story as well —"

Brianna cut in, "My sister, Medusa, was turned into the creature described in human mythology —"

"I remember Medusa — from a movie I watched with my dad — *The Clash of the Titans!*" Ethan interrupted. "In the movie, she was scary looking with snakes for hair, and looking directly at her would turn a man to stone. They killed her to use her head as a weapon to kill the *kraken* —"

"They got the snakes part right and the turning people to stone," Brianna interrupted, "but I can assure you — my dear sister — Medusa is alive and well. She is safely locked away in a temple in the lost city of Stonehenge. Her needs are tended to by three blind trolls that were captured with her. Only the blind can be in her presence without fear of being turned to stone."

"The only thing keeping those dreaded trolls in line are Medusa's threats," Daavic added. "Threats that she will heal their eyes — you see, Brianna and her sister are serpeneze, a species known for their powerful healing abilities —"

"A-a-and then — there's my p-p-poor — dear husband *Boris*," Bella interrupted, weeping in dramatic fashion. "*He* was abducted very recently — we still don't know what happened to *him* — it was shortly after we learned of the human boy who knew what *he should not* — so we naturally sent my *Boris* out to investigate and —"

"Yes Bella — we are all very saddened by your loss," Daavic interrupted, "but we do not want to delve too far into the specifics."

There was an uncomfortable tension in the room as Daavic cut Bella off.

"So what about you — what's your story?" Ethan blurted out his question at Alexander, immediately feeling guilty for his lack of tact. "I'm sorry — that didn't come out right."

"It's quite all right," Alexander said, putting Ethan at ease. "In many ways, mine is the most tragic of stories — I lost more than one family member that day and a best friend. I was married to a human woman — Tiffany was the love of my life. We had a child together, the only human-Caretaker hybrid ever conceived. He was only an infant when he was abducted by someone I thought was a friend — Victor Qruefeldt. In the process, Victor murdered our leader, Odin Ravenwood — it was the event that exposed the Grimleavers. Many years later, they abducted my wife, leaving her for dead in an icy land unknown to humans. Unfortunately — she could not be saved. There never was any rhyme or reason as to why they abducted her — after all, she was only human, she had no special abilities for them to exploit."

"What would the Grimleavers want with an *infant?*" Haley asked. "There's nothing to exploit there either."

"That is a question I have been pondering for many years," Alexander replied.

Alexander had a strange look on his face, like there was more to say, but he was holding something back.

"The only thing we've learned from these events is that when it comes to the Grimleavers there are many things we simply do not know," Daavic concluded.

"If I may interrupt, master Daavic — so I can take your orders for this morning's breakfast?"

"Certainly, Irvin."

"Most of you probably want the usual. Let me see if I remembered this right: Nicholas — one ripe blood turnip; master Daavic — two double-yolked eggs sunny-side up with waffled fish stick hash browns and a dash of pickle dust; Bella — one four-legged sausage chicken on pear skinned toast; Azron — three double-wide goat ham logs, a pile of applesauce potatoes, a barrel of dragon's milk, and a basket of buttermilk toad muffins; Brianna — a rat ham soufflé with mouse bacon sprinkles; and Alexander — a short stack of pancake leaves drizzled with melted peacock butter. Great choice, I must say, Mrs. Moonflowers delivered a fresh *Bisquick* tree just this morning —"

"Please — let me explain," Alexander interrupted. "Our menu must sound very strange to you." (The confused look on Ethan and Haley's faces must have been apparent.) "Our powers of evolution, allow us to create any sort of food your imagination might conjure up. I doubt you could come up with something that Irvin cannot whip up for you."

"*How is that different* from the Grimleavers?" Haley protested. "You evolve four-legged chickens and other strange things just for the sake *of your food?*"

"Oh, no dear — you've misunderstood," Brianna interrupted. "We grow all of our food organically, as plants: steak, chicken, sausage, bacon — you name it — it's all picked right off the plant it grows on. Everything we eat could be considered a vegetable, if you will. Now, if you want to get into a debate about plant rights, then that's a different matter — but we do have to eat."

"Our Mrs. Moongarden is quite the magician when it comes to growing things," Daavic added. "*Green fingers* I believe the humans call it."

"*Green thumb*," Ethan corrected, giggling.

"Go ahead and try the sausage or bacon," Daavic suggested. "I challenge you to tell the difference. Just feel safe in knowing that no animals were harmed for your breakfast."

The table broke out in laughter.

"So what do our valued guests want for breakfast?" Irvin asked.

"I think I'd like —" Haley paused, trying to think of the strangest thing she could imagine, "— how about an egg with three heart-shaped yolks, on a piece of toast that tastes like applesauce, and a glass of blue peppermint milk."

"The lady wants the Number Five," Irvin joked, jotting down Haley's order. "And what would Ethan Fox like to order?"

"I'll have," Ethan started smiling, "a piece of green chocolate toast, with two red caramel yolked eggs, on a bed of butterscotch lettuce leafs."

"The Sturgis Special," Irvin said, writing the order down.

"You've stumbled upon a family favorite," Alexander said with a surprised look. "Tiffany just loved the Sturgis Special. How on Earth did you dream that up?"

"I don't know . . . it just popped into my head."

"I will be right back with your orders," Irvin said, wandering back to the kitchen.

"Can I help?" Ethan asked, getting up from his seat and walking to the kitchen area with Irvin.

"The great chef Irvin needs no assistance," Irvin boasted as Ethan looked on. "I have flavors and spices that would even make *Emeril Lagasse* jealous — BAM!" he joked.

Ethan watched in amazement, as Irvin morphed new arms from his body as needed; they reached out to: stir, flip, sprinkle, and sort. He was cooking all of the dishes at once and needed no help doing so.

Irvin McGillicutty had mad cooking skills!

Out of the corner of Ethan's eye, a bowl of bright colorful cereal grabbed his attention. It was within an arm's length and it looked like his favorite cereal — *Fruit Loops*. He slyly reached over and snuck a few of the colorful frosty loops. He then turned away from Irvin to be sneaky as he popped the cereal into his mouth — but his delight quickly turned to disgust. This was not the sugary sweet flavor he'd expected, this cereal tasted more like rotten fish, and he quickly spat it out onto the floor.

"Ethan Fox ate grumpling food — Ethan Fox ate grumpling food!" Irvin began chanting.

The entire dining area was soon erupting with laughter.

Even Haley was laughing, as Ethan gulped down the glass of water Irvin had handed him.

"I thought you said grumplings ate *four leaf clovers*!" Ethan defended, staring at Daavic.

"I said — four leaf clovers are their favorite food," Daavic corrected, "but they like rainbow hoops too, especially Fish Gut & Snail."

Again, the table roared with laughter at Ethan's expense.

Moments later, breakfast was served.

"I can't believe it!" Haley announced. "This egg *really* does have three heart-shaped yolks!"

"Yeah — and my dessert breakfast, the Sturgis Special, beats the heck out of grumpling food!" Ethan joked. He then shot a warm look at Irvin, "It's the most delicious thing I've ever tasted Irvin."

"I can think of no better way to round out a good breakfast, than Pepper on the piano," Alexander said.

"Pepper on the piano —" Ethan repeated with a confused look on his face.

Suddenly, the piano at the edge of the dining area began to play. At first, it looked as if it was playing itself, but then a small almost invisible figure became visible sitting on the piano bench.

Ethan's gaze quickly met Haley's, as it became apparent that this song was familiar to both of them. It was the song Haley had been humming in her room the night before.

"Who's playing that — ?" Haley asked loudly, jumping out of her chair and walking towards the piano.

Curiosity had gotten the best of her.

"How do you know that song?" she asked.

The music abruptly stopped, as the small transparent creature jumped from the piano bench and bolted out the door to The Hall of Doorways.

Haley turned to Daavic with a sad look on her face, "Why did he stop? Where did he go?"

"Your sudden moves must have frightened him. Pepper is a very sensitive creature and for good reason — Pepper is — or I should say was — a taletaddler. He was abducted by the Grimleavers . . . they experimented on him for months before we finally found and rescued him."

"But didn't you say taletaddlers are invisible to all but the child they befriend?" Haley asked.

"Yes, I did," Daavic replied. "It was a bold move by the Grimleavers. It is very difficult to abduct something you cannot see. So the Grimleavers used Pepper's child friend as bait. They set a trap, forcing the child to tell them where Pepper was. The poor child was so frightened by their monster like appearance; he would have done anything they asked."

"What happened to the child," Ethan asked.

"In the end, the child's parents were killed and the child was left for dead," Daavic continued. "He was so traumatized by the ordeal that a Caretaker couple took him in. He lived among us for quite some time, until it was deemed safe to return him to the human world."

"What did you mean when you said, 'Pepper was a taletaddler'?" Ethan asked.

"The Grimleavers used their powers to transform Pepper into something they could use against us," Daavic continued, "an invisible monster we could not detect, but they were unsuccessful. No matter how hard they tried, they could not devolve the taletaddler into something evil. Taletaddlers are extremely resilient creatures. Yet in the end, when they were done — Pepper had been transformed — Pepper was no longer a taletaddler."

"What would an evil taletaddler do anyway — go around telling children to write *Stephen King* novels?" Ethan joked.

"ETHAN! It's not something to joke about!" Haley scolded.

"I'm sorry —" Ethan immediately apologized, his voice trailing off into silence.

"Anyway — enough storytelling — I think it's time to get on with the day we have planned," Daavic interrupted the uncomfortable moment of silence. "Irvin, please see our guests to the Front Room. Make yourselves at home — I will be along shortly to introduce you to Mrs. Moongarden."

CONFRONTATION

"Shnickyrooners and things like that," Irvin jabbered as they walked down The Hall of Doorways. "You ever notice that wherever you find winged skunk rats playing in the muddy popsicle drippings of fresh beetle dung there is always a piece of white pound cake dancing with a smelly old weasel troll?"

"I've never noticed that before Irvin, but that can't be a coincidence," Ethan replied, much to his delight.

"Here we are! The zeroth door on the left," Irvin said, opening the door. "Master Daavic will be along shortly."

"*They're coming for you — they are going to eat poor Pepper alive!*" the chants rang out as Ethan and Haley entered the Front Room.

Looking across the room as the scene unfolded, it was immediately obvious that RGB were up to no good again. But this time they had help. A teen-aged boy and girl with a brutish four-legged pet were yelling at RGB, egging them on. They were encouraging RGB to attack Pepper — encouraging them to be bad.

"Oh! No! —" Albert yelled, "a burning *fire-jay*!"

His forked tail slowly rose into the air above his head; a red fireball began to form between the prongs. Then, in an instant, the fireball shot out from the end of his tail and quickly transformed into a flaming red bird. The fire-jay began zipping around the room, swooping down at Pepper, as it screeched a menacing screech."

"And a swarm of horned *blugoats*!" Newton added, shooting a blue fireball from the end of his tail.

This one exploded into a swarm of tiny blue-winged goats.

"And don't forget about the *greenie meanie*!" Linus joined in, shooting a green fireball from his tail.

It turned into a large flaming green head. The greenie meanie resembled something out of a *Ghostbusters* movie, but this one had a very mean face and immediately began floating around the room, directing obscenities at Pepper.

"STOP IT — STOP IT THIS INSTANT!" Haley shouted angrily, breaking up the onslaught.

Startled, RGB and the teen-aged troublemakers turned to face their confronters — the three flaming apparitions quickly vanished in a puff of smoke.

"WHAT'S GOING ON HERE?" an angry Gruggins erupted, emerging from his box. "Who is disturbing my glorious sleep?"

Gruggins turned and directed his anger at RGB.

"What *mischief* are you up to now? *Teasing Pepper again*! I warned the three of you last time, *didn't I*? If you ever did this again, I would think up a very bad punishment!"

"Yes — master Gruggins, we remember — we are very sorry to have awakened your grumpness," a frightened Linus replied.

Newton and Albert nodded in agreement.

"Well if it does," Haley cut in, "I will personally make sure you all spend the night locked up with a box full of firelyte capsules!"

"No! Not firelyte capsules!" RGB cried out as they quickly joined hands and started up the staircase, "please — please — please, not firelyte capsules! We're allergic to firelytes . . ."

Their voices grew faint as they disappeared up the staircase.

"Well done," Gruggins congratulated Haley with a wink.

Gruggins turned his attention to the instigators.

"Blair Trabblemore," he continued, "I should have guessed you were behind this. Trouble seems to follow you and your boyfriend around. Take your *pet monster* and leave this room *immediately*! And I don't want to see you bothering Pepper again!"

Blair Trabblemore was of normal build for a girl her age, but that's where normal stopped. She wore a uniform of red and black fabric that wrapped around her body, arms, and legs like interwoven serpents. Her hair matched her wardrobe, crimson red strands braided with black. She had a pointed nose and chin, with eyebrows that curved upwards, over her dark brown eyes — she was a wicked looking young girl.

Blair Trabblemore was the original mean girl!

"NEVER YOU MIND — *grumpling*!" Blair exploded. "Caden and I were leaving anyway! But not because we're afraid of you! Malik hates the stench of humans!"

Blair directed her stare at Ethan and Haley.

Blair's boyfriend was Caden Stanley; a tall Nordic looking boy with blond hair, blue eyes, and high cheekbones. He towered over Ethan who was actually quite tall for his age. He was a good looking boy, but despite his good looks, there was something off about him — something sadistic — and that was what attracted Blair.

Caden's pet monster was not really a monster at all. Malik was a brutehound, a thick muscular dog like reptilian with stubby legs. He strongly resembled a pre-historic bulldog with razor sharp teeth.

"Step aside —" Caden said, purposely bumping into Ethan as they passed on their way to The Hall of Doorways.

Seconds later, Blair, Caden, and Malik exited the room.

"Who were those charming people?" Ethan asked sarcastically.

"Blair is the daughter of Roman and Silvia Trabblemore," Gruggins replied. "The Trabblemore family was once the headmasters of the Caretakers. But Roman's father, Gaylord, disgraced the privilege of his position. That was when the Council removed the Trabblemore's and replaced them with the Ravenwood family. A much better choice, if I don't say so myself."

"What Council are you talking about?" Ethan asked.

"There I go again, opening my big mouth," Gruggins replied. "Never mind nosey, I've said too much already. Are all humans as nosey as this one?"

The moment of awkward silence was suddenly broken by a whimpering sound coming from beneath the bench.

"Looks like our work here is not done," Gruggins said, pointing at the bench.

Ethan and Haley could barely make out the shape of a nearly transparent Pepper, curled up in a ball. He was cowering beneath the bench.

"It's okay — nobody is going to hurt you," Haley said softly as she approached the bench. "I'm sorry I frightened you in the Breakfast Room. It was beautiful music you were playing —"

"It's not working," Ethan interrupted.

Haley's hand quickly shot out to silence him.

"The song you were playing, I know it from somewhere," she began to hum the tune, "hmm-hmm hmm hmm-hmm . . ."

"It's working," Gruggins whispered.

A certain calm filled the air as Pepper began to unravel from the fetal position. He slowly emerged from beneath the bench and rose to his feet.

"Pepper, this is Haley," Gruggins introduced, "and this is Ethan Fox — they are the human visitors I'm sure you've heard about."

Closer up, they could see that Pepper wasn't completely transparent. Tiny black specks swirled around within the form of his body — it looked like flakes of pepper floating inside a molded body of clear *Jell-O*.

"Pepper cannot speak," Gruggins explained, "but he can communicate by manipulating the crystals within his body."

"Is that what those black specs are?" Haley asked.

Some of the specs began to move, arranging themselves into a word on Pepper's chest.

"Yes," Pepper replied.

There was a pause. Then —

The word quickly dispersed as a sentence took its place, "The black diamond crystals within my body are my only means of communication. Thank you Haley, thank you for rescuing me."

Standing this close, they could see that some of the black specs had arranged themselves into vague facial features on Pepper's head — Pepper was smiling.

"Hello, Ethan Fox — I am delighted to meet you as well," Pepper said, turning towards Ethan and politely extending his hand.

Pepper's hand felt like firm *Jell-O* as Ethan gently shook his fragile hand. It was like he was shaking the hand of a large peppered *gummy bear*.

"Hello Pepper, I'm happy to be meeting you as well," Ethan smiled.

"Humans might have some redeeming qualities after all," Gruggins mumbled, turning to Haley. "Good day, my dear child, it's off to quieter sleeping quarters for me. I have a nap to catch up on."

Gruggins bowed goodbye, then quickly popped up into the air, and fluttered towards The Hall of Doorways. The door mysteriously opened itself, allowing him to continue into the hallway undisturbed.

"I guess a backhanded compliment is as good as I can expect out of him," Ethan chuckled.

"Grumplings are quite grumpy at times, but Gruggins has a kind heart," Pepper explained. "He watches out for me and has been a very good friend."

"You've made friends with Pepper, I can see," Daavic said upon entering the room. "Time to say your goodbyes for now — I've spoken to Mrs. Moongarden, she will be more than happy to show you her life's work."

"Goodbye Pepper," Haley said, giving her new friend a gentle hug.

"Bye Pepper, I hope to hear more of your piano playing," Ethan added.

As they started towards the door, Ethan noticed that something in the Front Room had changed. The giant mirror was against a different wall, the one to the left of the door to The Hall of Doorways.

"Wasn't this mirror over there before?" Ethan asked, pointing at the empty space next to the chest of drawers.

"Yes it was — and it's been here — and over there — and over there," Daavic replied as he pointed around the room. "It just can't seem to make up its mind."

"Make up its mind — ?" Haley looked puzzled.

"Well — we've never moved it," Daavic explained, "nor has anyone ever seen it move — yet it moves just the same. It just can't decide where it wants to be."

As they made their way down The Hall of Doorways, Ethan was pleasantly surprised when Haley gently held his hand as they walked. The Hall of Doorways creeped her out as much as it did him.

"Just a little further to the Moongarden," Daavic said as they continued down the creepy hallway, "doors twenty-one and twenty-two on the right."

A moment later —

"Here we are!" Daavic announced, opening the huge double doors.

Looking inside, they could instantly see that this wasn't a room at all. It was an outdoor area with scattered clouds in the otherwise blue sky above. It looked like an organized tropical forest with dirt walkways and white picket fences dividing the various species of plant life.

"Breathtaking!" Haley said excitedly. "I've never seen so many colors in my life!"

"Pleased you like it — simply tickled," a silly sounding voice spoke up from behind a row of colorful shrubs. "Tending to troubled butterfly shrubs all day has certainly put a bee in my bonnet!"

Ethan and Haley walked into the Moongarden, following Daavic.

Ethan began carefully studying the colorful shrubs; they were covered with multi-toned green leaves of various shapes and sizes. But what really drew his eye, were the brilliantly colored butterfly shaped flowers that opened and closed — like a butterfly ready to take flight. The flowers were uniquely detailed; each one was colored differently than the next.

"There must be every color of the rainbow!" Ethan said in amazement.

"Indeed — but you'll find no rainbows here," the voice added. "The last time I allowed one in, it started a rainbow storm that lasted three days!"

"Rainbow storm —" Ethan repeated.

"Mrs. Moongarden, at your service," a woman emerged from behind the shrubs.

Mrs. Moongarden was a short pudgy woman with grey hair. She wore a colorful flowered bonnet on her head. She had rosy cheeks and a kind smile with circular lensed glasses on her round face — she looked like someone's grandmother.

"Hello, Mrs. Moongarden, I am Haley Hunt and this is Ethan Fox."

"More fun than a basket of daisies," she babbled as if talking to herself. "Human children are sure to cheer up the seedlings —"

Mrs. Moongarden sounded a bit loony.

"Now that the introductions are out of the way," Daavic interrupted. "I will leave you in the capable hands of Mrs. Moongarden. I shall return after she has shown you around."

Daavic disappeared down The Hall of Doorways.

"So — you adore my Lisa?" Mrs. Moongarden asked, looking at Ethan.

"Lisa?"

"The butterfly shrub you silly child, she told you her name was Lisa, didn't you listen?" Mrs. Moongarden chortled. "She is finicky that one, not always forthcoming. Any-who-de-do — if you like Lisa, you'll be simply tickled with what I have planned. Follow my footsteps and ask away, questions are the seeds of learning. But before we begin, I must warn you, do not wander off on your own."

A serious look suddenly crept over Mrs. Moongarden's face.

"Deadly things lurk where children wander freely, stick with old Moon-shoes and you'll be safe."

Moon-shoes was obviously a nickname she had made for herself.

"Follow me —" she said, as she started down a dirt walkway behind the butterfly shrubs.

Ethan felt a strange sense of déjà vu as he followed — taking in the wondrous scenery — it was like he'd been there before.

THE

MOONGARDEN

"First stop is Wendy — the withering froo," Mrs. Moongarden said as she slowed to a crawl, pointing to a gigantic colorful flower to the right of the path ahead.

"The flower of the withering froo contains forty-nine petals. It sits on seven giant shleaves that protect it from predators. The vivid blue serpentine pattern on the red petals is always separated by a thin band of black. If you ever see one, and the red and blue are touching, don't go near it! It's a dangerous impostor!"

"It must be the size of a small car — what kind of predator can eat that much?" Ethan asked, gazing at the giant flower from a distance.

"Good question — sowing those seeds already are we," Mrs. Moongarden smiled. "Do you see the yellow grape like fruit at the flower's center? Well — that happens to be the favorite food of the flying taber monkey. The froo uses the fruit to attract the taber monkey so it will be pollinated — very much like Earth's honeybees. Other creatures are attracted by the fruit as well, but unlike the taber monkey, they eat everything — flower and all. So the froo has come up with a defense."

Mrs. Moongarden paused for questions but when there were none, she went on. "I bet you're wondering why it's called a withering froo!" the excitement was evident in her voice.

"Yes — I was wondering," Haley replied.

"Ethan, would you be so kind as to pick one of those yellow fruits from the flower," Mrs. Moongarden instructed. "Go ahead, it won't bite."

Ethan slowly approached the colorful giant, but as soon as he got within ten feet, he was startled by its sudden movement.

In the blink of an eye, the leaves beneath the flower snapped shut, encasing it safely within the balled up leaves, shielding leaves — shleaves; then, the ball began to wither away as if the life were draining out of it. When the transformation was complete, it looked like a shriveled up ball of tree bark.

"Now that doesn't look very appetizing, does it?" Mrs. Moongarden chuckled.

"Is it dead?" Ethan asked, backing away from the ugly lump.

But as soon as he backed away to a safe distance, he had his answer, the green slowly returned to the giant leaves as they retreated back beneath the flower.

"And that is why it is called a withering froo!" Mrs. Moongarden concluded. "Thank you Wendy!"

As they continued down the path, Ethan's eyes were drawn to a small burning bush ahead, to the left.

"What is that?" Ethan asked, pointing at the small bush that was in flames — yet did not appear to be burning.

"Rose is a firelyte shrub," Mrs. Moongarden replied. "She stops burning every five years. When that happens, she will sprout twenty to thirty firelyte seeds, which will fall to the ground. Once the last seed has fallen, the flames return for another five years."

"We saw some firelytes in the Study," Haley said.

"You saw one example of how we use the infertile seeds of the firelyte shrub," Mrs. Moongarden corrected. "If the seeds are removed before the flames return, they are rendered infertile. Only infertile seeds become capsules and only capsules can summon a firelyte. In its normal life cycle, the flames always return, fertilizing the seeds, which sprout into new firelyte shrubs —"

"What's that smell — ?" Haley interrupted.

"Smells like bleach —" Ethan replied.

"Ozone —" Mrs. Moongarden corrected. "We're in luck, you two are in for a dilly of a treat!"

She was barely able to conceal her excitement.

"Follow me!" she said, hurrying down the walkway and taking the first right.

"The smell of ozone always precedes the dance, the dance of the trembling nomads!" Mrs. Moongarden explained, as she stopped at a fenced in group of small trees.

"Why are they fenced in like that?" Ethan asked.

"You're about to see for yourself why we have them in a pen," Mrs. Moongarden replied.

The trembling nomads were small penguin shaped trees that resembled mini-evergreens. Ranging from three to four feet tall, the trees had small arm like branches hanging at their sides. At their base, they had not one, but two small trunks which looked like little legs beneath the trees' branches.

"How cute, they look like little people," Haley observed, much to Mrs. Moongarden's delight.

"Why were they planted so randomly?" Ethan asked. "If you lined them up in rows they'd look like little soldiers — that would be cool!"

"Keep watching," Mrs. Moongarden whispered, smiling at Ethan's question.

Suddenly, the tiny trees began to tremble violently, as if shivering due to extreme cold. Then — all at once — their little arm like branches, rose up into the air as if shaking their fists at the sky. In an instant, their tiny tree trunks popped up out of the ground and the trees began running around their pen in random directions.

Ethan and Haley laughed hysterically as they watched the small trees run about the pen, bumping into each other, only to bounce off and continue in a different direction.

"They're like bumper cars!" Ethan cried out in laughter.

Then — as suddenly as they began — the nomads stopped all at once and their tiny trunks dug back into the soft ground. Happy with their new locations, their tiny arm like branches returned to their sides, and the trees sat silent.

"That was too cute," Haley said, still giggling at the dance of the trembling nomads.

"It is quite a hoot the first few times you see it," Mrs. Moongarden admitted. "As you can see, trembling nomads do not like being arranged in neat little rows," she winked.

"So what's next?" Haley asked, barely able to contain her excitement.

"Yeah — what's next? This place is awesome!" Ethan joined in Haley's enthusiasm.

"Well — I do have a few more exciting things to show you," Mrs. Moongarden answered.

She was pleased by the children's approval.

"Follow me —" she added, motioning down to a dark tunnel of plant overgrowth.

Moments later —

"Have you ever heard the story of *Jack and the Beanstalk*?" Mrs. Moongarden asked.

"Yeah — my dad used to tell me that one all the time!" Ethan replied.

They were approaching the light at the end of the plant tunnel, when Ethan began quoting a verse from the story, "*Fee, fi, fo, fum — I smell the blood of an Englishman — Be he alive or be he dead — I'll grind his bones to make my bread!*"

There was a pause. Then —

"You're not going to show us a giant with a taste for humans are you?" he joked.

"Not exactly," Mrs. Moongarden replied, as they emerged from the tunnel of foliage, "but I will show you the beanstalk!"

Mrs. Moongarden motioned towards their next stop.

When their eyes finally adjusted from the darkness of the tunnel, they were astonished by its size. It was enormous; the base of the beanstalk was several car lengths in diameter. The frame was formed from thousands of individual strands of intertwined vines — like a column of spaghetti hanging from a giant fork in the sky.

Ethan and Haley looked up into the sky to try to see where it ended.

"It disappears into the clouds —" Haley muttered.

"— just like in the story," Ethan finished.

"Well, I can assure you, no giants are going to climb down from the clouds to eat you," Mrs. Moongarden smiled.

"This is Lois — she is a skyclimber vine, named for obvious reasons. Notice how the leaves on her vines all have the same pattern?"

"Yes," Ethan and Haley replied nodding.

"Well that pattern is as unique as a fingerprint. No two skyclimber vines possess the same pattern, not that it matters for identification purposes — only a handful exist."

"In the whole universe — ?" Haley asked.

"Yes dear — this is a very rare plant indeed, an evolutionary oddity. It drops seeds only once every two hundred years, giving it almost no chance of a new one sprouting. Seven seeds are dropped from the top of the vine; each floats to the ground attached to a parachute sprout. Only if two or more seeds land within close proximity of one another, can a new vine sprout. The chances of such a thing is almost zero in the natural world, but sometimes cheating occurs and the seeds are gathered and sold as magic beans — like in the story. Once planted, the seeds grow fast and a new vine will reach the clouds within a day or two."

"Has anyone ever climbed it?" Ethan asked.

"The Ravenwood boys tried when they were young, but they were punished and told to never do it again."

"So nobody has ever been to the top?" Ethan asked again.

"Nobody from down here, but there are occasional sightings of somebody crawling around up there — it's a bit of a mystery," Mrs. Moongarden sighed.

"And that doesn't scare you?" Haley asked.

"No — my dear — fear of the unknown is a human trait," she replied. "Why would I concern myself over something I have never seen and has never threatened me?"

"Enough with all this scary talk," Mrs. Moongarden said in a lighthearted tone.

It was obvious Mrs. Moongarden was trying to change the subject, but Ethan was fine with that — something about the sky climber gave him the creeps.

Farther down the dirt path, the walkway ended at what resembled a small circular courtyard. At its center, a beautiful white fountain stood in a grassy area with six unusual looking plants around it. The grassy fountain area was surrounded by a wide brick walkway.

"Looks like a park up ahead!" Haley announced.

As they approached, the rest of the courtyard came into view. Beyond the fountain, to the right, was a larger grassy area with a white picket fence. Inside, a willow tree swayed in the breeze, partially obscuring a statue of a young woman that stood in its shade. Beyond the fountain, to the left, sat the remains of an old stone structure; part of a crumbling castle tower with a single entrance — it looked dark and creepy inside.

"I've saved the best till last — the dancing angel flowers are my personal favorite," Mrs. Moongarden said, pointing at the fountain.

The plants around the fountain looked like an ordinary variety of flower species at first glance. They had large green leaves at the bottom with long thick stems protruding up several feet.

Ethan moved in closer to examine the flowers at the top of the stems.

Actually, they didn't look like flowers at all. They looked more like dying lumps of tree bark.

"Are you sure these aren't withering froo flowers?" Ethan joked.

"I'm happy to hear you've made the connection, Ethan Fox. In fact, the dancing angel flower is a relative of the withering froo. But unlike the withering froo, it is not predators that scare the dancing angels into hiding, dancing angels only emerge under specific environmental conditions."

Mrs. Moongarden pulled her ELMO device from her pocket. "Fortunately, I control the environmental conditions within the Moongarden."

She paused, tapping at the screen.

"First — I'll give them a little water to play in," she said as a fine mist began to spray from the fountain.

"Next — we simulate their favored conditions," she continued, tapping away at the screen.

"Midnight —" she said as day quickly turned to night before their eyes.

"By the light of a silvery moon," she sang with a final tap of the screen.

Suddenly the soft silvery light of the moon lit the night's sky.

"And now — we wait," she whispered.

"Reminds me of camping trips with my dad," Ethan whispered to Haley.

The sound of crickets chirping filled the night air.

The lumps at the ends of the flower stems suddenly began to move, changing shape as if standing at attention. Delicate wings began to take form, as the lumps slowly unraveled into the form of oddly shaped butterflies. Within moments, all of the stems were budding with activity; on each stood a delicate butterfly like creature exercising its wings — they were getting ready for takeoff.

Next, the brownish grey color of their wings began to disappear; a brilliant yellow glow quickly replaced the dull colors. As they completed their color transformation, the glow became more intense, as if they were being illuminated from an internal light source. Then — one by one — the dancing angels began to take off into the night's sky, their transformation complete, the dance had begun.

Ethan and Haley were almost hypnotized by the spectacle.

The dancing angels no longer resembled butterflies, they were much more graceful. There was fluidity to their motion, like jellyfish swimming in water, only different. It was as if their bodies were changing form as they swiftly danced above the mist from the fountain.

As the dance proceeded, Ethan noticed something; the light illuminating their bodies was casting a circular glow over them where their heads might be. "They have halos — that's why they're called dancing angels," Ethan whispered, proud of his discovery.

"Very good — a dozen candied foxtails for you, but keep watching — the best is yet to come!"

Slowly the angels moved into a circular formation above the mist of water, they were moving in synchronicity. They kept this going for a while until suddenly; one of the angels broke away from the circle, swooped down into the mist of water and illuminated it from within — like a bird in a cage.

Ethan quickly noticed, as the angel danced around in its watery cage, something spectacular was happening.

As the mist of water droplets came into contact with the angel's body, they began to sparkle, bouncing off and falling to the ground in a shimmering cascade of gold dust.

"Pixie dust," Haley said, holding her hand out to catch some beneath the fountain.

"Gold dust," Ethan corrected, looking at the shiny specks in her hand.

"Dancing angels do attract their share of leprechauns," Mrs. Moongarden smiled.

Ethan continued watching as the caged angel swiftly left the watery mist to rejoin formation above the fountain.

The dance continued for some time. One by one, the angels took turns dancing in the water, each one showering a rain of gold dust into the fountain until it was overflowing onto the surrounding grass. By the time the dance was finished, the ground around the fountain looked like it was covered in golden snow. The dance ended as the last angel rejoined the circle formation, and then they swiftly returned to their stems and withered back into ugly lumps.

"That was awesome — don't you think?" Ethan asked, turning towards Haley.

But Haley was not there.

"She couldn't have lost interest in this — ?" he wondered.

"NO HALEY! NO!" Mrs. Moongarden screamed.

Ethan turned to see what was wrong.

Haley was near the white picket fence, kneeling down next to a vine that poked out from beneath the fence. She was holding a small colorful ball about the size of a golf ball.

Ethan watched as Mrs. Moongarden quickly ran at Haley as she began to rise. Haley had a wide sadistic grin on her face. He could tell something was wrong with her; it was like she was in a trance.

Mrs. Moongarden reached her just before she could put the ball into her mouth, and in one swift motion swatted the ball from Haley's hand. Another quick slap across her face seemed to break her from the trance.

"W-w-what happened — ?" Haley asked, confused as to what had just happened.

"You were in a trance or something," Ethan replied, rushing over to her side.

"You *almost* ate the fruit of the petrified wood berry vine!" Mrs. Moongarden snapped, panic-stricken.

Mrs. Moongarden was distraught.

"I-I-I'm sure I removed all the fruit yesterday . . . and pruned back the vines . . . I-I don't k-k-know how this could have happened. . . ." she rambled, blaming herself.

"What would have happened if she ate it?" Ethan asked.

"The same thing that happened to dear Pandora over there," she replied, pointing at the statue under the tree.

As Ethan studied the statue, he could see that it was much more than just a statue. It was a wooden carving of a young woman holding an open box; she had the same sadistic grin on her face that Haley had just minutes ago. Leafy vines protruded from the statue's base, in all directions, each ending in a nest in which the fruit would normally sit. But it was more than that he figured out, Pandora was the vine, she had been petrified and transformed into a plant. He shivered as he came to realize what had almost happened to Haley.

"So she was a real live person?" Ethan asked.

"Her name was Pandora," Mrs. Moongarden continued, still distressed, "she stumbled upon a petrified wood berry in a box . . . she was snooping where she should not have been."

There was a moment of silence. Then —

Mrs. Moongarden snapped out of her hysterics as she went on. "A petrified wood berry is so uniquely colorful that most species cannot resist the urge to touch it. Once touched, it releases an enzyme that causes the urge to eat it. The urge is so overwhelming that the anticipation quickly causes a powerful euphoria, slipping the victim into a trance. It's only a matter of time before the victim consumes the fruit, immobilizing them where they stand. The victim turns to wood, petrifies, and soon begins to sprout new vines. The whole process only takes a couple of hours — it really is quite miraculous."

"So tell me, Ethan —" Mrs. Moongarden now sounded serious, "did you see where the fruit landed when I swatted it from Haley's hand? I *must* track it down before someone else stumbles upon it."

"Is this what you are looking for?" Daavic's voice called out as he emerged from the dark tunnel of foliage.

As he walked towards them, it became apparent that he was holding the colorful fruit in a gloved hand.

"Mrs. Moongarden — I trust such a *careless* and *dangerous* oversight will not happen again!" Daavic scolded, tossing the deadly fruit into the fenced in area well out of reach.

"Master Daavic — I assure you — I have no idea how this happened, I took every precaution," Mrs. Moongarden apologized profusely.

"Well — obviously not quite enough."

"I'm so-so sorry sir, I can't imagine —" Mrs. Moongarden continued, pausing for a moment. "It's fortunate, you showed up to find it — with gloves no less. . . ." her voice trailed off.

Mrs. Moongarden turned towards the children.

"I hope you enjoyed our little tour," she changed the subject. "Too bad it ended with such sour apples — please drop by anytime. I will definitely get to the bottom of this," she finished, glaring back at Daavic.

"I had a wonderful time," Haley said, walking over to give Mrs. Moongarden a hug.

"Me too, I definitely want to come back and see more," Ethan added. Following Haley's lead, he too, walked over and gave Mrs. Moongarden a hug.

"You are excused Mrs. Moongarden — I have one more thing to show the children — your services are no longer required," Daavic coldly dismissed her.

Mrs. Moongarden choked back tears, as she hurried down the dark path Daavic had emerged from just moments before.

THE SECRET
WISHING WELL

"Okay, now that we're finally alone, can I let you two in on a little secret?" Daavic asked. "Actually, a very big secret — it's something I've never told a soul — so you better be sure you're up to keeping it."

Ethan and Haley looked at each other in agreement. Their curiosity was getting the best of them. They both nodded an affirmative yes.

"Great — I had hoped to pique your interest — you are in for a treat of spirit and mind!" Daavic said excitedly. "Not even Mrs. Moongarden knows all of the secrets of the Moongarden."

"Many, many years ago, when we were nearly your age, my brother and I would play in the Moongarden. There came a time, when we decided that we had explored everything — we had become bored. Until one day, my brother had an idea, let's climb the sky climber."

Ethan and Haley gasped as they both looked up into the sky at the mammoth vines. They were enthralled by his story.

"We didn't get far — we were only a hundred feet up before Mrs. Moongarden caught us. She was livid, yelling up at us. She was going to fetch our parents; we would be punished to the fullest. We quickly climbed down before she could return with our parents. We hid out in the ruins of the old stone tower."

Daavic paused pointing at the nearby ruins.

"It was the obvious place to hide, nobody ever ventured into the ruins because of the stories. . . ."

Ethan and Haley's eyes followed Daavic's hand. They were hanging on his every word.

"Stories — ?" Haley sounded frightened.

"Old tales that the ruins are haunted," Daavic replied. "Many claim to have heard voices coming from the ruins, but that day my brother and I didn't even consider the old tales. We must have hidden out for an hour before we started poking around inside, and that's when we discovered it — a secret hidden wishing well. Very clever how it was hidden actually, it's right here in plain sight."

Daavic motioned around the fountain area.

Ethan and Haley scanned the area; they were perplexed by his story.

"Right here in plain sight —" Haley repeated, "that sounds like a riddle."

"You sound skeptical — well I had hoped you would want to see for yourself," he said.

"Yes we do," Ethan quickly said.

"Follow me —" he smiled, "I can assure you — there are no ghosts inside."

Daavic started towards the stone ruins.

The circular structure was obviously part of a tall tower constructed a long time ago — it looked like the first few floors of a thirty story high rise. The top was uneven, as stones had crumbled away; yet it was flat enough to give the impression that there might be some sort of platform up there. As they entered the dark interior, it took a moment for their eyes to adjust; the room was very dimly lit, light from the entrance and a few missing stones barely penetrated into the interior.

"As you can see — it's very dark in here," Daavic continued. "So naturally, after an hour hiding away, my brother and I began to get a bit spooked. We began prying at the stones on the walls to see if any would come loose and let more light in — and that's when I found this!"

Daavic pulled a stone from the back wall of the structure. A pink glow suddenly began to emanate from the small cubby hole he had exposed in the wall. He reached in and pried a small oddly shaped rock from within it. Embedded into each side of the rock were initials, carved from a glow-in-the-dark pearly pink material — a "D" on one side and a "V" on the other.

"We were quite surprised to find this," Daavic said, holding the rock out so Ethan and Haley could see it clearly.

"So what would you imagine we did next?" he teased.

"I don't know . . ." Ethan and Haley said at the same time.

It was like they were in a trance together, staring at the mysterious rock.

"Look at the irregular shape — where would you imagine it goes?" Daavic hinted.

It suddenly dawned on Ethan; he had seen this shape before, when they entered the dark room. It was the same shape as one of the holes in the wall where a stone was missing.

"It goes there!" Ethan said excitedly, pointing at the hole in the wall where a small column of light peaked into the room.

"Very good," Daavic congratulated, handing Ethan the rock. "Here — you do the honors."

Ethan wasted no time making his way to the hole in the stone wall. It only took one try; the rock was a perfect fit as he slid it into place.

Then something strange happened — the rock and stones around it began to change: first merging together, flattening out into a smooth square panel embedded in the stone wall; then a pattern of five, evenly spaced concentric circles, etched themselves out exposing a pink glow beneath the black panel; and finally, more etching as glowing pink symbols began to appear evenly spaced within the circular bands. When the transformation was completed, it looked like a glow-in-the-dark pink dartboard with symbols instead of numbers.

"What is it?" Haley asked.

"Some sort of selection dial — or lock of some kind — we never were quite sure."

"Do you know what those symbols mean?" Ethan asked.

125

"No — they are part of an ancient language only understood by a select few. We only tried a few combinations before we hit pay dirt."

Daavic walked to the panel and began spinning the dials, lining the symbols up in a specific combination. When he finished with the final dial, the pink symbols began to blink, and then something else strange happened. They could now see the entire room clearly and it seemed to have changed. But it was odd, the room had not gotten any brighter, it was more like they could suddenly see in the dark.

"I can see all of a sudden," Haley said.

"Me too," Ethan followed.

"Dark light — my brother, Damien, used to call it."

Daavic smiled, he apparently had some fond memories of his brother.

The oddities did not stop with the new lighting scheme; however, the room had changed too. A staircase was now clearly visible, spiraling up the inner walls of the silo structure, and disappearing into the darkness.

"Those stairs weren't there before," Ethan pointed out. "Where do they lead — ?"

"Let's find out — shall we?"

Daavic motioned towards the foot of the staircase.

There was no railing, so they ascended up the narrow stone steps slowly. The dark light seemed to follow, keeping things lit all the way up. When they reached the top of the stairs, they found themselves standing at the end of a long dark tunnel. The dark light did not work here, all that was visible was the bright light at the end of the tunnel, and it looked like daylight. The creepiness of the tunnel helped to speed their progress down its long dark walkway and soon they were emerging into daylight.

"What the —" Ethan rubbed his eyes as they adjusted.

"How did we end up here?" Haley cut him off.

They were back in the circular courtyard area; it was as if they had just stepped back out the entrance to the stone ruins. It was exactly the same, except for two things: the fountain was no longer at the center of the courtyard, it had been replaced by a magical wishing well; and the ruins were gone.

"I present to you — the secret wishing well," he motioned.

Ethan and Haley quickly ran over for a closer look with Daavic following closely behind them.

The wishing well was marvelously crafted; it looked as if it had been carved from a single giant chunk of pink pearl. Solid gold trim and an exquisite assortment of inlayed black diamonds decorated the pearly pink shell adding detail to its brilliant craftsmanship. The pearly pink shine glimmered in the sun and from some angles even throwing out cold bluish hues.

"It's so *beautiful!*" Haley gushed.

"Yes — so it is," Daavic said, "but my brother and I found even more reasons to appreciate it — more than merely for its sheer beauty."

Daavic had walked up to the edge of the well and slowly began turning the solid gold handle of the well's crank. As the crank turned, the solid gold rope attached to it slowly began gathering on the spindle — he was pulling something up.

"No surprises here!" Daavic laughed, as a golden bucket and ladle emerged from the well attached to the end of the rope.

Ethan and Haley looked disappointed; they must have been expecting something else.

"This is the reason I've brought you here — it is my treat to you!"

But Ethan and Haley were speechless.

Daavic tried to ease their disappointment and went on. "To drink from the well is spiritual — it will enlighten your soul and strengthen your spirit! You simply must try it!"

"I don't know," Haley hesitated, "we don't really know anything about this well."

Daavic had already scooped up a ladle full of water from the bucket and had handed it to Ethan, who was more than willing to gulp down a mouthful.

"That was *very good*!" Ethan smiled wide. "I mean — it was *great* — here Haley, you have to try it — I did!"

He had already refilled the ladle from the bucket and was holding it out to her; in fact, he was almost insisting.

Haley reluctantly took the ladle from him and slowly began sipping from it. Tiny sips quickly became larger sips and soon the ladle was empty.

"You were *right* — that was *fantastic* — unlike anything I've ever had before!" Haley's smile widened like Ethan's.

Ethan and Haley, both, suddenly felt light headed as a strange sense of déjà vu overtook them. It felt just like the moment they had first met. And then the feeling subsided, giving way to a calm feeling of euphoria.

"I feel great!" Ethan announced.

"Me too — can I have another sip?" she asked.

"Oh — no — my dear," Daavic smiled.

He was lowering the bucket back down into the well when he paused to explain, "Always remember, too much of a good thing is most often not a good thing, and so it is with the powers of this well. Besides, I think we've stayed in the Moongarden's secret room long enough, we don't want people to start hearing voices."

Daavic laughed.

"Moongarden's secret room —" Ethan repeated, pondering. . . . "So if someone is near the ruins when we are in here, they could hear our voices?"

"Muffled voices — my brother and I ran some experiments. It's a perfect explanation for the stories of the haunted ruins."

"If we're in a secret room — then how do we get out?" Haley asked. "We came in over there," she pointed to where the ruins used to be.

"Simple — my dear — step outside the circle."

Daavic walked towards the dirt path at the edge of the circular courtyard. As he reached the edge of the brick walkway, he turned to Ethan and Haley, smiled, took a step backwards, and vanished into thin air.

"Where did he go?" Haley looked surprised.

"He stepped outside the circle! Let's go!" Ethan motioned for Haley to follow him.

Following Daavic's footsteps, Ethan and Haley made their way to the outer edge of the circular brick walkway.

Haley was eager to exit the secret room and quickly hopped out of the circle, disappearing as Daavic had.

Ethan turned around for one last look and was startled by a sudden sound.

"Mmmmmmm grrrrrrrrrr sllllllllll," the soft muted voice was unintelligible.

It sounded like it was coming from the direction of the wishing well.

"I must be hearing things," he said to himself.

Officially creeped out, he quickly jumped outside the circle, joining Daavic and Haley.

AN OCEAN

OF TROUBLES

After their tour of the Moongarden, Daavic escorted Ethan and Haley back to the Map Room for another meeting with Jordanna. She evidently had questions, hopefully something to shed light on what the Grimleavers would want with Ethan.

As they strode over the invisible floor, for the second time, Ethan treaded softly. He was obviously worried about falling through; it was a long way down. But walking in mid-air did not seem to bother Haley, she made her way eagerly. She was adjusting to life at The Residence much quicker than him.

"Please — have a seat," Jordanna greeted as they reached the crow's nest at the top of the stairs.

"I take it your time with Mrs. Moongarden was pleasant?" she asked, as Ethan and Haley sat beside her.

"It was great — the trembling nomads were my favorite," Haley replied.

"Danielle loved the nomads as well, the similarities you share with her run deep — I wonder . . ." Jordanna said, reaching into her robe to retrieve her ELMO device.

But they were quickly interrupted by a sudden burst of noise. Alarms were sounding as the Map Room came to life.

The lighting dimmed as Jordanna eased back in her chair, advising Ethan and Haley to do the same.

Soon the crow's nest had again vanished into thin air, and a detailed map of the globe enveloped the room. This time, there were two bright red dots flashing on the globes surface — something was happening.

"Tell us what we're looking at," Jordanna commanded to no one in particular.

"Troubles in the world's oceans headmistress — the Pacific to be specific," a cold calm male voice answered.

Ethan and Haley were witnessing the Caretakers in action.

It was evident who Jordanna was talking to, the Map Room itself. The Map Room was some sort of powerful computer or intelligence that was connected to and aware of everything on Earth. The sophistication of such a thing was mind boggling.

"Get me in contact with Fin, they must be aware of this at Poseidon," Jordanna ordered.

"Certainly headmistress," the voice replied.

Suddenly, an image popped up in mid-air in front of them; it was a large holographic 3D window into a control room of some kind. A strange creature in the room was looking down at charts spread out on a table in front of him. He looked up and began to speak.

"Fin Drenchler reporting headmistress — we've been expecting your call. Very disturbing events have transpired. The human world is aware and alarmed, as they should be."

Fin looked like a colorful amphibious humanoid. Large orange eyes, on a deep blue frogish face with fish-lips, and protruding finlike ears. He had long and wide webbed hands and his smooth shiny skin looked wet.

"So what have we got?" Jordanna asked Fin to elaborate.

"First we have this," Fin waved his hand as a new window popped up in front of them; this one showed a live television feed of a human news channel.

"Early this morning, Washington beach goers were *shocked* and *amazed* by what they discovered on this beach behind me," the reporter began. "A pod of dead killer whales washed ashore during the night, but the story only begins there," the reporter teased. "As the morning has unfolded, the death toll has been climbing, as whales continue to wash ashore — one hundred eleven at last count — a super-pod of orcas. But it's not the large death toll that has the experts baffled — it's the *strange* and *mysterious* way in which these animals died — some of them apparently bitten in half. You heard that right — killer whales — the apex predator of the ocean — did battle with *something* — and lost. It's no wonder why locals here are beginning to talk of *sea monsters!*"

Jordanna gasped at the gruesome scene, as the news camera panned down the long stretch of beach. As far as the eye could see, mangled orca corpses littered the beach; many with deep wounds where large chunks of flesh had been ripped from their bodies. Jordanna was visibly disturbed by this news.

"Judging by the look on your face, it appears you've come to the same conclusion as we have," Fin began. "I suggest a face to face meeting with your team to discuss a plan of action. We have reason to suspect Grimleaver involvement, but that's a matter better discussed in person, we believe they may be listening."

Fin's paranoia seemed to alarm Jordanna even more. It was the first time anyone had ever suggested the Grimleavers might be spying on the Caretakers.

"Agreed, better to err on the side of caution, so let's cut this short," Jordanna now shared Fin's paranoia. "We will send an under-party at first sun. I will contact the outpost."

"Perfect headmistress, but I have one more item to discuss, a special request if I may be so bold."

"Which is?"

"I would like Ethan Fox and the girl to accompany the under-party to Poseidon. I believe it very important that they make the journey as well."

Fin's request was cryptic and against protocol, but Jordanna trusted him immensely.

"Very well — I will make the arrangements."

The holographic windows disappeared as the line of communication was broken. Jordanna wasted no time contacting the outpost.

"Get me commander Triplin, at once," she commanded.

A new holographic window popped up quickly, but this time, a pale man with a black and white Caretaker robe answered.

"Adam Triplin here, how may I serve you headmistress?"

"Has anything out of the ordinary occurred recently?"

"Well, they . . . have been hungrier than normal; we even had to catch extra fish for them yesterday. Otherwise it's been quiet as usual —"

"And all three are accounted for?" Jordanna interrupted.

"Yes headmistress, I saw them myself, less than an hour ago."

"Then we must have missed one, it's been so long, why now . . ." her voice trailed off, she was deep in thought.

"Report back immediately if anything unusual occurs," she cut it short.

"Well —" she hesitated, "it looks like you two are in for an adventure." Jordanna had an uneasy look on her face.

Ethan and Haley were awakened early the next morning and escorted to the Study where the team would assemble. Jordanna greeted them with her usual warm smile before announcing her plans to them.

"The team will consist of Daavic, Brianna, and Alexander who will be accompanied by the two of you," she began. "We will use book travel to transport our team to a secluded beach. A team of Seakeepers will join our team and escort us to Poseidon; a secret palace at the bottom of the ocean. Seakeepers are the ocean dwelling arm of the Caretakers and Poseidon is their Residence."

"What's book travel?" Haley asked after the briefing.

"Sorry — I sometimes forget you are new to our ways," Jordanna apologized for the oversight.

"Do you see all of the books in this room?" she began. "Well — they are organized in a very special way. Most of the books you see are stories or reference books — our history here on Earth. But do you notice one bookcase in particular that stands out amongst the rest?"

"That one — !" Haley was quick to respond, pointing at the bookcase nearest the giant fireplace at the end of the room.

All of the books in that bookcase looked the same; withered old brown books with glimmering gold lettering.

Ethan quickly took notice; these books all looked just like the one his dad had hidden in the cubby hole behind his bookcase.

"What's different about those books?" Ethan asked, suddenly very interested in the conversation.

"The books on those shelves are all portals," Jordanna replied, pulling one of the books from her robe. "Portals to special places; some imagined, some real. Today's journey will begin here," she concluded, holding up the brown book so Ethan and Haley could see the shiny golden letters:

Tunnel Beach

"Tunnel Beach," Alexander's voice read aloud as he and the rest of the team entered through the in-door. "It's been quite some time since I've journeyed to Poseidon."

"Never been myself," Daavic added, "but I've always wanted to see it. Thank you for accepting my request mother."

"Don't be foolish, you were the natural choice Daavic. Your father would have expected no less. You should cherish the experience."

Ethan and Haley had never seen Daavic and Jordanna interact before; there was a strange dynamic going on, like it was forced. They had both lost everything the day Damien had destroyed their family. One would have expected a much closer bond.

"You've already been briefed on the situation," Jordanna summarized. "Once you arrive at Tunnel Beach, Fin's team will meet up with you; from there you will follow their orders. We are traveling into their world and will respect their boundaries, so follow protocol."

"All this talk of protocol, taking humans to Poseidon breaks protocol, mother!"

Daavic seemed unhappy that Ethan and Haley were going.

"Enough Daavic — never question the headmistress' authority in my presence again!" Alexander scolded.

"Alex is right Daavic, you've overstepped —" Brianna added.

"You always were the one to question authority Daavic," Jordanna cut in.

"Yet I'm the good son, mother — Damien was your favorite — but I am the good son!" Daavic protested.

"That you are . . ." Jordanna's voice trailed off.

There was an uncomfortable moment of silence. It was obvious that Daavic's comments had hurt his mother's feelings. Tears were welling up in her eyes but she quickly gathered her emotions.

"Let's get on with it," Jordanna ordered, "join hands and form a circle around me."

Jordanna was embracing the book, holding it close to her chest, as the team joined hands around her: Ethan, Haley, Alexander, Daavic, Brianna, and back to Ethan to complete the circle.

"Now close your eyes. You will begin to feel sleepy, but that's okay. Don't fight it — just let it take you away."

Jordanna looked down and read the title of the book one last time aloud:

Tunnel Beach

She then began to open the book slowly. Bright beams of light peeked out from behind the cover as she flipped it open. Jordanna stared into the light as it shined onto her face. Suddenly, she snapped the book shut, and when the light subsided, the team was gone.

Jordanna was alone in the Study.

JOURNEY TO
POSEIDON

Ethan woke up under the shade of a small canopy of trees. The trees ran along the outer edge of a tropical rainforest that nuzzled up against a secluded beach. Haley was sitting in a smooth patch of grass nearby, staring at him as he slept.

"Finally — I thought you were never going to wake up," she joked at the first sign of him stirring.

"Where are we?" he was groggy, still feeling the effects of book travel.

"Tunnel Beach — don't you remember?" Haley suddenly sounded concerned.

Ethan struggled to his feet and quickly began studying his surroundings. The sight of Daavic, Alexander, and Brianna standing on the beach jogged his memory.

"Of course, Tunnel Beach . . . the brown book . . ."

His response put her at ease.

"Haley, do you remember what I told you about my parents — how they were acting strange?" he whispered.

"Yes, after you remembered the poem, they began acting strange, and you think they were hiding something," she whispered back.

"Well — I left something out — I forgot about the book. It looked just like Tunnel Beach and the rest of the portal books in the Study. My dad had one. He hid it in a secret cubby hole behind his bookshelf at home."

"Maybe we should tell headmistress Jordanna when we get back to The Residence, she seems trustworthy?"

"I don't know," he shrugged, "if I can't trust my own parents, I'm not sure there is anyone I can trust — except for you."

Ethan and Haley's conversation was cut short as Alexander began walking towards them. Daavic and Brianna were holding their ELMO devices up in front of them as they looked out to sea.

"They must have spotted something," Haley said as Alexander neared.

"So how's our boy, finally up?" Alexander asked, smiling at Ethan in his usual friendly manner; his calm demeanor quickly put Ethan at ease. "First time is always the hardest with book travel, but you'll get used to it. Haley here took to it like an old pro."

"Have they spotted the Seakeepers yet?" Haley asked, watching as Daavic and Brianna scanned the horizon.

"Yes — we need you at water's edge. They are on their way and will be arriving shortly."

As they walked out onto the beach, Ethan took in its beauty for the first time. It was a long, fan shaped, stretch of beach with golden brown sands that melted away into rich emerald waters. At each end of the beach, long arms of foliage covered rocks reached out into the ocean waters creating a wide cove.

"They're entering the shallows now!" Daavic announced as they reached the edge of the surf.

Ethan and Haley began scanning the waters, curiously looking for any signs of the approaching Seakeepers.

"I see something — there they are!" Ethan shouted, pointing off at the horizon.

Something had just entered the cove and was stirring up the water as it quickly approached. There were several of them, making high arching leaps out of the water, as they swam towards the Caretaker under-party. As they got closer, Ethan could clearly see what it was that was approaching.

"They're dolphins!" he shouted.

"Hydromorphs," Brianna corrected.

The small pod of five dolphins continued towards the under-party. They swam into the shallower waters near the beach, before pausing for a moment. Then, all at once, the dolphins charged forward with the surf — beaching themselves in the process. As the surf receded, the dolphins began to transform, their bodies slowly rising up off of the wet sand as they morphed into humanoid form.

"Hydromorphs are the shape-shifters of the sea," Brianna explained as Ethan and Haley watched the transformation.

They displayed an impressive array of metallic colors when the process was complete; each of the hydromorphs had adopted their own unique color scheme. Fin Drenchler was immediately recognizable; he was the deep blue one with yellowish highlights.

"Welcome — I trust your trip to Tunnel Beach was uneventful," Fin greeted the under-party as he and two of the other Seakeepers walked onto the beach.

The two that remained behind in the surf, looked like they were on alert, scanning the area. They were much larger than Fin, deep green in color, and their thick scaly armored appearance gave them a much more menacing look. These two reminded Ethan of *The Creature from the Black Lagoon* — they were obviously there for security detail.

"I'd like you to meet my wife, Lyn and our son, Gil."

Lyn was much more petite than Fin and her features less masculine. Instead of the rigid finlike ears Fin had, she had small floppy protrusions — they looked like tadpoles attached to the sides of her head. She was brilliantly colored, every color of the rainbow was represented on her body, arranged in an incredible assortment of color gradients — it looked like reef camouflage.

Gil looked like a much smaller version of Fin, except for his color scheme; white with random splotches of greens and blues with hints of gold. He was about the same age as Ethan and seemed to take an immediate liking to Haley; smiling and eyeing her in an obvious display of affection.

"The bubble should be arriving at any moment!" Fin announced.

No sooner had he said the words then a small disturbance began to emerge from the water. Many feet from shore, a hole was forming in the water; it quickly grew larger, pushing towards the beach, until finally forming two walls of water that began to part further. It was like two invisible walls were pushing the water apart, creating a sandy wet walkway to a tunnel in the water that was now clearly visible.

"I will accompany you inside," Fin said, motioning towards the tunnel. "The rest of my team will swim alongside."

"A swim sounds so refreshing — might I join them and swim along as well?" Brianna asked politely. "At least until we lose the light — I do have some amphibian traits after all."

"Feel free," Fin replied, "join us inside whenever you're comfortable."

Fin led the under-party down into the tunnel; it looked like they were entering a giant capsule of air somehow held in place under water. When they stepped inside, their feet left the wet sand of the beach and set down on a firm buoyant surface — it was like they had just stepped onto a giant waterbed.

"We'll only have to walk to the first bubble-port," Fin explained. "From there we've installed a series of depth portals. It's a fast drop off out here — so it won't be far."

As they walked along inside the capsule of air, it quietly slid along with them as they progressed deeper beneath the water's surface — they were driving the giant underwater bubble with their footsteps.

The crystal clear water surrounding the bubble allowed them to see everything; it was a beautiful underwater seascape where plant and animal life were thriving in the tropical waters. Alongside the bubble, Brianna and the Seakeepers gracefully swam along, following the protective bubble. Brianna's long snakelike body was perfectly adapted for swimming underwater; she looked like a cross between a mermaid and a giant sea snake.

The Seakeepers had transformed back into dolphin form and swam as a small pod. Except for Gil, he had transformed into a handsome human looking boy in swimming trunks; only his big webbed hands and feet gave him away as something else. He began swimming around the outside of the bubble, performing stunts in hopes of gaining Haley's attention. When Haley finally took notice, he stopped, following alongside the bubble motioning for her to come closer.

"What does he want?" Haley smiled at Gil's obvious flirtation.

As she approached him from inside, he began to blow bubbles from his nose. But instead of rising to the surface, these bubbles floated sideways in the water, and began to slowly change shape into small seahorses. The seahorse bubbles hung in the water for several seconds before dissipating into tinier bubbles that quickly headed for the surface.

"That's so cute — how does he do that?" Haley cheered; she loved his shape bubble trick.

Gil continued for several minutes, blowing shape bubbles of all sorts: fish, birds, whales, mermaids, and finally the grand finale, hearts that broke into smaller and smaller hearts.

Gil was smitten with Haley — that much was obvious.

"What's the big deal? It's just a bunch of bubbles," Ethan grunted under his breath.

Someone was getting jealous.

"Okay son — enough flirting with the young lady," Fin broke in on the fun. "We have reached the sea cliff and will be descending very quickly from here."

Gil quickly minded his father, morphing back into a dolphin and rejoining the other Seakeepers.

Brianna took this as her queue as well. Swimming up to the exterior of the bubble, she slowly pushed at the invisible wall, separating the water outside from the air within: first one arm, then the other, followed by her head, body, and tail. It was as if she were climbing out of a reverse water balloon, but not a drop of water spilled through in the process.

"Nothing like a refreshing swim," Brianna said, "but I do like to see where I am going — so I thought it best to rejoin you now."

Brianna was dripping with water, but as each drop hit the floor of the bubble capsule, it was quickly absorbed into the surrounding ocean.

As they passed the edge of the underwater cliff, the submersible bubble angled downwards, and slowly began descending into the black depths below — it was like they were walking down a steep invisible staircase. It didn't take long for darkness to come, but as the light from the surface slowly vanished, the Seakeepers began to light the way. Their bodies began to glow — a bright bluish glow — lighting the bubble from the outside in.

They continued under the guidance of the Seakeeper escorts until reaching their destination. In the darkness of the deep, it was hard to see much of anything, bioluminescence didn't account for much light. But what they could see as they got closer looked like a giant black cube hanging still in mid-water; it was much larger than the bubble they were in. The Seakeepers in the water quickly disappeared beneath the cube taking their light with them — it was now pitch black.

The bubble continued forward, straight at the cube as if on a collision course, but when the time came there was no collision. The bubble slowly melted into the black cube, opening up a hole in its side where a bright light from within lit up the scene. The bubble continued to disappear into the side of the giant cube, taking the under-party inside with it. As the last few inches of the bubble disappeared into the cube, the hole in its side closed up, leaving only the darkness of black outside.

They found themselves standing in a brightly lit room. The other Seakeepers had already made it inside and had transformed back into their humanoid form. It looked like they were in a large furnished apartment with an instrument panel at the base of one of the black walls. Even from the inside, it looked like they were in a giant box; there were no apparent doors or windows anywhere.

"Bubble ports share a dual role," Fin explained. "They are often used as remote quarters for much of my team, which is why they resemble living quarters, because they are."

Fin walked over to the instrument panel and began hitting buttons.

"From here — it is merely a series of tunnels from bubble port to bubble port," Fin continued.

The wall above the instrument panel came to life under Fin's command and a giant map of tunnels quickly appeared.

"The yellow line shows our path — only four depth portals away, but the changes in depth will be extreme. Soon we will be at Poseidon — let's get started, shall we?"

Fin punched one final button.

A large circular tunnel opened up at the base of one of the smooth black walls. The interior of the tunnel had the same look and feel as the inside of the bubble they had just arrived in. It was dimly lit by the same bluish hue the Seakeepers had cast earlier, yet there was no apparent light source.

As they began walking, the tunnel angled down at an increasingly steep angle, until it became impossible to stand. The slippery surface they were on quickly turned the tunnel into a slide; they began zipping down its steep embankment. They slid for several seconds before slowing down as the tunnel leveled off at the end; they were at the entrance to another cube shaped bubble port.

They repeated the process three more times, each time journeying deeper and deeper into the depths of the ocean abyss. As their slide down the final tunnel slowed to a crawl, things began to get brighter; the blackness outside the tunnel began to lighten to a dark green color.

Rising to their feet, the under-party and their Seakeeper escorts continued down the long tunnel; it continued to get lighter as they rounded a bend. As the tunnel straightened out, they could begin to see where the light was suddenly coming from; a huge dome of light rested on the sea floor — it looked like a giant snow-globe half buried in muck and lit from within.

"What is that — ?" Haley asked.

"Looks like a city or something . . ." Ethan replied.

"Not a city — Poseidon," Daavic whispered.

The tunnel made an abrupt right turn towards the dome of light, they were about to enter Poseidon. As their path straightened out for the last time, the under-party could finally see the light at the end of the tunnel as they continued down a long straightaway. As they reached the light, they could see that there were no walls or barriers to speak of, only a dome shaped barrier of light encompassing the environment within. It was like walking from night into day with a single step. Stepping into the light, they could see the tunnel they were in kept going; only now it was brilliantly lit — they were in a tunnel inside a giant aquarium.

"This is more colorful than the Moongarden!" Haley announced excitedly.

It was like they were back at the surface, at a tropical coral reef, only more spectacular. The water was so crystal clear, they could see as far as their eyes would allow. The fine golden sand on the ocean floor was the perfect canvas for the abundant sea life to glide above — like an artist's brush. There was an odd assortment of sea-life: giant seahorses that were nearly big enough to saddle up, schools of V-shaped rays that gracefully swam in unison, and strange sea creatures of all shapes, colors, and sizes.

"I've never seen most of these sea creatures before," Ethan whispered to Haley.

He was surprised, there were animals here he hadn't seen on the Discovery channel.

"No human has ever seen any of the creatures here," Daavic pointed out.

"Look Ethan — mermaids," Haley eagerly pointed out as a group of three gracefully swam by.

"Hydromorphs actually," Fin corrected, "that was the form we originally took when we first arrived in the Earth's oceans. But a few unfortunate human sightings convinced us we would blend in much better as porpoises —"

"How much farther to Poseidon?" Daavic interrupted.

"I thought this was Poseidon?" Haley asked, motioning at the surrounding environment.

"That's Poseidon!" Gil smiled at Haley, he was pointing upwards, down the tunnel ahead of them.

As the tunnel began to angle down at an incline, the under-party could look out through the ceiling and see what was in front of them. There it was, Poseidon, and it was more breathtaking than what they had seen already.

Sitting atop a small mountain, half embedded into its side was a shimmering pink structure, a palace carved from an enormous pink pearl that was still partially intact. It looked like the palace structure was never fully completed, but that was part of its allure as the spherical surface of the pearl abruptly ended where the palace began. It looked like someone had cracked open a giant round egg and erected a castle inside.

As they made their way down the incline, the tunnel abruptly ended at the base of a steep set of stairs, leading up the side of the mountain to the palace. It didn't take nearly as long as it looked like it might. A few short minutes later, they had arrived. At the top of the staircase, they found themselves in a foyer leading to a much larger room.

The inside of the palace was as breathtaking as the outside. Everything was sculpted from the polished pink pearl: doors, tables, chairs, staircases, and banisters; even the internal structure of the palace had been carved — the entire palace was one piece, carved to the finest detail.

They entered a large room with high ceilings and a grand staircase that fanned out at the bottom and forked at the top. Tall spiral columns decorated the interior of the room, from floor to ceiling, as if they were inside a giant seashell.

"Given the enormity of the situation — I think it wise that we get started immediately," Fin announced, excusing the rest of his team. "Please, follow me to the briefing room."

Fin motioned to the double doors to the right of the staircase. As they entered the room, it quickly became apparent that the Seakeeper briefing team was ready and waiting. They were sitting at a long pink boardroom type table that was built into the polished floor.

Fin introduced his team of two to the under-party, Brooke Troutland and Marlin Trollwell.

Brooke was petite, similar in appearance to Fin's wife, but her colors were much more girly-girl; subdued pinks and whites with brilliant magenta highlights that made it look like she wore lipstick. Brooke was the Seakeeper in charge of the Pacific Ocean detail.

Marlin was Fin's right-hand man, he coordinated all Seakeeper operations, monitored human communications, and reported everything back to Fin. Taller and thinner than the other Seakeepers, Marlin looked like a different species of hydromorph. He had longer arms and legs and much bigger webbed hands and feet. But the most obvious difference was the shape of his head, a long smooth teardrop shape that forked at its tail end.

As Ethan stood gazing at Marlin, he noticed a stark contrast in his dull grayish coloring compared to the rest of the Seakeepers. But then it dawned on him, Fin was suddenly sporting the same drab color as well.

"What has happened to your coloring?" Ethan asked, directing his question at Fin.

"Like most sea creatures, our colors fade after prolonged periods out of water, it's unavoidable," Fin explained.

The contrast was most noticeable as Fin took his place at the head of the table, next to Brooke Troutland who sat to his right.

"Let's get started," Fin ordered as they took their seats at the table.

"Over the last two days, several disturbing events have taken place in Earth's oceans," Marlin began as a large map suddenly appeared on the wall. "Even the humans are keeping some of this a secret. Brooke will share the details. . . ."

"The first event took place here," Brooke began to explain as she stood and pointed to one of the flashing red dots on the map. "Roughly a day and a half ago, a United States naval submarine went missing. They were able to send out a distress signal that we intercepted . . . alerting us to the disaster. . . . The navy has kept it a secret, but launched a clandestine search for the missing sub."

"The humans are always losing track of their naval ships," Brianna pointed out, "what's so alarming about that?"

"I'm getting to that," Brooke continued. "Fortunately, we were able to locate it quickly . . . we have cloaked it . . . the humans will never find it now. But our findings were alarming. The vessel had been attacked — pierced and shredded down the entire length of its hull — there were no survivors."

"Certainly no Earthly creature could penetrate the hull of a submarine," Alexander spoke up, he sounded concerned.

"Exactly, you are catching on to our point," Fin agreed.

"The second event began here," Brooke pointed to the second red dot. "This is where it fed on a super pod of Orca's, Earth's apex predator. The humans know something . . . terrible is lurking in their seas."

"But it can't be —" Alexander gasped.

"It can only be," Fin cut Alex off in mid-sentence. "Someone has released a kraken!"

"But that can't be — Jordanna contacted the outpost — all three pups are accounted for!" Alexander protested.

"Yet the evidence remains," Fin continued. "Only a kraken could wreak havoc like this in such a short period of time. But there's more — we've tracked it to the Mariana Trench —

we've discovered a series of tunnels it has been excavating. It appears to be searching for something."

Ethan and Haley remained quiet, afraid to ask any questions. They could sense the tension in the air as everyone remained silent, pondering what they had just learned.

"How do the Grimleavers figure into this?" Daavic broke up the silence. "You told the headmistress that you have reason to suspect Grimleaver involvement."

"Yes, that —" Fin sighed. "That involves other unfortunate events . . . and a Seakeeper secret that even the Caretakers are unaware of. Many, many years ago, back when Ryvias was headmaster, a Seakeeper named Newt Dripmore went missing."

"Dripmore . . . I recall hearing that name . . ." Daavic murmured.

Daavic stirred in his seat; he appeared visibly shaken by the mention of his father. The rest of the Caretakers listened in silence.

"I had just taken over as leader of the Seakeepers," Fin continued, "I was handpicked by Ryvias himself. Anyway — I had reason to believe foul play; either Newt had joined the Grimleavers or he had been abducted. I did not know which. So against Seakeeper protocol, I took it upon myself to share our secret with Ryvias, a secret no Seakeeper had ever shared before. But I am about to share it again with you — the blood of a hydromorph is transmorphic —"

"Transmorphic —" Brianna interrupted, "no wonder you've kept that a secret."

"What is transmorphic?" Ethan asked.

Curiosity had finally gotten the best of him.

"It means," Alexander replied, "that if the Grimleavers ever got a hold of a hydromorph — we could end up fighting an army of shape-shifting vampires —"

"Not exactly," Marlin interrupted. "It's not quite that bad, the effects are limited, and they wear off after a couple of hours. Regardless, it is still not a weapon we want the Grimleavers to add to their ever expanding arsenal."

"Exactly, which is why I chose to tell Ryvias, I trusted him immensely," Fin added. "I had a missing hydromorph — abducted or not — there was a good chance the Grimleavers might learn our secret — the Caretakers had to know as well."

"But nothing ever happened . . . we are only learning of this now . . . you still haven't answered my question, how do the Grimleavers fit in?" Daavic ranted.

"Newt Dripmore never was found," Fin began, "we still have no idea what became of him, and the Seakeeper secret died with Ryvias — so I let it stay that way. There was no reason to risk telling anyone else, until now. So to answer your question — two weeks ago, two more hydromorphs went missing, Sal and Sil Finley, they were husband and wife. They were abducted by the Grimleavers — they know our secret — there is no question in my mind now."

The map on the wall disappeared, there were no further questions, and the briefing was over. As the meeting adjourned, Ethan let out a deep yawn that quickly made its way around the table.

"Looks like today's journey has taken a lot out of you all," Marlin broke up the silence. "Understandable, depth porting can be hard on the body. You will need rest to adjust."

After a bit of small talk, Marlin explained the arrangements to the under-party, "You will be shown to your quarters where you can nap, wash up, or just relax. It is three o'clock now and dinner will be served at six o'clock sharp."

Marlin then began ushering everyone out of the briefing room.

"Ethan Fox — could I have a private word with you?" Fin asked, waving him back in.

"I don't think that's such a good idea!" Daavic protested.

"I assure you, I've cleared it with the headmistress," Fin insisted.

"Very well," Daavic backed down as Alexander and Brianna glared at him.

Fin's talk with Ethan lasted only fifteen minutes. Afterwards Fin directed him to his quarters. Up the staircase and to the left, the door would be labeled Ethan Fox — the Seakeepers had kept it simple.

As Ethan arrived at his quarters, he was surprised to see Daavic arriving at his, too; he was coming down the hallway from the opposite direction. They exchanged a quick glance before entering their respective rooms.

This time, Ethan wasn't so surprised to see an exact replica of his bedroom at home, but now he had a waterbed! It didn't take long for him to notice that this room had an ELMO device as well, he could talk with Haley.

"So what did Fin want?" Haley asked as soon as she heard his voice. "Why did he want to talk to you alone?"

"I-I'm sorry Haley, I can't talk about it —" Ethan tried to explain.

"Fine —" she interrupted, "I'll see you at dinner — Gil's going to show me around — at least he'll talk to me!"

Haley's reply was followed by the sound of her door shutting, she had left her room.

The rest of the night was uneventful, dinner was short and quiet; the under-party was extremely exhausted. Marlin was right, depth porting did take a lot out of the body, and tomorrow they would do it all again, in reverse — they would be returning to The Residence.

A DAMIEN
SIGHTING

The next morning, following their return to The Residence, Ethan was awakened by the sound of Haley's voice.

"Ethan — are you awake? Wake up Ethan — Ethan wake up!" she pleaded.

"I am now," Ethan sat up to shake his grogginess.

"We've been invited to the Moongarden — a note was slipped under my door. Did you get one?"

He looked to the floor beneath his door and saw a green leaf folded up into an envelope. He unfolded the leaf and pulled a piece of parchment from inside, it read:

You are hereby cordially invited to bear witness to the uniting of two in the joys of matrimony. Percy, the Pear tree has asked for the branch of Alicia, the Apple tree. They are to be wed at a time yet to be determined.

Preparations are underway, and Moon-shoes requests the assistance of two able-bodied human children. If Ethan Fox and Haley Hunt are so inclined, would you please report to the Moongarden ASAYGT — Doors 21 & 22 on the right, no escort necessary.

"A pear tree is going to marry an apple tree! Oh boy, Mrs. Moongarden is a whack-a-doodle. I wonder what ASAYGT means — ?" Ethan puzzled after reading the note.

"As Soon As You Get This — I think . . ." Haley replied.

"How do you know — ?"

"I'm not sure . . . I just do," she said, sounding sure of herself.

Ethan quickly threw on some clothes and met Haley outside her room in The Hall of Doorways. He knew she would not be happy if he kept her waiting in the creepy hallway.

They quickly made their way down The Hall of Doorways to the Moongarden where they were greeted by a small garden gnome as they entered.

"You must be the human children," the small dwarf said. "My name is Grubner Trowel — I'm one of Moon-shoes' seven little helpers, happy to make your acquaintance. Come, right this way, she has been expecting you."

Ethan and Haley followed the foot tall dwarf into the Moongarden; he looked like one of *Snow White's* seven little friends. He led them down a pathway to the right and through a row of tall bushes where they came to a clearing. Mrs.

Moongarden was there, she was in a small meadow busy doing something under the shade of a tall apple tree.

"Wonderful! I knew I could count on the two of you," Mrs. Moongarden greeted. "But I'm afraid you've sprouted a bit early. Irvin was not supposed to deliver the invitations for another hour — naughty boy that Irvin."

As Ethan and Haley got closer, they could finally see what Mrs. Moongarden was up to. She was ironing, hundreds of small *Barbie doll* sized wedding dresses. To the side of the table sat a large bin full of tiny ruffled white dresses. One by one, she was spreading them out on the table and ironing the wrinkles out of them.

"I've yet to press them all — but a sneak peak can't hurt," Mrs. Moongarden smiled.

She unzipped one of the dresses she had pressed. She then stepped onto a small ladder where she reached up into the apple tree and slid the tiny dress over one of the apples.

"The real work will come after I've pressed the dresses — but you can see why I need help with the fittings," she said.

"We'd love to help," Haley smiled at Mrs. Moongarden as she secretly nudged Ethan in the ribs with her elbow.

"I'm afraid it will be some time before I am ready for you. But I've sent for Irvin, maybe you'd like to accompany him to the market. He'll be running errands for old Moon-shoes."

"Shnickyrooners and things like that," Irvin began his familiar rant as he stepped out from behind the bushes. "Butterfly trolls always meet their doom on the bald head of a flaming water hippo, and they never even get to lick the rosy lizard dew from the field of dripping rock monkeys."

"Yeah, I saw that on the Discovery channel," Ethan joked.

This got a laugh out of Grubner, the garden gnome; he laughed like a squirrel.

"Irvin McGillicutty at your service, what does Mrs. Moonflowers desire?"

"I need some things from the market Irvin, here is a list," Mrs. Moongarden replied. "The children will accompany you. I'd like you to show them around and make them feel at home."

The market wasn't far, just a few doors down The Hall of Doorways, the tenth door on the right. When they arrived, Ethan and Haley were not at all surprised to see a winding yellow brick road as Irvin opened up the door. A small sign at its beginning read: Market Square this way↑.

Market Square was just around the first bend in the road. It looked like a giant flea market in the middle of a town square. Masses of people gathered around produce and fruit stands. There were tents filled with all sorts of goodies. Many of the people looked human, but just as many non-humans were present, bartering and bidding on items from the various merchants.

The surrounding town was U-shaped, only the yellow brick road led in or out. Small shops and cafés decorated the outer edges of Market Square, many with quaint outdoor seating areas where patrons could enjoy a snack and beverage. Irvin was quick to take advantage of one such area, buying Ethan and Haley each a sugar-pickle soda before he ran off to fetch Mrs. Moongarden's items.

"Sit tight, Irvin will be back in a flash," he said before disappearing into the masses.

Ethan and Haley were sitting at a table outside a small café at the edge of town. "Tip of the U" it was called. At first, they sat quietly sipping their drinks and gazing at the odd assortment of beings in the crowd.

"Sugar-pickle soda sounds nasty but it tastes great!" Ethan announced after sipping from his drink.

He was trying to break the ice.

"Haley — I-I'm sorry I got you into all this, it's my fault the Grimleavers —"

"Don't be ridiculous, Ethan," she cut him off. "I'm glad I saw you on the boardwalk. I don't know where I'd be without you, I have you to thank for my being here. . . ."

She began to sob.

"I'm the one who should be sorry . . . I only went with Gil to make you jealous. It's okay for you to have secrets, I —"

"Haley — isn't that — over there — isn't that Daavic —"

Ethan interrupted her confession.

"— sitting at the table over there with those two creatures, they look like trolls," he finished.

"Yeah — it looks like him," she replied. "I wonder what he's doing here."

Daavic was sitting at an outdoor table across the town square from Ethan and Haley. He was at a sister café called "The Other U Tip," sitting with two forest trolls. They seemed to be in a deep discussion.

"He must be telling them jokes, they sure are laughing it up," Haley observed.

"Funny, I've never thought of Daavic as a jokester, maybe it's Damien and those are his wives," Ethan joked.

"E-E-Ethan," Haley whispered, she suddenly sounded terrified. "That can't be Damien — Damien is over there and I hope he didn't hear you."

Haley's hand was trembling as she pointed a few tables over.

Damien was sitting right near them; intensely focused on watching his brother.

Ethan and Haley sat motionless, watching Damien watch Daavic, they were afraid to move a muscle.

Suddenly, Damien snapped out of it, jumping from his seat as if he could feel someone watching him. He paused for a moment as if pondering something, then turned to Ethan, nodded recognition and rushed off into the crowd.

"Ethan — we should go tell Daavic, he might be able to catch him!" Haley insisted, jumping to her feet ready to take action.

But when they looked over to where Daavic had been sitting, he was gone, and so were the two trolls.

By the time Irvin returned, Ethan had convinced Haley to keep the Damien sighting a secret for now. She had insisted upon at least telling Jordanna, but he pleaded with her. There were too many questions and he didn't know who to trust — something didn't feel right about the whole thing. He had other reasons of course, ones that he could not tell Haley about, but for now Fin's secret was safe.

Irvin had finished the errands for Mrs. Moongarden and was excited to have time to show Ethan and Haley around

Market Square. But after the Damien sighting that was the last place they wanted to be, so Ethan made up an excuse. He told Irvin that it was Tuesday; only on a Friday could a human be shown around Market Square after consuming sugar-pickle soda.

Irvin was tickled to be let in on such human secrets, but Mrs. Moongarden would not be ready for them yet. So he would escort them to the Front Room where they could wait there or hang out in the Study.

"You're expected for duty in one hour, don't be late!" Irvin ordered as they followed the yellow brick road.

A GIFT FROM
JASPER

Irvin escorted Ethan and Haley as far as the Front Room; he was in a hurry to deliver Mrs. Moongarden the items from her list. They were surprised; it appeared they had an hour to roam freely about The Residence, wherever they pleased. Not that they would venture very far, not knowing what was around every corner was quite scary; after all, The Residence was a very creepy place.

"Let's go to the Study — I'd like to see what kinds of books are in its library," Haley suggested.

Ethan agreed. He too was curious about the Study's vast collection of books, and why his dad seemed to be in possession of one from the special bookcase.

As they entered, they noticed Daavic sitting at the large desk near the candelabrum. He quickly stopped what he was doing, locked something away in the desk drawer, and jumped to his feet. Obviously startled by their arrival, it was quickly apparent that whatever he was doing was for his eyes only.

"So — to what do I owe the honor?" Daavic greeted them politely.

"Mrs. Moongarden is expecting us in an hour. We had some time to kill so we thought we would browse the library — if it's okay with you?" Ethan replied.

"Certainly, just stay clear of the portal books," Daavic warned. "We wouldn't want you to end up in a dark hole somewhere, now would we? I've business to attend to so you're on your own till I return."

Daavic left the Study; Ethan and Haley were alone.

As Haley began perusing the book shelves, Ethan made a beeline for the bookcase with the portal books.

"Ethan! We've been warned about going near those!" Haley protested.

"Don't worry — I'm not going to touch anything, I just wanted to take a look."

Ethan began studying the gold lettering on the spines, whispering the titles:

Frosthaven Gully
Nimble Narrows
The Straits of Borealis

Haley walked over to help, she began reading from her eye level down while he began reading in the upwards direction.

As he reached the higher shelves, he could no longer read the titles, they were too high. So he slid the nearby bookcase ladder over and began to climb. He quickly scanned the shelves as he climbed higher; when he reached the top he noticed something.

"That's strange, the top shelf is different," he muttered. "The titles are all written in symbols, like the ones Daavic showed us in the Moongarden's secret room — and there's a book missing."

Haley had just finished reading the titles down to the floor and looked up for the first time.

"Ethan — get down from there! You're scaring me!" she yelled, startled at how high he had climbed.

Ethan rejoined Haley at floor level; his curiosity had been eased for now.

Haley made her way back to the normal book shelves and began browsing the titles again; maybe she would find some interesting reading in Caretaker lore. As her eyes wandered across the shelves, scanning the titles, something caught her eye.

"Ethan, come here, look at this," she called, pulling a book from one of the shelves and holding it up.

Ethan read the title aloud:

Tales of Avian Bravery —
The Story of Wormfreid

"Wormfreid — that name again . . ." he pondered. "He must be some kind of hero judging by the title."

"Ethan, hasn't anyone ever told you, you can't judge a book by its cover," Haley joked.

They were interrupted by the sound of the in-door opening and slamming shut. It was Daavic and he did not appear to be in a good mood. Haley quickly returned the book to its shelf and turned to greet him.

"I'll be needing the use of the Study," he said. "Please, accept my apologies and run along. I'm sure Gruggins will be more than happy to entertain you in the Front Room."

They wasted no time exiting the Study to the Front Room. Even a deep emotional conversation with Gruggins sounded better to Ethan.

The Front Room was quiet as Haley approached Gruggins' box.

"Gotcha!" Gruggins growled, popping out of his box and scaring Haley half to death. "Oh — it's only you. Sorry my dear, hope I didn't frighten you."

"That's okay — we're just waiting around for a while. I just wanted to say hi," Haley smiled.

"Been sensing a critter on the loose," Gruggins explained. "Thought it was a tribe of nibblewarts passing through the first time I felt it. Passed through just a moment ago — but I'm on to it now, a very tricky critter this one."

"Well — we're just going to hang out for a while, if that's okay?" Ethan asked.

"Whatever — just keep your eyes open and holler if you see anything," he replied before disappearing back into his box.

"Looks like that mirror has moved again," Ethan pointed out; it was now standing up against the staircase.

"I wonder what's up these stairs anyway," he added, walking over to the foot of the staircase.

"Ethan — we shouldn't go up there! We don't know what we might find!" Haley warned, running over to stop him.

But she was too late. He had already started up the stairs and was halfway to the next floor by the time she got there. He continued all the way to the second floor, looking around as he stood at the top of the first flight of stairs.

"Ethan — get back down here *now!*" Haley yelled angrily.

"There's another hallway that way," he said, pointing to the right. "Looks like a huge dark room straight ahead," he continued, "and another room over here," he pointed to his left as he started into the room.

"ETHAN! What are you doing? Get back here!" Haley screamed as he disappeared into the room at the top of the stairs.

Then — she could hear him talking to someone.

"It's you — how'd you get here? I thought you —" Ethan's voice suddenly became silent.

"GRUGGINS! GRUGGINS! *Something's happened to Ethan!*" Haley cried out at the top of her lungs.

Gruggins quickly emerged from his box and fluttered over to Haley. Together, they climbed the staircase, Gruggins riding on her shoulder.

"Don't you worry — Gruggins won't let anything harm you. I'm sure Ethan Fox will be fine," he comforted her as they arrived at the top of the staircase.

When they entered the room, it was empty except for Ethan; he was unconscious, flat out on the floor. Haley rushed over to his side and knelt down beside him. Gruggins hopped off her shoulder onto Ethan's chest and quickly began examining him. He was thorough; looking at his feet, hands, side, and even backside after asking for Haley's help to flip him over.

"Curious . . ." Gruggins said, he was pondering something very deeply. "That might explain a few things. . . ." he added, stuffing something into his pocket.

"What? What's wrong with Ethan?" Haley pleaded as tears streamed down her face.

"Oh, don't worry about him. He'll be okay, very sleepy but quite all right," Gruggins explained with a comforting smile.

Gruggins hopped back up onto Haley's shoulder and produced his handy blowgun out of thin air. "This'll wake him up long enough to get him to his room, but then he's gonna need a long nap." He blew into the blowgun as a dart zipped from its tip landing squarely in the meat of Ethan's arm.

Ethan was groggy when he woke up. He could remember nothing after climbing to the top of the stairs. The trip back to his quarters was quick with Haley's help. She draped his arms over her shoulder and acted as a human crutch while Gruggins rode along on his shoulder for moral support.

No sooner had they plopped him down onto his bed, then he began to snore — Ethan was out like a light.

It was finally time to join Mrs. Moongarden for Alicia's fitting, so Gruggins graciously volunteered to escort Haley down The Hall of Doorways. She would help Mrs. Moongarden but Ethan would have to sit this one out.

* * *

Ethan could hardly see as he slowly made his way through the cold blistering sandstorm. Not sure where he was, or where he was going, he pushed forward as if guided by an invisible force. He had the strange feeling that he was being watched, but that was impossible in such conditions. As he continued along, the winds began to subside. The heat of the sun quickly made its presence felt, and soon the wind had stopped completely.

Ethan was standing in a vast desert; tall dunes of sand decorated the landscape. As he scanned his surroundings, he quickly saw that he was being watched, by deep blue eyes, thousands of them peeking out from within the dunes of sand. Yet he was not frightened, the eyes dotting the desert landscape seemed to give him an odd sense of calm.

"Who are you? Why am I here?" he tried to communicate with them, but they said nothing, the desert was still.

A disturbance in the sand nearby suddenly commanded his attention; something was pushing up from beneath. He watched in silence as sand poured off a large hatch that swung open from beneath the sand. The figure of a man slowly emerged, ascending up a staircase within the desert bunker; the man was tall and wore a hooded yellow robe.

As the man strode across the sand, he seemed to be completely oblivious to the eyes in the desert sand watching him. He was unaware of Ethan's presence as well; the man appeared to be alone. He quickly stopped walking and knelt down to pick something up from the sand. As he stood, Ethan could see what it was, a brown book with gold symbols that shimmered in the desert sun.

A bright flash blinded Ethan's eyes and suddenly he was in a different place; it was windy again, the sound of a nearby willow tree whistled in the air. The ground was mostly dirt with patches of crabgrass, the man in the yellow robe lay dying from deep wounds, blood was pooling beneath him.

Ethan could not move; it was as if his feet were cemented to the ground. All he could do was watch as a three foot tall blue bunny approached walking on two feet. He quickly recognized Jasper and tried to get his attention, but no words would come out of his mouth as he tried to speak — not a sound.

Jasper knelt down next to the dying man and gave him a hug. Jasper was crying as the man began to stir; he reached into his robe and pulled out the brown book, handing it to Jasper as he took his last breath. Yellow spots slowly began to appear on Jasper's blue fur; Ethan could feel that something significant had just happened.

Suddenly, Ethan was back in his bedroom at home, standing in the middle of the room. Jasper was in the room with him holding the brown book in his hand, holding it out for Ethan, pleading for him to take it. The movement of a shadow on the wall caught Ethan's attention, it was being cast by something or someone behind him, but he could not bring himself to turn around. The shadow slowly came into focus as it grew taller, Ethan could see what it was. It was a tall devilish figure of a creature with thick swooping horns — Ethan was terrified!

*   *   *

Ethan burst out of bed, trying to catch his breath from the terrifying nightmare he just had. Sweat was pouring from his forehead; he pulled back the sheets from his bed to wipe the sweat from his brow, and that's when he saw it. Under the covers, lying down near the foot of his bed was a withered old brown book with golden symbols. He didn't know what to make of it, had the dream been real?

Still in shock from his nightmare, he was not sure if he was seeing things or not, he needed to speak to Haley. As he reached for the ELMO device on his dresser, he noticed something else odd. His pocket tote was larger than how he had left it; someone had opened it and forgotten to close it back up — someone had been snooping in his room.

"Haley, are you there?" Ethan spoke into the ELMO device. "I need to speak with you now!"

"Yeah I'm here, you missed it Ethan, the fitting was so spectacular —" she began to gush.

"Haley!" Ethan interrupted, "I need to talk to you now, could you please come over to my room."

The serious tone in his voice must have alarmed her; she was over in a flash. He sat her down on his bed and went over his nightmarish dream in every detail. At first she tried to comfort him, telling him everything would be okay, but he wasn't done.

"Haley, I'm not finished — when I woke up, I found this in bed with me," he blurted out as he held the book up to show her.

"That looks like one of the portal books, how did it get here?" She looked surprised.

"I don't know, but someone's been snooping in my pocket tote too," he replied.

"Do you think that could be the missing one?" she asked.

Haley was rubbing the black infinity ring on her finger.

"I don't know — but I sure don't want to open it."

Ethan set the book down in his lap.

"What's wrong with your finger?"

"I'm not sure . . . my ring, it feels strange, like it just turned into a snake and is slithering between my fingers."

Suddenly the book came to life as the cover flipped itself open. The yellowish pages seemed to be glowing as they flipped from page to page — like a card dealer shuffling cards. Finally, when it was done, the pages all flopped back over and the book was sitting in Ethan's lap opened to page one.

"Look Ethan — something's written on the first page — it's the poem, The Eyes of the Desert Sand."

Now that the book was open and they had not suddenly been transported to a mysterious world, Ethan was no longer afraid of it. He began flipping through the pages.

"The pages — their blank," she said.

"Yeah — all but the first one," he added. "But look at this, it looks like there were pages before the first one, but someone ripped them out."

Wisps of yellowish light suddenly began to waft up from the book's pages and disappear like wavy clouds of golden smoke.

Ethan quickly pulled his hands away as the book again took over.

The pages began to flip, forward then backward, as if the book were searching for a specific page. It settled on the first blank page. Writing began to appear at the bottom of the blank page as if written by the pen of an invisible author; it was being written backwards, and it was another poem:

Cruel Intentions

It lurks in shadows and hides from the light,
With cruel intentions it feeds on fright.

An evil plan with dreams so dire,
The Silent Forest will burn with fire.

To find the key things must unfold,
At a grumpling's feet the secret's told.

Four portals locked away so tight,
Unlock the door to begin the fight.

A path has been given, in deception brave and bold,
Heed our words of warning; believe not the book of gold.

Ethan and Haley were in shock as they read the words. They did not know what to do or who to turn to — none of it made any sense. What was the Silent Forest? What were the four portals? And how had Ethan ended up with this mysterious poem book?

They talked for hours discussing what to do about the mysterious book, but all they had were questions, no answers. Ethan was still not convinced there was anyone he could trust other than Haley. So for now, they decided to keep the whole thing a secret. Ethan and Haley had a lot to think about.

THE GALLERY OF THINGS REMEMBERED

The next morning, Ethan woke up bright and early; he couldn't sleep anymore and had something he wanted to surprise Haley with. When he returned to his room, another note had been slipped under his door. As he pulled the note from the envelope, he got a brief whiff of a fragrant scent; he didn't remember smelling it before, but it somehow reminded him of Jordanna. The note read:

Dear Ethan,

I feel we've made very little progress in discovering what the Grimleavers are up to and why you've been lured to The Residence. A new discovery has been brought to my attention and I feel that we have much more to discuss.

Please gather Haley and meet me in the Front Room ASAYGT, I have something to show you two.

Sincerely yours,

Jordanna Ravenwood

Ethan wasted no time entering The Hall of Doorways to knock on Haley's door. They had stayed up rather late discussing the strange events of the previous day. But he was eager to get a move on, they had things to investigate. When she opened her door, she was already dressed, ready and waiting — evidently as eager as he to start the day. The plot was thickening, they were both bound and determined to get to the bottom of things.

When they entered the Front Room, Jordanna was standing next to the giant mirror. It had moved itself again, this time to the right of the front door at the base of the staircase. Jordanna was studying the symbols around the outside edges of its frame, the same sort of symbols Ethan and Haley had seen twice before.

"That was fast," Jordanna smiled as she turned to greet them. "I'm so glad you've rushed over, time is of the essence."

"Your note sounded important, and my curiosity was piqued," Ethan said.

"Well then, let's get started shall we — please, follow me," Jordanna said, motioning at the wall across the room.

As she opened up the door to the left of the front door, a cool breeze rushed by, giving Ethan and Haley chills. Inside was a dimly lit hallway that curved to the left. There were no lights, doors, or windows; but the light from the room at the end of the hallway was strong enough to light their way.

They emerged into an enormous rectangular room with very high ceilings and scaffolding around its outer edges. It looked like a brightly lit arena with white canvas walls ascending eighty feet straight up. Hundreds of paintings were being painted, randomly scattered along the walls — like postage stamps on a giant poster. Small elf like creatures hung from ropes that dangled from the scaffolding; they were watching and monitoring the paintings for something.

"Welcome to The Gallery of Things Remembered," Jordanna announced, motioning about the room. "The Gallery catalogues happenings . . . past and present . . . some important . . . and some not so. . . ."

As Jordanna explained the Gallery, a small portly elf walked up to greet them. He wore a black suit jacket with worn blue jeans and red sneakers. Much older than the rest; he had grey hair and reading glasses perched upon his long pointed nose.

"I'd like you to meet our curator, Dorkin Drumbles," Jordanna introduced politely. "Dorkin and the rest of our Gallery workers are forest elves who've volunteered to help out. Forest elves are uniquely adapted for hanging in trees — we'd have a heck of a time otherwise."

"Help out we do," Dorkin spoke up in a quirky voice that reminded Ethan of *Yoda*, "monitor the artwork, collect and mount for display, very important work it is, to determine relevance. . . ."

As Ethan listened to Dorkin, he began to scan the paintings on the walls.

Many were already finished, but many were in the process of being painted — by the hands of invisible artists it appeared. Next to each unfinished painting, an elf hung from a nearby rope, patiently holding out a palette of paint as floating brushes magically dabbed from them, painting away on the enormous canvas. Finished works were being collected by other elves, cut away from the walls where the white canvas would magically grow back.

"Finished pieces are collected and taken for determination. . . ." Dorkin added, motioning towards the floor area of the enormous room.

The floor of the room was split into two areas: one where a large team of elves mounted the finished works into frames; while the other half of the room was being used as a staging area. Finished works were put on easels where three white haired old women would study them. The three hunched over old hags wore black robes — they looked like witches.

"Over here . . . we make a determination as to the piece's significance," Jordanna began to explain, pointing at the staging area. "If they are deemed of importance, then they are moved to a viewing room, otherwise they are catalogued and stored away in Gallery vaults."

"I don't understand — what purpose does the Gallery serve?" Haley asked. "Who is creating all those paintings? And who determines what is important and what is not?"

"All good questions," Jordanna replied, "we had similar questions when we arrived. The Residence was here long before the Caretakers were put here, by a higher power shall we say. The Gallery was empty when we arrived; its walls were blank canvases. Then one day, paintings began to appear. Shortly after that the three old hags arrived; they'd been sent to review finished works, to determine important pieces we must keep. . . . That's the short version anyway."

"That is why I sent for you headmistress, significant it is, the new painting!" Dorkin was tugging on Jordanna's robe with obvious excitement.

They walked to the other side of the room where a corridor to an adjoining room was suddenly visible. It was a dimly lit showroom with hundreds of paintings prominently displayed on the walls. As they entered the room, Ethan and Haley were quickly taken with the paintings; each one was brightly lit by a set of small spotlights. The paintings appeared to be in no particular order, but many were accompanied by a small golden plaque attached to its frame, engraved with a caption.

Ethan read one of the captions aloud:

The Great Dinosaur Hoax

It was a painting of giant reptilian lizard creatures resembling dinosaurs, but they were walking erect and looked intelligent.

Haley read another nearby caption:

The Butterfly Nebula

"It's beautiful!" she gushed.

This was a painting of outer space, a colorful gaseous nebula sparkling with stars. The stars were arranged into a complex pattern, shaped like a butterfly with intricate detail. Surrounded by the vast darkness of space, random stars and spiraling galaxies dotted the exterior. But in the lower right corner, off by itself, was a small cluster of planets encased in a white translucent Chrysalis.

Ethan and Haley curiously gazed from piece to piece as they continued into the viewing room. It was a long curved room with no end in sight; paintings covered every inch of every wall and disappeared around the bend into the distance.

Ethan read from another golden plaque:

Who Really Built the Pyramids?

He stopped for a second look; this one really grabbed his attention. It looked like a picture taken from atop a hill; the foreground was tropical and flush with plant life. The hill looked down upon a vast desert; pyramids were being built in the distance. Giant carved stone blocks were being carried down a long winding path that trailed off to the distant build site.

But what was captivating Ethan, was who it was carrying the stone blocks — they were ants. Giant ants standing erect, each the size of a dog; they were in groups, hoisting the blocks up and carrying them down the trail one at a time.

"I never saw that on the Discovery channel!" he joked.

As they rounded another bend, it appeared they were approaching the end of the road. The paintings stopped up ahead and only blank walls continued. They reached the last few paintings when Dorkin stopped in his tracks as he pointed up at one; it was covered from view with a sheet.

"This painting it is headmistress Ravenwood!" Dorkin was trembling with excitement.

As Jordanna slowly unveiled the painting, a sense of panic overwhelmed Ethan and Haley as they stood holding their breath. Anticipation gave way to relief as they let out a collective breath, this was no big deal. It was a painting of both of them on the boardwalk at the precise moment they had first spotted each other. Ethan was holding his hand up to block the sun so he could see her and Haley was staring back at him.

"But what does it mean?" Haley asked. "We already know how Ethan and I first saw one another."

"Sometimes it's not immediately obvious, but significant just the same," Jordanna replied. "Study the picture — is there anything else that looks strange to you? You both seem pretty focused on each other in the picture, oblivious to everything else around you."

"Look at him," Haley said, pointing to a strange man in the painting. "It looks like that creepy man is watching Ethan."

"Indeed," Jordanna said.

The man was sitting on a nearby bench, his hands deeply planted in the pockets of his full length brown overcoat. He wore a black leather wide brimmed hat and dark sunglasses. He was obviously trying to conceal his identity.

"I don't remember seeing him," Ethan said, "and it was warm that day, nobody in their right mind would wear an overcoat."

"Very well, I would like you both to study this painting," Jordanna said. "Come back tomorrow if you need to. Think about it as you lay down to sleep. Sometimes the subconscious mind can be a very powerful tool."

They stood staring at the painting for a few more moments but nothing came to mind.

On the way out of the viewing room, Ethan and Haley continued to scan the beautiful artwork on the walls. Several familiar pictures drew their attention along the way: a giant pink pearl, a village of grumplings, a blue taletaddler with a man in a yellow robe — that one really caught Ethan's attention.

They exited the viewing room and made their way across the Gallery floor and down the corridor to the Front Room.

"Well, it seems we didn't learn anything new after all," Jordanna said, sitting down in a chair near the middle of the room, next to a small coffee table.

The phantom bubble hung in the air motionless above the coffee table.

Haley followed Jordanna and sat down as well, across the coffee table from where Jordanna sat.

Ethan began to study the narrow black carpet running under the table. It ran from the front door all the way across the room to the marble slab against the far wall. A curious smirk began to form on his face as his eyes followed the carpet to the front door.

"So, if this is the Front Room," Ethan announced as he took a few steps to the door, "then what's in the front yard?"

Ethan turned the knob and yanked the door open. A bright light shined into the Front Room as his and Haley's eyes grew wide in surprise.

"Well — it looks as if our secret's finally out, now we have much more to discuss," Jordanna said.

THE FOUR
PORTALS

Outside the front door to The Residence was an odd place indeed; as far as the eye could see, a black and white checkerboard plane stretched off in all directions — like an endless tiled floor. The sky was blue; it was a bright sunny day but no sun was visible. Giant spooky trees lined the horizon; they looked dead, contorted leafless branches reached up at the sky as if they died in agony. But that was just the landscaping, the yard furniture was even stranger; four shiny metallic spheres hovered several feet above the checkered plane just outside The Residence.

"What are those — ? Ethan asked, pointing at the basketball sized orbs.

"They are portals," Jordanna replied.

The four spheres hovered side by side in a row, each levitated by an electric field of a different color: one red, one green, one blue, and one yellow. Jolts of electricity emanated from holes in the plane beneath, blasting up like miniature lightning bolts, causing each sphere to glow its respective color.

"Portals — portals to what — ?" Ethan asked staring at the portals. "I'm going to take a closer look."

Ethan stepped through the doorway, but he didn't make it very far. As he stepped across the threshold, it was as if an invisible force was reflecting his body back into The Residence. He ended up back in the Front Room as if he had just stepped through the doorway from the other side.

Ethan was confused.

"Well — it appears you've discovered the lock, it's still working," Jordanna smiled, trying to lighten the mood. "Please — let me demonstrate. . . ."

A small rubber ball suddenly appeared in Jordanna's hand. As she stood up and tossed the ball through the doorway, it disappeared for a second before zipping back into The Residence — it was as if someone had thrown it back from the other side.

Watching the lock in action seemed to alleviate Ethan's confusion.

"So you see, the doorway to the four portals is locked, nobody can use them," Jordanna explained.

"The four portals — did you say the four portals?" Ethan asked as his gaze met Haley's.

Haley seemed as shocked as Ethan.

"Yes I did — please, let me explain — we have much to discuss," Jordanna replied, motioning for Ethan to join her and Haley at their seats.

Brightness from the sunny-less day outside was lighting up much of the Front Room. A column of light strode along the narrow black carpet from the half open door. Colored beams of light reflected off the metallic spheres creating interesting patterns that danced along the carpet. It looked like a large centipede had walked along the carpet in boots and left a colorful trail.

Ethan studied the curious pattern as he slowly closed the door before joining the girls.

"What you saw were portals — portals to the four elemental worlds of the Chrysalis," Jordanna began to explain. "They are the Caretaker home worlds of Hades, Ceres, Atlantis, and Zephyr."

"I was right, they are aliens," Haley whispered to Ethan.

"As I said before, we are more like distant cousins," Jordanna corrected, "but please — there is so much to explain."

"The elemental worlds are a coalition of planets united under the Chrysalis and governed by a Council of Elders. Tens of thousands of years ago, the Council of Elders was visited by The Designer; they were told to select four members from within the Council, one for each of the elemental worlds. These four members would leave the Council forever, they would be bestowed with unimaginable powers; they'd become the Creators."

"Creators — Creators of what — ?" Ethan asked.

Ethan and Haley were enthralled by Jordanna's story.

"Of Earth," Jordanna replied.

"The Designer had created something as well — the human race which needed a home world of its own. So the Creators were chosen, Zamalador form Hades, Vraitor from Ceres, Stravis from Zephyr, and Driveous from Atlantis. They were given a schedule and a list of requirements — The Designer had even chosen a barren desert planet from which they would start. The Designer had very specific demands for what Earth would be like, only when they were all satisfied would the new world be pulled into the Chrysalis."

"You keep talking about that . . . what is the Chrysalis?" Haley asked.

"Good question," Jordanna smiled. "The Chrysalis is a metaphysical barrier of life energy generated by the elemental worlds; it surrounds our planets and any we chose to pull inside. Think of it as an invisible enclosure that protects everything within it."

"Protects them from what — ?" Haley asked.

"From The Designer's mortal enemy, of course," Jordanna replied, "the ultimate source of evil in the universe, The Destroyer."

Jordanna's response visibly shook Ethan and Haley. They didn't want to image anything more evil than the Grimleavers.

"But its okay," Jordanna continued. "The Destroyer cannot survive long within the Chrysalis, and doesn't make it a habit of showing up here."

It was beginning to make some sense: the emblem on the Caretaker robes; the strange candelabrum; and all the red,

187

green, blue, and yellow coloring. It was all representative of the four elemental worlds of the Chrysalis, and Earth was inside the Chrysalis.

"But why is the door to the four portals locked?" Ethan asked; getting back to the subject matter he was more curious about.

"Another good question, and another long answer I'm afraid," Jordanna replied.

"The Creators left the portals as a gift to the Caretakers. It would allow us to visit our home worlds and keep the Council of Elders informed. But then, long after the Creators were gone, something unexpected began to happen. Creatures from our worlds began to show up on Earth, where they would wander about freely in the human world. It was only a few at first, but then they started coming in greater numbers, it became a Great Exodus; a problem we could not deal with alone, so the Creators were forced to return to Earth."

Jordanna stopped to clear her throat. Looking from Ethan to Haley, she paused as if waiting for questions. When there were none she continued.

"It was apparent we could not send them all back, the creatures wanted to be on Earth. So we chose the next best thing. Caretakers began rounding up the creatures while the Creators created environments for them; small worlds within your world, sharing some of the same spacial confines as Earth, but not visible to the human world. It worked great, human sightings of non-Earthly creatures began to decline and everything was back to normal. But in the end, when the Creators left for the second time, they saw the error in their ways and decided to lock the portals so such a thing could not occur again."

"So the Caretakers, they're stuck on Earth — they can never go back?" Haley asked.

"Never say never, my dear," Jordanna replied, smiling at Haley's concern. "They did leave us clues in The Book of Creators. But it warns, the portals should only be unlocked at a future time that will become clear as things unfold."

"The Book of Creators — is that the big gold book in the Study?" Ethan asked.

"Very good — yes it's the one on the pedestal in the Study."

"And the other books —" Ethan persisted, "the portal books, why do the ones on the top shelf all have symbols instead of letters?"

"Ethan, have you been snooping, my dear boy?" Jordanna laughed as if she had expected no less. "The books on that shelf comprise a special set, a very special set indeed. The symbols are from a secret language, a language only known by the Creators. Even I can't read what is on those books — no Caretaker can."

Jordanna was being very honest with Ethan and Haley, and they were really beginning to like her, and trust her.

"Mrs. Ravenwood —" Haley said; then paused to look at Ethan with a serious look on her face.

"Jordanna," Ethan interrupted, "I think we have some secrets we need to share with you. We know what the Grimleavers are after and the Silent Forest is in danger."

THE

HELL GIANT

Jordanna was very surprised at Ethan's mention of the Silent Forest. She listened intently as he described his scary dream from the previous day. Ethan retrieved his pocket tote and began to unravel it as he neared the end of his story. When he was done, he reached inside and paused for a moment.

"I was soaked in sweat," he explained, "so I pulled back the sheets to wipe my face, and that's when I found this — !"

Ethan pulled the brown book from his pocket tote and held it out for Jordanna to see; the golden symbols practically glowed in the dim light of the Front Room. Jordanna gasped in shock, she was obviously not expecting this.

"We thought it might be the missing book from the top shelf," Haley said.

"May I — ?" Jordanna asked, holding her hand out.

Ethan quickly obliged, handing the book over to Jordanna. But as soon as it left his hands — something strange happened — the glowing gold symbols slowly faded away leaving only the worn brown cover.

A calm smile began to form on Jordanna's face as she handed the book back to Ethan.

"No, this book is not from the same collection," she said. "This book is very unique, and it appears that Ethan Fox has been chosen."

Once back in Ethan's grasp, the golden symbols quickly returned to the book's cover. He opened it up and turned to the first two pages. He showed Jordanna the poems and described how the book came to life, writing out the second poem before his and Haley's very eyes.

Once Jordanna had read the poem and digested it, she sat silently for a moment pondering things.

"For now," Jordanna began, "I think it better that we keep this between us, not a word to the others, do you understand? You've been chosen Ethan Fox. You and Haley must accompany my team to the Silent Forest. We must investigate."

She pulled her ELMO device out and went on. "This is headmistress Ravenwood, will Daavic Ravenwood, Nicholas Knight, Gruggins McGhee, Azron, and RGB please report to the Study at once — this is a priority one emergency!"

Jordanna rushed Ethan and Haley into the Study where they were quickly joined by the others. The team members were curious; it was not every day they were called to duty under such circumstances. Jordanna briefed the team, telling them only that a confidential source had informed her that the Silent Forest was in grave danger, they must investigate immediately.

"But certainly you're going to tell us more than that . . . mother!" Daavic protested. "Like where this information came from? Who is this secret source?"

Daavic peered at Ethan.

"Daavic, you've got to stop questioning authority, it'll be your undoing," Nicholas interrupted; his voice was gruff, almost whispering. "If your mother is keeping secrets, she has good reason. You have to trust that. . . ."

It sounded like even Nicholas was not totally convinced.

"For the first leg of your journey, you will book travel to Blind Man's Bluff," Jordanna continued. "You will camp there tonight. I will contact Borealis and send for Sol. He will join you there and fly the party down to the clearing in the morning, the winds are favorable then. Any questions?"

"Mrs. Ravenwood," Haley asked, her hand raised into the air. "What is the Silent Forest?"

"One of the hidden worlds I spoke to you two about earlier," she replied. "It is home to many of the creatures that came to Earth during the Great Exodus. But most importantly, it is where the grumplings were moved to after the Greenfield Massacre. That is why I'm sending Gruggins; he will act as our liaison."

The other Caretakers in the room were surprised. Jordanna was talking openly to Ethan and Haley about things they were not supposed to know.

"I've shown them the portals," Jordanna confessed, "and told them of the Creators, the Chrysalis, everything. . . . It was my decision and mine alone. I take full responsibility."

The silence in the room was deafening as they pondered Jordanna's revelation.

"Daavic, you will take care of RGB," she continued, "keep them balled up unless they are needed. Unleash them only on Nicholas' command. Gruggins, you will ride along on Ethan or Haley until it is safe. Azron, you are our brawn, protect the others and see that they return unharmed."

"Mrs. Jordanna?" Linus interrupted as RGB's collective arms raised into the air.

"Yes, Linus," she replied.

"Do we have to stay balled up? We will behave! Kepler may be in the Silent Forest! We need to keep our eyes out for Kepler!"

"Very well — but you must remain balled up until you reach the bluff, then you may take your natural form."

RGB's dedication to their fallen comrade broke Jordanna's heart. Happy with her answer, RGB quickly morphed into little balls so Daavic could gather them up for book travel.

"Now then," she continued, "let's get on with the mission — nightfall is merely hours away on the bluff — we've no time to waste."

Jordanna held out her hands and a portal book magically appeared in them. It read on the cover:

Blind Man's Bluff

The team quickly gathered around Jordanna and began joining hands in a circle: Ethan, Haley and Gruggins, Nicholas, Daavic and RGB, Azron, and back to Ethan.

The second time book traveling was much easier for Ethan; he woke up with the rest of the team this time. They were on a flat clearing at the edge of a very high, very steep cliff. It looked down over a vast ocean of trees, as far as the eye could see, lush greenery stretched off into the horizon. Two hours had passed and dusk was rapidly approaching by the time Sol arrived.

"Sol has arrived! Our old friend is here!" RGB cried out, alerting the team to his arrival.

RGB had been standing at cliffs edge, scanning the horizon ever since they arrived and taken their natural forms.

Ethan followed Haley and Gruggins over to see what RGB were looking at below. But it wasn't in the forest they were looking, it was just above it, and it was beautiful.

They were looking down on an enormous bird of prey as it effortlessly soared above the forest; it appeared as if he was trying to tickle his belly with the tips of the trees. Flashes of orange from the setting sun glistened off his silver feathers as he glided towards them. As he approached the cliff, he angled up and began a steep ascent. He continued the climb flapping his enormous wings only a few times on the way up.

When he reached the crest, Ethan and Haley finally got an idea of exactly how enormous Sol was — his wing span was nearly forty feet. They backed away as Sol landed on the edge of the bluff. The last flap of his wings caused a strong gust of wind to blast across the summit as he came to rest.

"Sol! RGB has missed you! Happy to see you again," RGB greeted, hopping up onto his back.

Sol turned his head and gently nudged Albert, Linus, and Newton with his giant beak. The affection among them was mutual.

"What kind of bird is that?" Ethan whispered as they studied the giant raptor.

"Sol is the last of Earth's mighty thunderbirds, very powerful creatures they were," Nicholas replied, walking up behind them. "Terrible betrayals nearly led to their extinction, if not for Wormfreid —"

Nicholas paused before going on. "Anyway that was a long time ago and a story better left for another time."

"Sol, we are happy to have you, hopefully we will not need your help once again," Nicholas greeted. "This is Ethan and Haley. I'm sure the stories of Ethan Fox have made it to Borealis by now."

Sol nodded a bow of acknowledgement.

He was a tall majestic creature standing nearly as tall as Azron. The dark edges on his silver feathers made his shiny metallic finish look like giant fish scales. His head was donned with black and bronze feathers that grew in a cool pattern — like he was wearing the helmet of a modern warrior.

Giant eagle eyes the size of saucers, peered back at Ethan and Haley over his yellowish beak that hooked to a sharp point at the end.

CHAPTER SEVENTEEN

As Ethan gazed down at his enormous claws, he was reminded of *Jurassic Park*, Sol's talons were larger than a velociraptor's.

Day quickly gave way to night. It was cold at the top of Blind Man's Bluff, so the team gathered around a campfire Daavic had made. The top of the summit was a base camp of some sort. Oval huts that looked like giant half buried eggs surrounded the fire pit — there were even a couple large enough for Azron and Sol. After a dinner of grilled steaks — Caretaker style — the team retired to their cozy quarters. Tomorrow would be a full day.

The team emerged from their quarters, early in the morning, when the wind currents were favorable for the glide to the clearing. Sol would take the team down on his back; the mighty thunderbird was plenty strong to carry them all but it would take two trips. Azron would have to be carried down separately. Sol would take the rest of the team first and return for him.

Ethan and Haley were excited.

Sol had been saddled with a strange looking leather contraption with straps that they would hang onto for the glide down. The team was in place, sitting two wide across Sol's back: Ethan and Daavic in front, and Haley with Gruggins and Nicholas in back. RGB would glide down on their own, alongside the mighty thunderbird.

Sol took two steps to the edge of the cliff and leapt off, they were airborne. The view was beautiful as they soared over the lush green forest. Ethan and Haley watched silently as forest drifted by beneath them only to be replaced by new forest. A strong wind at their backs pushed them along like they were on an invisible conveyer belt. RGB were effortlessly gliding alongside at first, but then decided it was time to play.

"Weeeeeeeeeeeee," Linus yelled out, as he sped ahead — it was like he had a rocket attached to him.

"Woooooo Hooooooo," Newton and Albert followed.

It looked like they were playing tag in the sky, as RGB chased one another around, doing somersaults and loop-de-loops around Sol.

The glide lasted about seven minutes before they sighted the clearing; a small kidney shaped meadow that tapered off at one end. Sol made a quick decent setting down gently in the middle of the flat grassy meadow. The team quickly dismounted and with a few flaps of his massive wings, Sol was off to fetch Azron. The return trip to Blind Man's Bluff would take time against the strong winds, so Sol's return would be delayed. But the team could waste no time, they would enter the Silent Forest immediately.

At one end, the canopy of forest trees surrounding the meadow formed a cave like enclave; it was the entrance to the Silent Forest. Daavic led the way as they entered; RGB were at his side with hands joined as they followed along. Ethan and Haley were behind them. Gruggins rode on Haley's shoulder, while Nicholas brought up the rear.

As they ventured deeper into the shady forest, it quickly became apparent where the name came from. It was completely silent, not a sound could be heard. It was not until someone decided to speak when Ethan understood what complete silence really was.

"Well — it looks as if mother has sent us on a wild goose chase," Daavic said.

But when he spoke, his lips moved but there was no sound. It was as if the rest of the team were hearing him telepathically. It was absolutely silent.

"It is a large forest, we must explore it all to be sure," Nicholas ordered.

Thin beams of sunlight peeked through the thick cover of trees dotting the forest floor. The floor of the Silent Forest was marvelously decorated by colorful vegetation. It was unlike anything Ethan had ever seen. As he studied the strange forest, he noticed that some of the trees had large ear shaped appendages attached to them, going up both sides of the trees — like a ladder for a very odd tree house.

"The Ears on the Forest Trees . . ." Ethan thought to himself, remembering his father's sketches.

There was no animal life to speak of, at least not visible on the forest floor, nor in the trees above. The only evidence of life was the ears on the forest trees and strange cocoon like huts that hung high up in the trees.

The team ventured deeper and deeper into the beautiful lush forest. It seemed empty but then something alarming happened. An explosion of sound roared out, breaking the serene silence, it was coming from up ahead on the path they were following. Creatures began to appear: forest trolls, sprites, gnomes, and various other species were rapidly approaching on the path — like a mini-stampede. They were running from something.

"This is very disturbing!" Nicholas yelled out above the noise; his voice was no longer silent. "Something must have breached the canopy — no sounds should be heard within the Silent Forest!"

Suddenly the sound grew deafening as they got closer to what was causing the commotion. The forest up ahead was burning. Trees were being effortlessly ripped from their roots and tossed aside in flames.

"It is what we've feared — I'm afraid — a hell giant!" Nicholas yelled out.

The hell giant was an enormous fire creature nearly as tall as the forest trees. It looked like an evil giant firelyte with devilish horns and piercing black eyes. It was raining down fire onto the forest floor as it walked across the large clearing of embers it left in its wake — the canopy had been breached.

"We've got to stop it before its done irreparable harm to the forest!" Nicholas yelled.

"Yes but without Sol that will be impossible," Daavic argued, "and without Kepler, the three pyrodevlins will not be able to contain it for long!"

"Yes — but Sol should be along shortly!" Nicholas insisted. "We need to unleash RGB now! Have them pull the hell giant into the middle of this clearing! If Sol sees it from above, he will join the battle! It's our only option!"

"But that's a ridiculous plan!" Daavic argued. "You'll be sending RGB to their deaths!"

"Give them the order! Release them now!" Nicholas ordered.

Daavic hesitated for a second, but then obeyed, bending down to give RGB their orders.

RGB wasted no time, springing into action, darting out into the black clearing of embers that smoldered where lush forest once stood. Then all at once, the pyrodevlins raised their forked tails up over their heads, while small balls of fire began to grow between their prongs. Fireballs then shot out the ends of their tails, trailing out colored streams of energy that remained attached to the pyrodevlins. The fireballs wrapped themselves around the hell giant's arms and legs as they hit. RGB had lassoed the giant fire beast and were pulling it towards the clearing.

"It looks like it's working, but Sol had better get here fast!" Daavic yelled. "The three of them won't be able to hold him for very long!"

Ethan, Haley, and Gruggins watched from the edge of the clearing as Nicholas and Daavic ran out alongside RGB. They were amazed at how powerful the small pyrodevlins were as they wrestled the hell giant out into the clearing. But they were tiring quickly as the giant fire creature flailed back and forth trying to break free from their grasp.

One of the giant's arms suddenly broke free; Albert had lost his grip, the red energy lasso streaming from his tail disappeared. Albert quickly struggled to conjure up another fireball. The hell giant swung his free arm violently, catching a tall tree at the edge of the clearing, just as Albert lassoed it with a new stream of energy. The tree was falling.

Ethan and Haley didn't even see that the tree was slowly falling towards them, it would crush them.

Suddenly a shadow glided by overhead as Sol swept down into the clearing. Azron quickly jumped from Sol's back and ran towards the falling tree; he saw that Ethan and Haley were in grave danger. He arrived just in time, catching the giant tree just before it could smash down on them — Azron had saved them.

Sol quickly swung back into action as well, flapping his mighty wings to gain altitude above the monster as RGB continued to pull the hell giant into the clearing. Sol continued to hover above the creature, flapping his wings harder and harder, as he slowly drifted closer to the hell giant. As the flapping intensified so did the strong wind he was now generating. Soon thunder and lightning began to ring out from above.

Sol was creating a storm above the hell giant and it was hurting him. It was obvious RGB were tiring, the color was beginning to drain from their bodies, and their lassos were growing thinner as they continued to struggle against the beast. But Sol's storm was intensifying as well and together they were slowly defeating the hell giant.

Then in one last act of defiance, the monster wriggled an arm free, lunging up into the sky taking a swipe at Sol. He connected, hitting one of Sol's wings and almost knocking him out of the sky. But Sol was too powerful and quickly regained control. A few more flaps of his mighty wings and it was all over; the hell giant had nothing left and quickly melted away into the clearing as rain poured down from above. When it was all over, a giant firelyte diamond the size of a pumpkin was all that remained of the hell giant.

Ethan and Haley were standing at the edge of the clearing in shock. Azron garnered all his strength and tossed the giant fallen tree aside. If not for him, they surely would have perished.

"Thank you Azron, you saved us," Ethan managed, walking over to thank the gentle giant.

But as Ethan neared Azron, he spotted something in the forest, it was Damien and he was holding something. They looked like giant firelyte capsules the size of baseballs; he held one in each hand.

"IT'S DAMIEN! HE'S HERE! HE DID THIS!" Ethan yelled at the top of his lungs as he pointed Damien out to the others.

Azron, Nicholas, and Daavic quickly sprang to action giving chase to the retreating culprit, as RGB and Gruggins stayed with Ethan and Haley. Sol continued to circle overhead. Several minutes later, they returned empty handed, Damien had escaped.

"Well he knows we're on to him," Nicholas said, "I don't think he'll be back any time soon. And now that the forest creatures have been alerted, they'll be attacking anything that doesn't belong in the forest. He won't be able to surprise them again."

"Exactly," Daavic agreed, "but speaking of forest creatures, I didn't notice any grumplings in that stampede."

"That is because there are no grumplings," Gruggins said, "I have not sensed them since we arrived — the grumplings have left the Silent Forest."

"Yet another mystery to unravel," Nicholas said. "Regardless, I think our job is done here. We should head back and prepare for our return. There is much to tell the headmistress."

As the team headed back into the forest, Ethan turned to take one last look at the aftermath from the battle that had just taken place. He looked skyward to wave at Sol, just as the mighty thunderbird headed into the sunset, and then he saw it. A single giant feather floating towards the ground, it would land somewhere deep inside the Silent Forest.

DEADWOOD
SALOON

The team had returned from their harrowing experience in the Silent Forest. Jordanna called them to the Study so they could report their findings. She invited Alexander and Brianna along as well. It was official; Damien had joined the Grimleavers and was trying to burn down the Silent Forest. Ethan had seen him flee into the forest with two hell pods; if he had unleashed the other two hell giants, the forest would surely have perished.

"But why — ?" Jordanna mulled. "What reason would he possibly have for burning down the Silent Forest? And where have the grumplings gone? They wouldn't have left on their own, they are far too afraid of the leprechauns."

"Agreed headmistress," Alexander said. "It seems that the deeper we delve into this mess, we are only left with more questions."

"Yes, more questions," Jordanna agreed, "but I do have an answer to one question. I know what the Grimleavers are after."

Jordanna's admission was a surprise to everyone in the room, everyone but Ethan and Haley.

"More information from your secret informer — *mother*?" Daavic asked snidely.

"Actually yes," Jordanna replied, "it appears the Grimleavers want to unlock the door to the portals."

"But how could you possibly come to know this?" Nicholas protested.

He was obviously beginning to side with Daavic.

"We have never infiltrated the Grimleavers," Nicholas continued, "yet you are telling us information that could only come from one of them. Who is your source? It is highly irregular for you to keep such things from us."

"Yet special circumstances demand special treatment," Jordanna continued. "I'm sorry Nicholas, just trust that my source is a legitimate one."

"I must agree with Nicholas, you are breaking protocol," Brianna objected.

"Yes mother — and I fear you may be involving yourself in something that could get you hurt, or even killed," Daavic added.

"The headmistress has never given us reason to question her," Alexander jumped to Jordanna's defense. "We must trust her judgment."

"Mr. Sturgis is right," Gruggins joined in, "the headmistress is an honorable woman. You must honor her as such."

"I was afraid of such a reaction," Jordanna continued, "but I must insist that we move on for now — I have more disturbing news. I heard from Fin while the team was away, there has been a theft at Poseidon; several items were removed from the storage locker. Whomever did this, used our presence there as a distraction — the items were stolen while Fin and his team were busy with us."

"Do they know what was taken?" Daavic asked.

"They are in the process of doing a full accounting. Fin will report back when he knows more. But we all know important items were moved to Poseidon hundreds of years ago; items that were kept in the storage locker. It was the one place we were sure the Grimleavers could never reach."

"Yes — which is why there was never any locks installed," Alexander added. "There has never been a crime of any kind at Poseidon. I fear something sinister is afoot, the Grimleavers are becoming more and more bold with each passing day —"

"Yes, and that is not all," Jordanna interrupted. "After speaking with Fin, I thought more about what we learned at Poseidon. It made me recall the uneasy feeling that came over me after I last contacted the outpost. I tried to contact commander Triplin again, but could not reach him. We've lost contact with the outpost. A team will depart for Kraken Island first thing in the morning to investigate."

The reaction in the room was one of stone silence. Azron and RGB had been watching quietly as had Ethan and Haley. But now the rest of them were quietly pondering the realities of the situation.

Breaking up the silence, Jordanna went on. "I have yet to decide who will accompany me, but I will send word in the morning."

"You can't be suggesting," Nicholas pleaded. "This is an even bigger break from protocol. No headmaster has ever been on such a dangerous mission."

"You will hear my decision in the morning," she continued, ignoring Nicholas' pleas. "Until then, might I suggest a trip to the Deadwood Saloon? A new batch of dragon's breath arrived yesterday. You all deserve a break."

"That sounds like a marvelous idea," Brianna said. "I haven't had a dragon's breath in ages. I could use the clarity."

"Just make sure you all turn in early," Jordanna ordered. "Some of us will have a full day ahead of us tomorrow."

After Jordanna left, the group decided they would take her up on her offer. A trip to the Deadwood Saloon sounded like a fun departure after what they had all been through. Daavic declined the team building experience; he said he had important matters to attend to. Gruggins had adjourned to his box. Ethan and Haley would join Azron, Brianna, Nicholas, Alexander, and RGB — they were in for the time of their lives.

*   *   *

The trip to Deadwood was not far, the twelfth door on the right down The Hall of Doorways. Ethan and Haley had never felt so safe walking down the creepy hallway. Azron and the rest of the team were there to protect them.

"Deadwood Saloon — it doesn't sound like much of a place for kids," Haley said as they reached the twelfth door on the right.

"It does get its share of shady characters, but don't let the name fool you," Brianna said. "A fine establishment it is. Owned by Jewels Stoodlemeyer — been a Caretaker mainstay ever since Jewels took it over."

Nicholas opened up the twelfth door on the right; it was another outdoor area, a small town right out of the old west. Night was falling as they entered Deadwood; they were standing on a dirt path that angled left and widened to the road into town. To the right, tumbleweeds and hilly plains rolled off into the distance ending at the edge of a mountain range. Directly in front of them was a hill with a narrow dirt path that winded its way up to a dark house at the top.

"That's a spooky looking house," Ethan said, looking up at it. A candle burned in the picture glass window next to the front door; the curtains were slightly drawn making it visible.

"Dakota Drakelan lives up there," Alexander said. "The old codger rarely even pokes his head out anymore. Dakota was an old time Caretaker, used to be our best and some say most powerful. He's retired now, but you can't fault him for keeping to himself; the things . . . he's seen are better left in his head, that's why he's holed up in that old house."

They turned left on the dirt path and began into town. It was a small town, a row of joined together old west style buildings on each side of the dirt road. The road came to a dead end at a large red barn at the end of town — it looked like a place where horses would be kept only there were no horses. As they reached the edge of town, a crowd could be heard whooping it up inside the building on the left. Outside the old fashioned swinging doors, a large sign protruded out from a post in front of the building, it read:

DEADWOOD SALOON

Azron entered first, swiping the swinging saloon doors open with a push of his giant hand. The doorway was tall but he still needed to bend down to avoid bumping his head. As they entered, the crowd inside suddenly got quiet as everyone turned to see who they were. But the distraction was short lived and quickly went back to chatter.

RGB quickly set off on their own; darting over to a small round table in the middle of a large seating area. They proceeded to jump up onto the table and danced around in circles, chanting.

"Dragon's breath — dragon's breath — dragon's breath," they sang.

"Follow me, there's a table at the end that should accommodate Azron," Brianna said.

They followed Brianna down to the end of the L-shaped bar where it bent right. There was another seating section at the end with much larger tables and some Azron sized chairs.

"Dragon's breath everybody?" Brianna asked. "I'll give Blakelyn our order —"

"Do they have sugar-pickle soda?" Haley interrupted.

Somehow drinking something called dragon's breath did not sound palatable to Haley.

"Sure dear — I'm sorry — I sometimes forget, you look so much like her," Brianna replied. "Same for you dear?" she asked, looking at Ethan.

Ethan nodded, also happy there were other choices.

Blakelyn Wentworth was the barmaid at the Deadwood Saloon, having four arms made her perfectly suited for such work. She was a beautiful woman with flowing red hair, deep blue eyes, and more suitors than most women could deal with. She was a petite quadroll like her mother Bella, but had a charming friendly demeanor, unlike the brash chattiness her mother so often exhibited.

Ethan began to study the patrons sitting at the bar as they awaited their order.

At the end of the L, a small gnome with curly hair and glasses stood on a barstool looking up at a television mounted on the wall. He was watching *NFL football* and drinking coffee. Next to the gnome, sat three chubby human looking men, one medium and two large; they were watching football too.

"Scoooooter — this is Jimmy's seat," the large one with glasses said; he was standing up to show the other two, there was a plaque on his stool, it read: Jimmy's Stool.

"Jimmy loves his stool — nobody sits where Jimmy sits — Sparkie tried once, but nobody sits in Jimmy's stool," Jimmy ranted; he was talking about himself in the third person.

The other two ignored Jimmy's rant and ordered another round of dragon's breath.

Ethan giggled as he watched the silly exchange, but the glare shining off the balding domes of Sparkie and Scooter made him look away.

Further down the bar, on the other leg of the L, sat three brute quadrolls — the male counterpart to Blakelyn's species. They were fawning all over Blakelyn. The brutes of the species were much larger, with four muscular arms; but they were not nearly as attractive as the females. Their features were rough, short bunched hair, large pancaked noses, and high protruding foreheads — they looked like a cross between a caveman and a boxer.

Brianna returned to the table with an oversized goblet of dragon's breath for Azron. Blakelyn followed with three more goblets and two glasses of sugar-pickle soda. After a quick introduction, Blakelyn returned to the bar. It was a full house and there were three rowdy pyrodevlins for her to deal with next.

A thin white fog wafted from the goblets of dragon's breath. Ethan stood up to peek inside Azron's enormous goblet, a glowing purple liquid bubbled beneath the fog. It looked much less appetizing than the crisp green hue of sugar-pickle soda.

"A toast," Alexander said, raising his goblet into the air, "to the successful dousing of a hell giant — that must have been quite the sight to see."

Everyone clanked their glasses together and began gulping away.

"Ahhhhh — nothing like the clarity that comes from that first sip of dragon's breath," Nicholas said. "I've been a fool, to question the headmistress like that. I've been letting Daavic sway my opinion."

THWACK-THWACK-THWACK!

A thunderous sound erupted from the end of the bar, startling Ethan and Haley.

It was the gnome; he was clapping his hands together making the loud thundering noise, THWACK-THWACK-THWACK! It was annoying everyone in the saloon, especially Jimmy, Sparkie, and Scooter who were sitting next to him covering their ears.

"Don't worry — it'll die down," Brianna said, "it's only Cyrano our resident thunder gnome. He's happy because his team scored."

"Tinx — need a light over here!" Sparkie yelled out as the noise subsided.

Tinx was a winged pixie dragon about two inches tall and four inches long. Her lizard textured skin was peach colored with white swirls — like on a fancy textile. Sparkie held a white stick with a small pouch at the end. He was holding it up in front of his face and wanted it lit on fire. When Tinx heard her name called, she quickly fluttered over and landed on the bar in front of Sparkie.

"Are you sure Sparkie?" Tinx asked in a concerned tone. "This is your third one. Are you having girl troubles again?"

"Lighter up!" Sparkie insisted.

"Don't tell me, you went out with another drama mama," Tinx said as she winked at Sparkie and shot him a flirting smile.

She then breathed a stream of fire at the pouch and made a hasty retreat. The pouch smoldered for a second and then exploded in Sparkie's face, leaving him soot covered and splintered from the shattered stick.

"Woooo Hoooo!" Sparkie yelled as Jimmy and Scooter laughed hysterically.

"Looks like those three are getting lizard faced again," Azron laughed.

At first, Ethan hadn't noticed. But now that Azron mentioned it, he could see that Jimmy, Sparkie, and Scooter's faces had changed in appearance. Scaly leathered skin was beginning to form lines and ridges on their faces. They were beginning to look lizard faced — it was a vast improvement Ethan thought.

"Is something wrong with them?" Haley asked, suddenly concerned.

"Oh no, my dear," Brianna began to explain. "Dragon's breath tastes nasty but it is perfectly harmless. We drink it because it gives us clarity — it frees our minds from unwanted distractions and helps us see our mistakes. But one can only have so much clarity — so we normally limit ourselves. It is a fine line, but once it's been crossed, the hideous flavor turns to euphoria. It's simply the most wonderful flavor you could ever taste. That's when the side effects begin to kick in."

Brianna paused to laugh, shaking her head, pointing at the three reptilian faces.

"Brianna could tell us many stories about dragon's breath —" Nicholas began.

Brianna quickly shot Nicholas a look, stopping him in mid-sentence.

"Is Blakelyn any relation to Bella Wentworth?" Ethan asked, watching the three brutes at the bar vie for her attention.

"Hard to believe isn't it," Alexander replied. "She is such a beautiful creature, nothing like her mother."

"The complete package," Brianna added. "She has pledged herself to the man who can put a ring on every finger — her fingers of course."

"Those numbskulls drooling over her have been trying for ages," Azron joined in. "But their too dense . . . collected only a dozen rings between them. . . ."

"The Rumpner brothers," Brianna continued, "Grant, Billie, and Pierre, they aren't the sharpest knifes in the drawer. But they've loved Blakelyn for a long time — been fighting over her for as long as I can remember. So she made the silly pledge to stop them from fighting."

"Smart girl — she'll never have to make good on it anyway," Alexander smiled.

"Rumor has it, her heart is pledged to another though," Brianna said. "Gruggins saw it himself."

"What did Gruggins see?" Haley asked, eager to hear more about her little pal.

"It has been said that grumplings can see things, things not visible to other creatures," Nicholas explained. "It's like they possess an all seeing eye. . . . They have many hidden abilities . . . they only let us know of a few.

BONG-BONG-BONG!

A gong suddenly sounded. Patrons in the saloon suddenly began getting up from their tables and leaving the bar area. They were migrating to a large room in the back. It was set up like a small arena; thick netting separated it from the saloon proper.

"Looks like a challenge has been made," Alexander said. "A drone war is about to begin."

"A drone war —" Ethan repeated; it sounded like something from one of George's video games.

"Drone wars date back to our arrival on Earth," Alexander began to explain. "It is an evolutioner's game. Each player gets a drone and they take turns, evolving their respective drones into more advanced life forms. The winner is the one with the last drone standing; it's sort of a fight to the death."

"That sounds horrible!" Haley protested.

"Maybe, but it is how we've honed our skills and stayed sharp for thousands of years," Alexander explained. "I guess we all have our dirty little secrets."

After his quick explanation, Haley wanted no part of watching the drone war. Instead, they stayed in the saloon area and gossiped about more of its patrons. Brianna had a wealth of stories to tell, people watching in the Deadwood

Saloon was apparently one of her favorite pastimes. By the time the patrons started filing back into the bar area, it was time to retire for the night. Tomorrow would be a long day for some of them.

They exited through the swinging doors of the Deadwood Saloon, stopping at the edge of the wooden walkway for a breath of fresh night air. Brianna stepped down off the sidewalk and turned around to say something, but quickly stopped dead in her tracks.

"N-n-no — it — it can't be —" Brianna struggled to spit out the words; she was pointing at the saloon sign.

"What's wrong?" Ethan asked as he looked up at the sign. "It's just a big old raven."

"That's not a raven," Nicholas corrected. "It's a grimtailed dread and wherever one is sighted — darkness follows. . . ."

DARKNESS
FOLLOWS

Upon closer inspection, Ethan could see that this was definitely not a raven; it was much larger and looked more dead than alive. An opaque white film covered its eyes like that on a dead fish. Its feathers were mangy and tattered, especially near the tail which looked like it had been put through a shredder. The only evidence that this bird was alive was the beating of its heart, visible through a gaping wound in its abdomen — grimtailed dread was a fitting name for this creature.

"Brianna — contact Jordanna at once, I'll fetch RGB!" Alexander began barking orders. "Azron, you and Nicholas stay here with Brianna — keep a watch out and protect the children at all costs!"

The Caretakers quickly jumped to action. Brianna pulled her ELMO device out to call Jordanna. Azron and Nicholas took up positions next to Ethan and Haley while Alexander ran back into the Deadwood Saloon.

CAW-CAW — the grimtailed dread let out two piercing shrieks, bobbed its head, and took flight.

It sailed past the old house on the hill and was over the plains when it happened. The dread suddenly disappeared, replaced by a swirling grey vortex in the sky, it was growing quickly. A strong wind began to gust from its black center as it grew larger — it looked like a small hurricane turned sideways in the night sky. Tumbleweeds began to blow through town as the wind gusts grew stronger, and then as quickly as it had started, the wind was gone. An eerie calm took over — even the sounds within the saloon had died down.

"Yes . . . something bad is going to happen . . . we'll do what we can . . . but send the security detail at once!" Brianna finished talking with Jordanna just as the wind had subsided.

Alexander rushed out through the swinging saloon doors. RGB were right behind him eager for action. Everyone was staring up at the swirling vortex. The stillness in the air was unsettling, like the calm before the storm.

Then, in an instant, loud noises began to erupt from the center of the vortex as creatures began flooding out from its blackness: vampires swarmed the sky, gliding on their enormous bat-like wings; vicious flying monkeys carried stones; and large vulture like birds with horns were mounted with trolls on their backs, the trolls wore armor and were armed with staffs that glowed blue with electricity. They were being dropped off on the plains outside of town. They were amassing an army and this was the ground assault — Deadwood was being attacked.

"Chances are they've come for Ethan, he and Haley will stay with me!" Alexander continued to give orders. "We will force their hand — they will have to bring the fight to us! Brianna, you and Nicholas concentrate on the air assault. Azron can handle the trolls on the ground. I will shield the children. RGB, stay near me and handle anything that gets by their defenses."

Alexander took Ethan and Haley by the shoulders and guided them into the street. When they reached the middle of the dirt road, he directed them to kneel down. He then raised his arms into the air, holding his palms toward the sky; a glowing shield of light began to form in the air above his out stretched arms. It grew brighter and larger as he slowly spread his arms out and down to his sides in a wide sweeping motion. He was forming a dome shaped shield around them, all the way to the ground — he had generated a shielding force field.

RGB took position around the outside of Alexander's shield, forming a tight perimeter. Nicholas spread his large angelic wings and swiftly took to the sky. Brianna and Azron started down the road out of town. Brianna took her position in the middle of the road at the edge of town. Azron continued onto the plains to greet the approaching trolls.

The flying monkeys started the assault, hovering overhead and dropping large stones from above. Azron dodged and swiped at the stones with his massive hands as he continued towards the trolls. Nicholas swooped in behind the attacking monkeys ripping the wings from any he could catch up to. Brianna had a unique attack of her own: the tube like worms on her head stood up and pointed skyward and began to glow; green pulses of light shot at the monkeys' eyes blinding them instantly; with each shot, the worms would lose their glow and then begin to rejuvenate. RGB joined in, shooting fireballs at the monkeys as they continued the onslaught. Any stones that made it past their defenses, harmlessly bounced off Alexander's protective force field.

As Azron neared the army of trolls, they began leveling their staffs and sending jolts of blue electricity at him. But the giant was far too large; it did little more than anger him. Azron swiftly closed the gap and began swinging his arms wildly like giant clubs. Trolls were flying everywhere — they were no match for Azron. Wave after wave of monkeys and trolls continued their attack, but they were out gunned, it was futile.

The vampires were next to join in, they had been hanging back and watching from above as the battle below unfolded. Brianna and RGB were taking care of the monkey assault so Nicholas focused on the oncoming vampire attack. While vampril strength was no match for a vampire's, the wings of a bat were no match for the wings of an angel either. Nicholas knew his advantage would be agility, so he would play to his strengths.

The vampires began their descent, one by one in single file, diving towards Alexander's shield — they were after Ethan Fox. Nicholas was over the plains above Azron when the vampires began their attack, so he quickly started a steep climb to intercept them. He'd climb above them and attack from behind. RGB would have to handle the vampires at the front of the line; however, Nicholas could greatly reduce their numbers from behind.

Nicholas was picking the vampires off one by one. He could dive faster than them, swooping in and grabbing them from behind, and breaking their wings before they were even aware of what was happening. It wouldn't kill a vampire, but the plunge to the ground would crush enough bones to take them out of action for a while.

The first few vampires in the attack formation had neared the shield and were dodging RGB's fireballs when something unexpected happened. The Grimleaver attack force made a sudden and hasty retreat. It was as if an unheard voice had called out to them. Instantly they turned around in unison and headed back towards the vortex.

The giant horned vultures began to swoop down and pick up the retreating trolls while the remaining vampires collected their fallen brothers. The Grimleaver attack force was quickly disappearing back into the vortex as the Caretaker security detail arrived. There was not much for them to do other than watch the retreating army.

Nicholas swooped in and landed beside RGB as Alexander lowered his shield. Brianna and Azron were running back to join them.

"I don't understand," Alexander said as Brianna and Azron arrived. "Why would they do this? They've never been so bold."

"My thoughts exactly," Nicholas agreed. "Why would they even try such a futile attack? They could never be a match for us here at The Residence."

The calm silence returned to the air as the last of the retreating Grimleavers disappeared into the vortex. A strong gust of wind sucked the tumbleweeds in the opposite direction as if all the air was being sucked out of Deadwood. The vortex was shrinking and within an instant it was gone.

Alexander pulled his ELMO device from his robe and quickly contacted Jordanna.

"The attack was thwarted without much difficulty I trust?"

"Yes headmistress, but how did you know it would be so easy?" Alexander asked.

"Because it was not an attack," Jordanna replied, "it was a diversion. Please report to the Front Room at once — your presence is needed. And bring the others."

The team quickly escorted Ethan and Haley through The Hall of Doorways to the Front Room. The sound in Jordanna's voice had them all very worried. They arrived to find Jordanna picking up pieces to Gruggins' box. It had been crushed and the Front Room was a mess.

"Daavic tried to stop him —" she wept, "there was a struggle and Daavic gave chase. But I'm afraid he's escaped to the Moongarden."

"Stop who? What happened here?" Alexander asked.

"Has something happened to Gruggins?" Haley interrupted.

"It was Damien!" Jordanna cried. "Gruggins has been abducted! Damien has him!"

LAIR OF THE
SPIDER GECKO

Everyone was surprised by the news of Gruggins' abduction. Haley took it especially hard. It was a very bold move for the Grimleavers to attempt such a pointless attack; they should have suspected something. But why Gruggins? If opening the portals was the Grimleavers end game, why take him, it didn't make any sense.

Daavic returned to the Study. He had chased Damien down The Hall of Doorways to the Moongarden but he had given him the slip there. Damien must have found a very good hiding place.

"I've made my decision," Jordanna began, "tomorrow we depart for Kraken Island. Nicholas will accompany me — Ethan and Haley will go along as well — the rest of the team will stay here and concentrate on finding Gruggins."

"But surely mother! Under the circumstances you can't be serious!" Daavic protested, "Such a small team, with human children, on what could be a very dangerous mission!"

"I must agree with Daavic," Alexander spoke. "Under the circumstances, I think it better we postpone this mission altogether."

"Now who's questioning authority?" Nicholas defended Jordanna's decision.

"I'm sorry, the decision has been made, I have my reasons," Jordanna interrupted. "It's more important than ever now, we must find some answers."

Jordanna dismissed them all. It was time to turn in for the night. Tomorrow would be a busy day for everybody.

Ethan woke the next morning, to once again find his pocket tote disturbed. Someone had been poking around in his room while he slept. But whom? Did it have anything to do with the recent events? It left an eerie feeling in the pit of his stomach.

Jordanna and Nicholas were already in the Study when Ethan and Haley arrived. Haley was reluctant to leave. She wanted to stay with the others and find Gruggins; but Jordanna convinced her otherwise. It was important that they stay with her for the time being — she would ensure their safety. They would once again use book travel, this time traveling to One-Two-Tree Island, a micro-island in the middle of the Pacific Ocean. Fin would send a greeting party to show them the rest of the way. Jordanna had made the arrangements.

* * *

This time Ethan was the first to awake, he was getting used to book travel. It was a calm sunny morning in the middle of the vast Pacific. Ethan was surprised to see where he was, One-Two-Tree Island was a small patch of sand no bigger than a living room; there were two tall palm trees in the center that crisscrossed halfway up. The only thing missing was the message in a bottle.

The others awoke shortly after Ethan. Fin's greeting party was expected shortly so they all began scanning the horizon. The water was as smooth as glass, which made it easy to see the approaching hydromorph as it breached the surface for the first time. At first, it appeared to be a lone dolphin, but as it neared they could see the dolphin was escorting something else. Four-wide bulges just beneath the water's surface disturbed the ocean calm like approaching speed bumps.

The dolphin surfed its way to the edge of the beach where it morphed in mid-swim, wading the last few feet. He introduced himself as Wilbert Frye. Wilbert was mostly yellow and white with subdued orange markings. He had the look of a mature adult but was much smaller than the others they had seen. Wilbert Frye was a pygmy hydromorph.

"Four seaskippers as requested," Wilbert said, pointing at the strange sea creatures he had escorted.

The seaskippers had stopped in the shallow water at the edge of the beach. They were blackish blue with brilliant red circle patterns scattered about. They looked like oddly shaped giant stingrays with longer wings and shorter bodies — like underwater stealth bombers.

"Anyone ridden a seaskipper before?" Wilbert asked, and then explained how.

Riding a seaskipper was easy. After all, they did all the work, the rider merely steps in, leans back, and steers. On the back of each seaskipper were two foot shaped crevices; the rider climbs aboard, steps in, and a lip like muscle gently grips the rider's legs like a lollipop. Once aboard, a thick padded flap of hyde folds up behind the rider giving them a platform to lean back on while two thick antennas join together in front to act as reins.

Ethan and Haley were not alone. Jordanna and Nicholas had never ridden a seaskipper before either. But after Wilbert's explanation, they would all soon be experts. Besides, they would not be required to steer, these seaskippers already knew the way to Kraken Island — they would ride on auto pilot.

They were gliding over the ocean as if skiing behind an invisible boat; the seaskippers skimmed along just beneath the water's surface. The seaskippers were fast, and before long they had lost sight of One-Two-Tree Island altogether. They were alone in the middle of the Pacific.

"How much farther?" Haley yelled over the noise of the seaskippers. "There's no sign of any land!"

Haley was beginning to feel uneasy.

No sooner had she uttered the words, it happened — a giant hole opened up in the water in front of them. It was several hundred feet away and large enough to drive a double-decker bus into. And the seaskippers were heading right for it.

"OH MY GOD! WHAT IS THAT?" Ethan screamed, pulling back on his seaskipper's reins, but his commands were ignored.

"Nothing to be alarmed at," Jordanna yelled back, "it's just the tunnel to Kraken Island!"

As they reached the edge of the giant hole, the seaskippers expertly navigated its riders into the tunnel. It descended into the ocean depths at a steep angle. The seaskippers spiraled down the outside of the tunnel, keeping their riders inside — like they were skiing down the inside of a giant straw. The tunnel leveled out to a dimly lit straightaway before finally angling back up towards the surface. It was quickly getting brighter as they approached the surface. The light at the end of the tunnel was visible, and so was a wall of water.

"Prepare for a water landing — we're gonna get wet!" Jordanna shouted.

The seaskippers stopped spiraling outside the tunnel and straightened out their paths as they neared the wall of water above. Each of the riders was on a different quadrant of the circular tube, one behind the other. Then one by one the seaskippers pulled away, un-lipping the locked feet of their riders, and catapulting them at the wall of water as they did.

They hit the water as if they had just jumped from a cliff. The water was clear and shallow and they were now in a small lagoon. The lagoon was surrounded on three sides by thick foliage, on the other side, a small beach ended at a steep cliff. The cliff was part of an insurmountable mountain range that circled the island.

"The only way to the island's interior is through that cave," Jordanna said, pointing up at the left side of the beach to a dark cave at the base of the cliff.

"We'll need sunlight crystals," Nicholas added. "I'll gather some while you and the children dry off."

Nicholas proceeded to the base of the cliff and began hammering at a large black bolder with a rock he had found. The bolder was soft. He quickly chipped off some large pieces and threw these against the cliff wall causing them to shatter. When he was done smashing rocks, he began picking through the pile of rubble he had created. He returned with four dirty crystals and proceeded to wash them off in the lagoon. They shimmered in the sun as he laid each out on a handkerchief he had spread out in the sand.

"Sunlight crystals store the sun's rays very efficiently," he said as Ethan watched with a curious grin.

The team had dried off; it was time to venture into the cave. Nicholas gathered up the sunlight crystals and handed each of them one, keeping one for himself. As they moved to the entrance of the cave, Nicholas disappeared inside for a moment, and emerged with four lantern enclosures. He opened one up and put his sunlight crystal inside, the others did the same.

"Sunlight crystals don't glow, they actually emit sunlight," he added as they entered the cave.

It was pitch black at first, but then the crystals fired up, lighting the cave wonderfully — it was like they each had a propane lantern. The cave was straight and narrow, but opened up wider as they reached a fork in its path.

"It is very important that we take the path to the right," Jordanna said. "Legend tells of a fearsome creature that lives deep within this cave — the path to the left is home to the fabled spider gecko."

They continued down the fork to the right but quickly encountered a problem. The path to the right was blocked, a cave in had occurred.

"Strange, there haven't been reports of any cave ins . . ." Nicholas pondered.

"Agreed," Jordanna said, "I'm afraid we should fear the worst. The mission just got a whole lot more dangerous."

"Yes," Nicholas agreed, "and we can't afford more delays. We'll have to chance the other tunnel — if we keep still we should be okay. The children will have to wait at the lagoon, it is plenty safe there. We will send for them once we reach the outpost."

Jordanna explained to Ethan and Haley the dangers of what they were about to do; it was far too dangerous to ask them to go along. They made their way back to the fork in the cave's path — Ethan and Haley would be okay heading back to the beach on their own. Nicholas and Jordanna would venture into the lair of the spider gecko. As long as they treaded lightly they should be all right. According to legend, the spider gecko slept most of the time anyway, but it always woke up hungry.

Ethan and Haley were back on the beach. They'd found a nice shady area to shield them from the now scorching sun. They were at the edge of the thick foliage at the end of the beach, under a small cluster of umbrella shaped trees near the cave's entrance. It had been about an hour since they split from the others and they were beginning to become impatient.

"Something's not right Ethan," Haley began, "why would Jordanna choose us to come along and then leave us here?"

"She explained it to us," he replied, "the other tunnel is too dangerous and she didn't want to put us at risk."

"Maybe she wanted it to be our choice," Haley argued. "She took a big chance bringing us — the other Caretakers were angered by her choice, but she said she had her reasons — remember?"

"The poem book," Ethan agreed, "when we showed it to her, she said I had been chosen — that's why she brought us!"

"They need our help, Ethan. Jordanna must have felt strongly about that or we wouldn't be here — we have to go after them."

Ethan and Haley wasted no time. They scooped up their sunlight crystals and headed back into the cave. They retraced their way back to the fork in its path and slowly ventured into the lair of the spider gecko.

They remembered Jordanna saying it was important to tread lightly, so they carefully measured every step making as little noise as possible. The cave opened up into a chamber the size of a small living room — large enough that their lanterns did not light the entire chamber. Ethan went left while Haley explored right. There was no sign of Jordanna and Nicholas but they must have come through the chamber.

"Ooooooh, Ethan, come here," Haley whispered from across the chamber.

Ethan could see by the light of her lantern what she had found; it was the skeletal remains of a human. He was pinned to the base of the cave wall in a sitting position, held there by webbing of some kind. The skeleton wore tattered clothes and clutched a jeweled knife in his hand like a pirate.

He hurried over for a closer look. The added light from his lantern lit up the wall even better. And then something else happened. A glittering patch of gold suddenly materialized out of nowhere — it was a circular pattern of gold dust on the cave wall above the remains.

"Look — someone must have put that there," Ethan whispered, pointing at the wall.

"Looks like it is covering something up," Haley observed.

Ethan began rubbing at it and blowing with his breath. The dust easily flaked away and fell to the cave floor. When he was done, they could see what was covered up. A black crest was embedded in the cave wall. He began prying at it with his fingers but it was no use, it was in too deep.

"Try this," Haley said, handing Ethan the knife she had just pried from the skeleton's hand.

Ethan went to work digging at the crest patiently until he finally wrested it free. Roughly circular in shape, it looked like four unique and independent symbols interconnected at the center — it was about the size of a cantaloupe and made from a hard black marble looking material.

"We need to keep moving," Ethan said, storing the knife and crest away in his pocket tote.

Haley agreed.

"It truly is the must have accessory for the on-the-go explorer," Ethan mimicked Irvin's words.

They continued to the end of the chamber where the cave narrowed to a tunnel once again. Not a sound was coming from anywhere in the darkness ahead, so they continued as quietly as possible. The tunnel went on for some distance before they arrived at the next chamber. There was a strange scent in the air that Ethan noticed as they entered. It was much larger than the last chamber — like a gymnasium with high ceilings. There were bunches of white oblong sacs stuck to the walls like giant bananas with rounded ends; a florescent bluish green light glowed from within, they were all over the walls of the giant chamber.

"They look like eggs of some kind," Ethan whispered as they tiptoed across the chamber floor.

"I'm getting a bad feeling Ethan, my infinity ring is crawling again," Haley whispered back.

They were standing in the dead center of the large chamber when it happened. Wisps of yellow light began to emerge from Ethan's pants pocket. The poem book was coming to life again; it was in his pocket tote.

Ethan quickly retrieved the tote and drew the string to open it — he was becoming an expert at it by now. He pulled the book out and rested it in his open hands. It quickly flipped to the first blank page where a poem wrote itself out backwards on the glowing page. It read:

Creepy Crawlers

Dark and dreary comes the night.
We lose our way in fear and fright.

Loud and crunchy noise prevails.
It all begins with slugs and snails.

Death that's black is all around.
So skip and jump don't touch the ground.

But if you run away with fear.
Creepy Crawlers will be near.

Ethan and Haley had just finished reading the poem when they heard it, a crunchy crawly sound. Something was rustling on the ground around them. Ethan quickly shoved the book back into his tote and held his lantern out. He bent down and took a few steps before they saw it, millions of creepy black bugs of all shapes and sizes were crawling over each other. They had surrounded Ethan and Haley and were closing in.

"AAAAAAAAAHHHHHHHHHHHHHH!" Haley let out a piercing scream that could have awakened the dead.

As Ethan held the light closer to the creepy crawlers, he noticed they backed off ever so slightly. So he began pushing forward making sweeping motions with his lantern.

Haley stopped panicking and joined in when she saw what Ethan was doing.

"Stop what you are doing," Nicholas' voice called out.

Nicholas and Jordanna had come to their rescue.

"It is very important that you listen carefully," Nicholas said. "Put your lanterns on the ground and stand between them. Stay completely still, do not move a muscle."

Nicholas and Jordanna had heard Haley's scream. They were standing on a ledge at the end of the chamber a few feet above — it was an entrance to another tunnel.

Ethan and Haley obeyed as Nicholas sprang into action.

He slammed his lantern against the cave wall, breaking free the sunlight crystal inside. In one smooth motion, he bent down and picked up the sunlight crystal, spread his wings and took flight. He circled twice over their heads to find the sweet spot in the mass of black death on the floor below. Hovering for a moment to gather strength, he found it, the perfect spot to launch his attack; he quickly broke into a dive and smashed the crystal down onto the cave floor with a forceful throw. It shattered into a blinding flash of light, igniting the layers of bugs into a blue inferno that quickly vaporized.

"It was foolish of you to come!" Jordanna scolded as Nicholas set down beside them.

Jordanna jumped down off the ledge and started towards them when something caught her eye — something they could all hear.

Ethan, Haley, and Nicholas immediately spun around to see what was making the creepy clicking sound.

It sounded like it was coming from the chamber entrance but it wasn't, it was above the entrance, another tunnel they had not seen before. High up near the ceiling it was emerging from a dark tunnel, an enormous spider gecko. From a distance it looked like a car sized scorpion with spider legs and gecko feet. It clung to the wall like a gecko as it slowly crept down the cave wall.

"Take the children — find a way up that shaft!" Nicholas yelled to Jordanna. "I'll hold it off with these and buy you some time."

Nicholas smashed the lanterns Ethan and Haley had put on the ground, retrieving the two sunlight crystals they held.

Ethan and Haley ran to the end of the chamber where Jordanna was waiting.

They quickly disappeared following Jordanna down the narrow tunnel; she led the way with the only remaining lantern. They arrived at another small chamber, it was dimly lit on one end by the luminescence of several bunches of spider gecko eggs. On the other end, a thin beam of light beamed down from a shaft that led to the surface — it was like they were in the bottom of a deep well.

Jordanna rushed over and began parsing the walls. She was looking for a way up.

"It can't be!" Jordanna cried.

Ethan rushed over to see if he could help.

She was bending down at the floor of the well. A rope ladder laid at her feet; it had been thrown in from above. They continued searching for a way up: a secret switch, a hidden ladder, or even grooves large enough to hold onto. But there was nothing. They had looked around for several minutes when they heard commotion from within the tunnel, it was Nicholas.

"I had hoped you'd be gone by now, I only stunned it!" Nicholas gasped emerging from the dark; his voice sounded dire. "It looks like we've run into a dead end — all we can do is stand and fight — can't say I like our chances."

"Can't you just fly the ladder up the shaft?" Ethan asked.

"My wingspan is too wide for the narrow shaft — I'd never make it off the ground —"

"Wait a minute!" Haley interrupted. "I have an idea . . . I know what to do. . . ."

She quickly ran to the far end of the chamber and pulled one of the squishy glowing eggs from the wall. It was the size of a zucchini and jiggled in her hands like it was filled with Jell-O. She squeezed the end with both hands and slimy green goo squirted out the other end. She continued squeezing until every last drop had oozed out.

"Don't ask me where I learned this . . . I have no idea. . . ."

Jordanna, Ethan, and Nicholas watched in disbelief as Haley slipped her arm into the empty egg sac.

It fit like a long sock at first but then something happened. It suddenly sucked itself snug against her skin and her arm began to change. It grew longer as did her fingers. Her fingertips began flattening out into suction cups. The egg sac was morphing into a gecko arm.

They watched speechlessly as Haley continued with her other arm and two legs. She was halfway up the shaft of the well before the others fully understood what she was doing.

"Jordanna, you and Ethan follow Haley, it will be coming soon," Nicholas said.

Nicholas grabbed the remaining lantern and shattered it for the last sunlight crystal.

Ethan and Jordanna were outfitting themselves with gecko limbs when they heard it — the spider gecko was coming.

The beast slowly emerged from the dark tunnel; it was blackish purple and had the face of a gecko with six black spider eyes. It had three tails that hung over its head like a scorpion, two short ones for spinning web and a long one in the middle for shooting dagger like spikes at its prey.

Jordanna and Ethan were gecko'd out and started up the shaft walls.

Nicholas jumped in front of the spider gecko to buy them more time. He threw the remaining crystal at its feet causing a blinding flash which filled the cave. The creature was stunned by the light and retreated back into the tunnel.

Nicholas quickly ran over and began squishing egg sacs to outfit himself with gecko limbs. He had just gotten the last one on when the spider gecko crept back into the tunnel. He started up the shaft wall; the spider gecko in hot pursuit, the race was on.

Ethan and Jordanna emerged from the top of the long tunnel. It was a bright sunny day out; if Nicholas could make it into the sun, the spider gecko would not follow. Haley had found a rope near the mouth of the well. She was tying it around a nearby tree when Ethan and Jordanna emerged.

Nicholas was a much better flier than wall scaler as he clumsily made his way up the vertical shaft wall. The spider gecko was closing in. Its three tails were spitting like machine guns; streams of web trailed out from the side spinners while spikes zipped out from the middle tail. A stream of web flew by narrowly missing his head but the next stream found its target ensnaring Nicholas' foot in its sticky grasp. Nicholas lunged forward breaking free but not without a price. His gecko leg was pulled off along with it and he was losing his grasp.

He was two-thirds of the way up when Haley finished tying the rope off. Ethan and Jordanna wasted no time helping Haley carry the heavy coil of rope to the edge of the well. Nicholas was struggling to climb higher. The spider gecko was nearly upon him when they dropped the rope down the mouth of the well.

"Grab on to the rope, we'll try to pull you up!" Jordanna yelled down as the rope fell into Nicholas' view.

The rope was just outside his reach, he was almost out of time. The spider gecko was bearing down on him when he made one last desperate move. He pushed down on the wall all at once with his gecko limbs; they nearly ripped off in the process. His lunge forward was just enough. He was able to grab hold of the rope.

But the spider gecko was not giving up; it made a final move of its own. It lurched forward, spitting two spikes from its long middle tail. As it did, one of them found its mark striking Nicholas in the meat of his thigh. The poison was spreading quickly; he was using his last bit of strength to hold on as the others hauled him up. By the time he reached the top, he had lost consciousness.

KRAKEN ISLAND

Nicholas was barely able to hang on, putting a death grip on the rope with his last bit of strength. He was unconscious when he reached the top of the well but Jordanna was able to patch him up. She removed the spider gecko barb and revived him with water from a canteen she had tucked away. He was still very weak, but vamprils have strong metabolisms, it would take the poison much longer than normal to do its damage.

"There's not much more I can do I'm afraid, my experience with vampril anatomy is limited," Jordanna said. "We need to get him to the outpost."

"I'm far too weak to fly, but if we can fashion a crutch or something, I will make the walk to the outpost," Nicholas said.

They were on a flat ledge at the top of a steep cliff that overlooked the interior of the island. To the left of the well shaft, trees and thick foliage climbed further up the encompassing mountain range.

Jordanna and the children searched the vegetation, finding a thick branch to build a crutch from.

To the right of the well shaft, a narrow path carved its way down the inside of the circular mountain range — like threads on a bolt.

Jordanna looked out over the cliff surveying the landscape, mapping out where they were about to venture.

The mountain range encompassed the islands interior like a giant bowl with a land locked lake at its center. There was another small land mass at the lake's center; an island within an island. A column of smoke was rising from it.

"Center Island —" Jordanna said, "it looks like the outpost is in trouble. We must proceed with caution — we've no choice, Nicholas will not last long without help."

They slowly made their way down the narrow path. Nicholas was doing as well as could be expected with the help of the crutch Jordanna had patched together. It took an hour to reach the bottom. The path ended on a small rock beach with a sign in the middle that read:

Private Notice from Center Island:

To raise the bridge of water, it takes a special stone. A five hopper will be required to make it ring the tone. Skip not once to see it through, it takes two skips from me to you.

"Sounds like a riddle," Ethan said.

"But what does it mean?" Haley asked.

"Looks like one of the new precautions commander Triplin was taking," Jordanna replied, "I'm afraid I was never told of it, only that extra measures were being taken."

"Well — let's see . . ." Ethan pondered, "if it is a riddle, it sounds like it's talking about skipping a rock. A five hopper is five skips — I used to skip rocks with my dad all the time."

Ethan began searching the rocks on the beach to demonstrate.

"There's a trick to it," he explained, "the flattest rocks skip the best."

Ethan picked up a medium sized rock; it was flat and shaped like a used bar of soap. He walked out near the water's edge and heaved forward with a healthy throw. The rock dug straight into the water without skipping a notch.

"Bad throw, not enough horizontal, needs to skim along the top," he explained.

Haley and Jordanna decided to join in, they were searching for rocks of their own. Ethan found a pile of slate shaped rocks. He was on his fourth unsuccessful throw before Haley found her first rock. She approached the edge of the water with a perfectly round golf ball shaped rock in her hand.

"You'll never skip that one, has to be flat," Ethan said.

"Ethan — are you forgetting where we are?" Haley challenged. "The sign says, 'a special stone' — haven't you noticed all of the rocks on this beach are flat?"

She launched an underhanded softball pitch at the lake. The stone bounced off the water's surface like a ping pong ball off a concrete floor — it was a three hopper.

"I just got told!" Ethan laughed.

"Here, give it a try," Jordanna said, handing Ethan a round ball of a stone.

He launched it straight up into the air, vertical rather than horizontal. It landed with a thud, hopping five times before sinking into the water.

The sound of a loud gong erupted from Center Island — it rang in their ears like a tone from a hearing test. The water started bubbling — like an overdone kettle on a campfire. Pillars of water began sprouting in the distance; one by one they sprung up, walking across the lake like the legs of a water giant. Two rows of columns stretched across the span of water to Center Island; they were shorter on each end like the piles of a bridge, and that's what they were. The finishing touches came in a rush. A short wall of water shot across the top of the bridge from the other side; it created a smooth glass surface of water that rested atop the piles. There were fish still swimming within the structure of the water bridge.

"We did it! A bridge of water!" Ethan yelled, running up the ramp of water onto the bridge.

It easily held his weight.

"Come on up!" he shouted as he stopped to turn around, but he quickly fell through splashing into the lake below.

Ethan swam back to the others as Haley looked back at the sign and began reading it again. A wide smile grew on her face — she was about to one up Ethan once again.

"It takes two skips from me to you," she said as she skipped out onto the bridge of water.

She continued up the ramp onto the water platform and kept moving, skipping around in circles.

"You're not supposed to stop, you have to keep skipping!" she yelled.

"Well done my dear," Jordanna said smiling, giving her a wink of encouragement.

It wasn't going to be easy for Nicholas, he was barely able to walk let alone skip across a long bridge of water. He was too weak to fly. But with the aid of his wings and the crutch together, he could lighten his weight enough to keep him skipping along to Center Island.

It was a long but uneventful journey across the bridge of water. They reached Center Island just as Nicholas began losing his mind.

"Shnickyrooners and things like that," he murmured, "Jimmy loves his stool . . . this is Jimmy's stool. . . ."

Nicholas was growing delirious.

The bridge dropped them off on a small flat of granite at the edge of a thick jungle. There was an opening in the trees; a well traveled path was exposed in the green wall of growth. Nicholas was running out of time so they wasted none in taking the path towards the outpost. Jordanna had no idea what they were about to come across but they were losing precious time.

They came out of the jungle at a wide dirt clearing. A tall set of trees at its center hid house sized huts in its giant branches. Bamboo stairways and bridges connected the seven tiers of huts; it reminded Ethan of a *Disneyland* tree house he had once visited.

As they made their way around the towering trees, a large bonfire became visible nearby; it was the source of the billows of smoke. There were bodies in the fire, vampire bodies; someone was burning their mangled remains. A woman was kneeling down, she was crying loudly while a tall man threw another vampire into the flames. They wore black and white robes like Jordanna, it was Adam Triplin and his wife Trudy — they were Caretakers.

"What happened here?" Jordanna gasped as they approached from behind.

Trudy was horrified, all she could manage was a whimper, but Adam was composed enough to answer.

"Sorry headmistress, it was the Grimleavers, they surprised us," Adam replied. "They killed nearly my entire staff before we even knew what hit us. They were disguised — disguised as us. They sabotaged communications and we were unable to fend them off — until they . . . came and killed the vampires."

"Who are they — ? Who came?" Jordanna asked.

"I-I-I don't know . . ." Adam replied. "They were unlike anything I have ever seen before. . . ."

Nicholas collapsed, he had run out of strength on the journey down the mountain, the poison was finally taking its toll. Jordanna rushed to his side as he lied on the ground. He was just about to lose consciousness when he said something.

"The vamprils, they are here —" Nicholas managed.

"He's been ranting deliriously," Jordanna said. "I thought we could find help for him here, but I'm afraid the Grimleavers have all but killed his chances."

Jordanna paused and began to weep for her friend.

"Ethan, check your pocket tote, the poem book," Haley interrupted; she was massaging her finger, her ring was slithering again.

Jordanna stood and turned towards Ethan. She could sense that something was about to happen.

Ethan retrieved the book like an old pro; no sooner was it resting in his hands than it once again sprang to life. Jordanna watched with keen interest as it flipped past the existing poems to the first blank page. Writing began to crawl up from the bottom of the page as usual. When it was done they all stood together reading it.

The Plight of the Vamprils

A proud but troubled species, secluded and alone.
Vampril wings take flight; they come to save their own.

Dark disturbing secrets, the story will be told.
Feeding on blood of vampires, so ruthless and so bold.

Devolved of spirit, weak of mind.
Like fallen angels, running blind.

The dangerous path they've chosen could surely be their end.
Two outcomes one forsaken, be it enemy or friend.

"This can only mean one thing," Jordanna said, kneeling down at Nicholas' side.

She bent her head down as if praying for a few minutes; it looked like she was in a trance. Then suddenly she stood up, opened her arms wide, and began to speak in an amplified voice.

"He needs your help — he will die without it. You may take issue with the Caretakers, but Nicholas has done nothing wrong. He does not deserve to die."

It was as if she was speaking to the entire island, her voice echoed through the distant mountains. At first the sound of her voice just trailed off into silence. Then suddenly sounds thundered from the distant mountains. Vamprils were taking flight, they were on Kraken Island.

There were seven of them. It took them no time to soar over the land locked lake. They landed in the clearing not far from the bonfire, they were all female vamprils.

"Very smart to be burning them," one of the vamprils said, pointing at the fire.

She was at the head of the pack; they walked towards Jordanna as if in formation.

"Valeska — it's nice to see you again — I only wish it were under better circumstances," Jordanna greeted, shaking the woman's hand.

They had angel wings and wore flowing white robes, but Valeska Vandercort was the tallest of the group. She was their leader.

"Tend to him before he dies," Valeska ordered the others.

They quickly rushed to Nicholas' side and began looking after him.

"Is this all of you?" Jordanna asked. "Where are the others? Where are your men?"

"I'm afraid we have a lot to discuss old friend," Valeska began. "After we left The Residence, we wandered the countryside — a roving band of vamprils. We didn't stay any place for more than a few days; we thought it best to keep moving. The men were sure there was a mole within the Caretaker organization — a mole that helped in Nicole's abduction. It was a grave mistake leaving The Residence, thinking we would be safer protecting ourselves from the Grimleavers. What we never considered was that the vampires they had created could hunt us so easily — they have a nose for vampril blood. They found us wherever we traveled. We were attacked time and again. We lost many to the vampires, only four of our men survived; they were gravely injured and are recovering now —"

"But you could have come back at any time," Jordanna interrupted.

"Vamprils are very proud, but also very stubborn," Valeska continued. "We thought we had found a place they would never venture to, but the Grimleavers have been busy. Their vampire army has a new weapon, hydromorph blood, and they are using it to shape shift."

"We received intel from Poseidon — Fin was speculating as much," Jordanna said. "But how did you find this out?"

"We've been here on the island, this was our quiet little hideout," she replied. "The vampires were disguised as

Caretakers. At first we wondered why the outpost crew was killing each other — we thought they had all gone mad. But when the hydromorph blood wore off, it became obvious what was happening —"

"He's coming around headmistress," one of the vampril women interrupted.

Whatever they had done to treat Nicholas appeared to be working. He was sitting up slowly.

But the happy reunion was interrupted by the sound of water splashing. It was coming from a nearby inlet on the other side of the trees. Jordanna and Valeska began walking towards the disturbance and Ethan and Haley followed.

"We've been taking care of the pups," Valeska explained. "Since the attack on the outpost, we've been feeding them."

They came to a small ramp — like a boat launch going down into the small bay. Two sea creatures were frolicking in the water, splashing around like seal pups. When they saw people approaching the creatures quickly swam to the ramp and began hobbling out of the water.

The kraken pups had cute adorable faces with large brown eyes and long lashes. They were dark bluish purple with the body of a small seal, but much longer. Their tails tapered at the end like that of an eel. A row of elongated pectoral fins helped them walk; they were floppy at the ends like immature tentacles.

"But where is the third?" Jordanna asked. "When I spoke with commander Triplin, he said they were all accounted for."

"As I was about to say —" Valeska replied. "We've been taking care of the pups for nearly a week. The attack did not just happen, it's been several days. The commander Triplin you spoke to was a Grimleaver — the real commander Triplin and his wife, were being held captive. Grimleavers made off with the pup. Some stayed behind to carry on the charade until . . ." her voice trailed off.

"The commander spoke of someone killing the vampires — did you see who it was — was it you?" Jordanna asked.

"It wasn't us, but I'm afraid I have more to tell you — I know who it was," Valeska replied. "I said that only four of our men had survived but that's not entirely true. There were eight men and seven women. But Romulas and three of the others left us, they've changed, they are vampin creed now."

"But why would your husband and the others turn?" Jordanna asked. "They were honorable leaders — Romulas was Nicholas' best friend."

Jordanna was very disturbed by the news.

"Vengeance —" Valeska replied, "they were angered at being hunted and unable to defend against the Grimleavers, and they became obsessed with vengeance. My husband figured out that we could sniff out the vampires as easily as they could us. So he and the others hatched a plan. They would leave us here where it's safe, hunt down vampires, and feed on them. They would turn vampin creed, it would make them very powerful — they are now a self sustaining army of four that will not rest until every last Grimleaver is destroyed."

"Oh, my — this is very disturbing news," Jordanna said. "We've always speculated as to what might happen if a vampril was to feed on a vampire — but vampin creed was only a theory."

"I'm afraid the reality is much worse than the theory," Valeska said. "They've changed, they are not thinking rationally. Their wings have blackened and eyes turned red, they've become monsters. I worry of what's to come when they run out of vampires to feed upon."

CHAPTER TWENTY-TWO

UNEXPECTED

GUESTS

Nightfall was coming quickly so they decided to stay at the outpost for the night. The tree huts were mostly untouched by the Grimleaver attack and would provide ample shelter for them all. Nicholas made a full and quick recovery after the vampril women tended to him. Together they helped commander Triplin finish burning the pile of vampire remains.

Ethan was confused, wondering why they didn't just burst into flames under the sun's rays — like in the movies. Jordanna explained that it was different in real life, real vampires aren't burned by the sun's rays; they avoid light because their eyes favor the darkness.

In the morning, they would bury the bodies of the outpost crew and repair the communication systems. Commander Triplin would remain at the outpost with Valeska and the vampril women; the others would return to The Residence. A team would be dispatched to relieve them and transport the injured vampril men back to The Residence — they would be safer there.

It was still early morning when they arrived at The Residence. Jordanna wasted no time; she was on her ELMO device making plans. She called for a full session meeting of the Caretaker Council; she had research to do so everyone was to meet in the Map Room in four hours. She dismissed Ethan and Haley telling them they could wander freely, but to stick to places they knew — she didn't want any unwelcome surprises.

Ethan and Haley headed back to Ethan's room so they could talk in private; there was a lot to discuss after the trip to Kraken Island. When they arrived, Ethan retrieved his pocket tote and pulled out the pirate's knife and mysterious black crest.

"This knife must be worth a fortune," Ethan said, examining its jeweled handle.

Haley was reading a note that had been slid under her door. It was from Mrs. Moongarden — a reminder that today was Percy and Alicia's ceremony.

"I'm more interested in the crest," Haley said as she finished reading the note. "Somebody hid it there for a reason — it's got to mean something."

"Yeah — you're right," he agreed, stuffing the knife back into his pocket tote.

Ethan held up the crest so they could see it in the light, but it slipped from his hand and fell to the ground. It landed with a heavy metallic ring — like he had just dropped an iron skillet. But it did not break; whatever it was made of was very strong.

They discussed their trip to Kraken Island for several moments before Haley had an epiphany.

"I wonder —" she pondered, "we might be able to find something out in the Study — it's full of reference books."

Ethan agreed.

Ethan returned the crest to his pocket tote and he and Haley headed to the Study. When they entered, RGB were there. They were arguing about something.

"No it doesn't — RGB stands for Really Great Blue!" Newton insisted.

"Rat Germ Blue maybe, but not very great!" Albert countered.

"Hey maybe it means Red Goat Baby," Newton replied.

"Or Red Geek Booty," Linus added.

"No — RGB definitely means Ranting Green Brat!" Albert shot back.

"That's enough," Haley interrupted, "you're all wrong, I know exactly what it means — Really Good Boys. So why don't you all be really good boys and quit your bickering."

"We're sorry," Newton said, surprised by the interruption.

"Yes — Miss Haley — we are sure you are correct," Linus replied.

"No problemo," Albert added.

After breaking up the argument, Ethan and Haley began scanning the titles of the reference books. They were looking for anything about knifes — or weapons — or symbols — or emblems; anything that might remotely point them in some direction. No sooner had they started, RGB started back up.

"Oh, yeah I remember," Albert said, "it means Rotten Grump-face Blue."

They started bickering again; it was not going to stop.

Ethan and Haley ignored it this time and continued scanning the reference shelves. Ethan's eyes quickly landed upon another title that stopped him in his tracks.

"OH MY GOD — Haley look!" Ethan said loudly, pulling a book from the shelf; it was titled:

Creatures of the Dark Realm
by Dakota Drakelan

"Dark Realm — isn't that what your dad's video game was about?" Haley asked.

"Yeah —" he replied.

"Maybe he knows this Dakota Drakelan or something?" she interrupted.

"That name sounds familiar, too . . ." he replied.

"It does, doesn't it . . ." she pondered.

"Wasn't that the name of the retired Caretaker — the one living in that creepy house on the hill?" he asked.

"Yeah — I think it was."

"So answer this question — how would my dad know a Caretaker?"

Ethan had an uneasy feeling about his latest find. But he ignored it for now so they could continue searching for answers. Haley found a book that caught her eye, it was called:

Weapons and Other Dangerous
Inventions of the Chrysalis

She flipped through the pages quickly, stopping on a page that looked familiar, it was a Lightning Lance.

"Look at this Ethan — it's the weapon the trolls used when they attacked Deadwood."

Ethan looked down at the page but his eyes were quickly drawn to something else — something on the adjoining page — it was Haley's infinity ring. They read over the paragraph next to the picture; the ring was a rift key, designed by someone named Heldrick Von Grim. The many uses of a rift key were largely unknown to the author, but it was rumored that most of its uses were for diabolical purposes.

"That doesn't give me a very good feeling either," she said. "Ethan, can I see the crest one more time?"

Ethan retrieved his pocket tote and pulled the black crest out for another look — maybe it would give them inspiration. The room suddenly got quiet, RGB had stopped their bickering, and were now standing straight up side by side looking at Ethan with wide eyes.

"Have you seen this before?" Ethan asked.

"How did Ethan Fox come to possess the Creators' crest?" Linus asked.

The three pyrodevlins hopped up onto the Study table, knelt down in a bowing stance, and held their hands out.

Ethan started walking towards them — they knew something about the crest. As he walked, his foot caught the edge of a throw rug which tripped him. He fumbled the crest flipping it up into the air as he fell to the ground. But the crest didn't fall; it stayed hovering in the air, slowly floating towards RGB.

Ethan and Haley watched in stunned silence.

As the crest reached the tiny outstretched hands of the three pyrodevlins, RGB each grabbed hold of a different quadrant causing it to glow brightly in their respective colors. They fell into a trance.

Ethan and Haley walked closer as RGB held the glowing crest above their heads.

The quadrants glowed bright red, green, and blue, the fourth remained black. Ethan reached the table first. As he neared, the black quadrant of the crest began to give off a faint yellow glow. And then wisps of yellow light began to emerge from his pocket.

"Ethan! It's happening again," Haley said, rubbing her infinity ring.

He quickly retrieved the poem book from his pocket tote and held it in his open hands. The book took over yet again, but this time something different happened. It didn't flip to the first blank page, this time it flipped to the torn out pages. The first torn out page slowly began to grow, it was reconstructing itself, and as it did the fourth quadrant of the crest glowed a brighter yellow. There was already a poem written on this page, it had been there before, it read:

The Odyssey Begins

The journey's just begun but evil's planned ahead.
Behold a Realm of Darkness to one day raise the dead.

Its minions lurk in silence among the breeding horde.
Awaiting the arrival of an evil dark Grimlord.

Creator from a chosen world this warming you must fear.
Trust in others you must avoid as darkness will be near.

But hope will run eternal, a savior will arrive.
A long lost hybrid child, feared dead but still alive.

Creator from a chosen world protect it at all costs.
A Moment in Eternity, will tell you when you're lost.

"What does it mean?" Haley asked.

"I don't know . . ." Ethan replied, "they all seem to have some sort of meaning, but they're very cryptic."

The poem book began to calm, its yellow glow dimmed along with the fourth quadrant of the crest. RGB snapped out of their collective trance and gently set the crest down on the table. It snapped apart effortlessly, the four symbols were now separate entities.

"It has begun Ethan Fox — it has begun," RGB chanted in unison.

"What's begun? What are you talking about?" Ethan pleaded.

"Red Gas Buffalo, that's what RGB stands for," Newton said with a menacing grin.

The bickering started up again. It was as if they could remember nothing that had just happened.

"What just happened?" Ethan asked, turning to Haley. "They're as batty as Mrs. Moongarden."

"The Moongarden, you just reminded me — we have to leave, Mrs. Moongarden is expecting us," Haley said, tugging at his arm.

Ethan gathered up the symbols and poem book and tossed them into his pocket tote as they hurried to the Moongarden — Haley did not want to disappoint her friend.

When they arrived, they were greeted by a young lady in a flowery sundress. She wore a bonnet like Mrs. Moongarden and looked like she could be her daughter.

"Hello, you must be Ethan and Haley, my name is Rosebud," she introduced herself, offering her hand to Haley first.

Rosebud escorted them to the small meadow where Haley had helped Mrs. Moongarden outfit Alicia. Each and every apple on the large apple tree was dressed in a small wedding dress. There were large and small white chairs set out in rows on the grass. A white stage sat beneath the two trees that stood side by side. Percy had been dressed as well, his pears each wearing a small black tuxedo with a bow tie. Mrs. Moongarden winked at Ethan as they approached.

"Thank you so much my little Moon-sprouts, I couldn't have done it without you two," Mrs. Moongarden greeted them.

Haley looked at Ethan in surprise, and then back at Mrs. Moongarden.

"Young Ethan Fox helped with Percy's fitting," Mrs. Moongarden said smiling.

"I wanted it to be a surprise," Ethan said.

"When did you find the time?" Haley asked smiling; she was pleasantly surprised.

The isles were filled with people, animals, and creatures of all shapes and sizes. Ethan and Haley recognized Grubner Trowel sitting in the front row with six other dwarfs. Dorkin Drumbles would marry Percy and Alicia. In addition to his curator duty, he was the Caretaker reverend as well — Dorkin wore many hats at The Residence.

The ceremony started with a song from Rosebud. She had a wonderful voice, and the crowd went wild when she was done. She exited the stage into a row of shrubs as she finished. The ceremony started a moment later as Dorkin took the stage. It went off without a hitch, Dorkin was an old pro at the pulpit, and he pronounced Percy and Alicia husband and wife to the applause of the crowd. The crowd noise subsided and then it happened — a terrifying scream filled the air; it was coming from the direction of the skyclimber vine.

A group of wedding goers rushed down the dirt pathway towards the skyclimber. It was Rosebud; she was kneeling at base of the giant vine sobbing.

"It was horrible . . ." she cried. "I saw him . . . climbing down the vine. He . . . jumped down and tried to attack me — it was Damien!"

The news of Damien being on the loose in the Moongarden frightened everybody. Mrs. Moongarden was not taking any chances; she would lock it down tight and send everyone home. The ceremony had been a success despite this sudden turn of events.

Ethan and Haley were escorted to their rooms. They were to stay there until further notice. Security would be alerted and the Moongarden thoroughly searched.

Ethan arrived at his room and decided to lie down; it had been an exhausting day, a nap was in order. He emptied his pockets out on his dresser: a set of house keys, a 49ers wallet, and his pocket tote. He was just about to lie down in his bed when he spotted movement out of the corner of his eye. It was his pocket tote, it was unraveling by itself, and something was moving around inside.

"You know kid, you're really starting to grow on me," a voice spoke up from within the small bag.

Ethan was stunned and couldn't take his eyes off the bag.

"I think I'm starting to like you," the voice said as a small green head emerged from the pocket tote.

"And a how do you do to you," Gruggins McGhee said with a smile.

CHAPTER TWENTY-THREE

FAMILY REUNION

Ethan called Haley over to see his unexpected guest. He told Gruggins that they were supposed to be keeping to their rooms — Damien was on the loose. But Gruggins insisted; they only had time for him to explain things once. Haley was pleasantly surprised when Ethan opened up his door.

"Gruggins! How did you escape? We've all been so worried," Haley gushed.

"I've missed you too, it's been longer than you know Danielle —" Gruggins paused, "— er — I mean Haley."

Ethan and Haley gave each other a glance. Gruggins was acting strange.

"Used the negative doors," Gruggins began to explain. "I've been with Ethan Fox since the day he arrived; had to sneak myself into that pocket tote before Irvin gave it to you. I remembered hearing from inside my box when Ethan got the tote. Haley got the copycat as well. Irvin darn near grabbed me instead of the copycat — I had to practically hand it to him —"

"I don't understand," Haley interrupted, "what are you talking about? And how could you be in two places at once?"

"Okay, I can see I've confused you, let me start over," Gruggins said. "The day you and Ethan arrived, a negative door sprouted up in The Hall of Doorway's — it happens from time to time, to bookmark an important moment. After Damien abducted me, I went through that door. I arrived in the Study just after Haley. I knew I had to beat feet to Irvin's room before Daavic called for him. If I could hide out in the pocket tote, I would be with you at all times. I could watch out for you both —"

"I remember now," Ethan interrupted, "it was you I saw in the room at the top of the stairs. You shot me with a dart."

"Well I couldn't have you blow my cover could I? Didn't want me to find me — so I gave you a little nap and cloaked myself on the wall," Gruggins smiled. "Imagine my surprise when I found my own blow dart buried in your butt!"

Gruggins pulled out a small golden dart with "G.M." monogrammed on the shaft.

"It confused me at first," he said, "but then I began to figure it out. I'd been sensing something outside my box — turns out, the 'tricky critter' I was after was me."

"It's all beginning to make sense," Haley said, "the mysterious person snooping in Ethan's room, his pocket tote moving around — it was you — you weren't snooping, you were coming and going."

"And you're the reason the gold dust suddenly became visible on the cave wall," Ethan added. "It must have been cloaked leprechauns gold."

"Very good, you're figuring things out very quickly," Gruggins reassured them. "We have a lot more to discuss, but I'm afraid I may have to ask you to break some rules. Do you trust me enough to do that?"

"Yes we do," Haley replied immediately.

Gruggins looked at Ethan with a questioning stare.

"I'm in if she's in," Ethan said.

"Great, then let's go, there's someone I want you to meet," Gruggins replied, hopping up onto Haley's shoulder.

They were reluctant to travel down The Hall of Doorways at first, since they had been told to stay in their rooms. But Gruggins had warned them, they may need to break some rules, so they followed his lead. It was a quick trip down the hallway to the twelfth door on the right. It was daylight this time when they made their way down the dirt road into town; the Deadwood Saloon was nearly empty when they arrived.

Ned Peppler, the daytime bartender, was sitting at one end of the bar reading a paper. The rest of the place was empty except for a stranger sitting in a dimly lit corner of the room. Gruggins directed them towards the stranger. As they slowly made their way through the empty bar room, Ethan got a strange feeling, and then he heard the voice again.

"Be calm Ethan Fox, breathe easy and stay calm, everything will be all right," the soothing voice within his head said.

It was the same voice he had heard at *Gothcon* when the two vampires were carrying him down the hallway.

As they approached the stranger, Ethan could see him more clearly as his eyes adjusted to the light. He was wearing a brown overcoat, a black wide brimmed hat, and dark glasses.

"It's the stranger," Haley whispered, "the one in the Gallery painting — the one watching you on the boardwalk."

Ethan was getting an uneasy feeling, but he kept replaying the voice in his head, "Everything will be all right. . . ."

They sat down at the table across from the stranger. His head was tilted down into his goblet of dragon's breath. Gruggins hopped down onto the table from Haley's shoulder.

"This better be worth it," Gruggins complained. "I've spent the better part of a week holed up in a stuffy pocket tote. Good to see you made it safely, seems like it's been forever."

"Forever for you, mere moments for me," the stranger said; his voice was soft but gritty and he spoke in a slowly measured tone — it sounded faintly familiar to Ethan.

The stranger's head slowly rose as he reached up to pull off his hat. Long stringy black hair fell around his face as he reached up with his other hand to remove his glasses. He slowly pulled off the glasses exposing his eyes, one was deep green, the other bluish grey with a crescent moon-shaped pupil — the stranger was Damien Ravenwood.

Ethan and Haley jumped from their seats in terror. They were about to start for the door when Ethan heard the voice again.

"It was me Ethan Fox," the calming voice spoke up in his head, "I am Damien Ravenwood — I was not there to harm you, it was I who saved you from the vampires."

It suddenly dawned on Ethan who the stranger sounded like, it was the voice he had been hearing in his head — Damien was his guardian angel.

Haley bolted for the door when Ethan sat back down.

"Come back Haley!" Ethan shouted. "We need to hear him out."

Haley stopped dead in her tracks, turned around, and looked at Ethan.

"We told Gruggins we would trust him," Ethan said. "Let's hear what the stranger has to say."

"But Ethan, we know he's bad — he tried to kidnap you," Haley pleaded as she took her seat at the table; she was staring daggers at Damien.

"No — he didn't," Ethan said, "he was the one who saved me — I didn't put it together before, but I see it now."

"I'm afraid you've all been misled about me," Damien said. "My brother has been very busy framing me — making everything appear to be my doing. He's done a masterful job up till now I might add, but he made one grave mistake."

"But we saw you in the Silent Forest, with two hell pods, you tried to burn it down!" Haley protested.

"Do you remember when you saw me at Market Square?" Damien asked. "I was watching my brother — he gave the forest trolls three hell pods. I was there to stop them. Unfortunately, I was too late, they were able to ignite one but I stopped them from setting off the other two."

"Daavic was joking with those trolls, they were laughing when he was talking to them," Haley countered.

"I'm afraid you misunderstood my dear," Gruggins corrected, "forest trolls don't laugh, it only looks that way when they are terribly frightened."

"Damien is telling the truth," Ethan said.

"At first I wasn't sure of my brother's motivation," Damien explained. "I sensed he was very disappointed so I watched him closely. He was looking for something in the Silent Forest and was very angry that it wasn't there. I thought about it long and hard, it finally dawned on me — the grumplings — the grumplings had left the Silent Forest."

"Daavic was the first to notice the absence of the grumplings," Gruggins added. "I sensed it the moment we entered, but he was the first to point it out."

"I know my brother well," Damien continued. "If he needed a grumpling for some reason and there were none to be had elsewhere, then Gruggins was in danger. So I took a huge risk. I snuck into The Residence to snatch Gruggins — forcefully if I had to. Luckily I beat my brother to the punch, barely; his Grimleaver buddies arrived shortly after I did. Daavic caught me in the act, only because he was there for the same reason — to abduct Gruggins McGhee. But imagine my surprise when the little bugger came along willingly."

"You went along willingly?" Haley asked, looking down at Gruggins.

"Yes my dear, I did," Gruggins replied. "Once I figured out that the critter I had been sensing was me, I knew something was coming. I could only be here and there if I

266

jumped timelines somewhere along the way. And since I hadn't done so yet I knew it was coming."

"It all makes sense," Ethan said, "I never really did trust Daavic very much."

"Okay so what if it is true, then what?" Haley asked.

"I have a question to ask you."

"*Which is?*"

"Has Daavic showed you the secret wishing well in the Moongarden?"

Ethan and Haley looked at each other and then nodded their heads.

"And I bet he had you drink from it as well."

"How did you know — ?" Ethan asked.

"That's not important right now, we'll get back to that . . . later —" Damien replied.

"Master Damien," Gruggins interrupted, "I'm afraid there have been other developments you should know about."

"Such as?"

Gruggins filled Damien in on the recent events Jordanna had been dealing with, things he had overheard from within Ethan's pocket tote: dispatching a team to Poseidon, the theft from the storage locker, the attack on the outpost, the missing kraken pup, etc. . . . By the time Gruggins was finished, Haley was chomping at the bit again.

"So what now — ?" she asked.

"Now we have a whole lot more to discuss," Damien replied, "Gruggins and I have a plan. . . ."

* * *

The Map Room was nearly full; Jordanna had called for a full session of the Caretaker Council. The bottom half of the spherical room was filled with seats. Hundreds of Caretakers looked on as Jordanna, Daavic, and the CAGE team — Azron, Alexander, Brianna, Nicholas, and Bella — floated above them.

"I've called this session," Jordanna began, "to bring you all up to date on recent events, things we've been investigating. We ask that you relay this information to your teams — as always we welcome any questions or input from each of you. Let me start with the Grimleavers — we have learned that the Grimleavers are plotting to open up the four portals."

A sound of muffled voices filled the room; the Caretaker leadership appeared to be surprised at Jordanna's revelation as well.

"But surely that would be suicide," a voice spoke up from the crowd.

"Not even the Grimleavers are that crazy," said another.

"Agreed," said Jordanna. "We all know The Book of Creators holds the key. The Grimleavers would never be so foolish as to try to remove it. And since they cannot defeat us here — why would they even consider such a thing?"

"And what are their motives?" Alexander asked. "Secluded from the elemental worlds, they stand a much better chance against us."

"Exactly," Jordanna agreed, "how could they possibly benefit from opening the portals? I've pondered these and many other questions for days. I have consulted The Book of Creators, it states simply: 'Before the portals are locked away a key will be made, the last thing through will hold the key' — it's been well documented. The Book of Creators was the last thing through the portals — the BOC holds the key. But the BOC does not stop there, it further lists specific events that must occur before the key can work — none of the events it lists have come to pass —"

"So it appears the Grimleavers are becoming more aggressive than ever before," Nicholas interrupted, "to accomplish something that cannot possibly be achieved."

"That's what's been bothering me," Jordanna said. "Either the Grimleavers know something we don't know — or The Book of Creators does not hold the key."

"You speak of blasphemy!" a voice yelled out from the crowd.

"Nonsense!" yelled another.

Heated conversation filled the room, the Caretaker Council was not happy with Jordanna's proclamation.

"Moving along!" Jordanna shouted to hush the crowd, "I've heard from Fin regarding the break in at Poseidon — all of the items taken were from Pandora's Bunker."

The crowd broke out in muffled discussion again.

"They are still investigating the specifics," Jordanna continued, "but so far it appears Stravis' journal was taken among other things."

Jordanna paused as the sounds of the crowd grew louder.

"THE COUNCIL WILL COME TO ORDER!" Alexander shouted heatedly.

"Fin also believes a kraken is on the loose," Jordanna continued again. "We sent a team to the outpost, it had been attacked, and the Grimleavers abducted one of the pups."

"But how could they attack the outpost? The security measures alone —" a voice spoke up from the crowd.

"The vamprils witnessed the whole thing," Nicholas interrupted, "they were hiding on the island. They confirmed another of Fin's suspicions, the Grimleavers have found a new weapon, they are using hydromorph blood to shape shift."

Muffled voices filled the room again.

"STOP! There's more!" Nicholas interrupted. "Many vamprils have been lost but some have gone rogue — they've become vampin creed."

The voices grew louder yet again.

"What would the Grimleavers want with a kraken pup?" a voice yelled out from the crowd. "Even they are not foolish enough to devolve an Earthly kraken."

"Another one of those, nagging questions I've been asking myself," Jordanna agreed. "What use would they have for a kraken pup?"

The question hung in the air as silence filled the room, and then another voice broke the silence.

"Isn't it obvious mother, they set it free to wreak havoc on Earth's oceans. They set it free so you would send a team to Poseidon."

The room stayed silent as the stranger in a brown overcoat slowly made his entrance. Ethan and Haley were at his side and Gruggins was on Haley's shoulder.

Then — Damien took off his hat and glasses.

The room immediately erupted in loud shouts as the crowd recognized his face — the face of the man who killed their beloved leader.

"SECURITY, TO THE MAP ROOM ON THE DOUBLE!" the sound of Daavic's voice rose above the crowd noise as he screamed into his ELMO device. "WE MUST ARREST THIS MAN IMMEDIATELY!"

Daavic was pointing at his brother, his face red with anger.

"I know what they've been up to mother!" Damien shouted as the room grew silent. "I can help —"

"I'm afraid I must agree with Daavic," Alexander interrupted, turning towards Jordanna.

"BY THE HEART OF WORMFREID MOTHER —" Damien shouted, silencing the room again. "I know what the Grimleavers are up to — I know what he's been up to!"

Damien stared into his brother's eyes.

"But Daavic must be dismissed from Council, what I have to say is not for his ears."

"SEIZE THAT MAN —" Daavic roared as security entered the room.

"WAIT —" Jordanna interrupted.

"But surely mother," Daavic argued, "you can't be considering —"

"He will get what's coming to him," Jordanna interrupted, "for killing Ryvias he will pay. But first, I will hear what he has to say."

"But mother —" Daavic protested.

"Daavic, you are dismissed!" Jordanna ordered.

CHAPTER TWENTY-FOUR

BROTHER

DEAREST

Daavic angrily slammed the door beneath the stairs. He had gone to his basement retreat after his mother dismissed him from the Map Room. He was still fuming from his brother's accusations. His mother seemed all too eager to hear Damien's nonsense. After all that time, what could his brother possibly have learned that would cause him to give himself up?

Daavic made his way across the Front Room and entered the Study through the in-door.

RGB were arguing over a book, tugging at it with their tiny hands like a three way tug-of-war.

"OUT! LEAVE THE STUDY AT ONCE!" Daavic growled.

RGB had never heard Daavic yell like that. They wasted no time dropping the book and rushing through the out-door.

Daavic walked across the Study to his desk. He took a seat and leaned back deep in thought. After a few minutes of contemplation, he reached into his robe pocket and pulled out a key. He unlocked the desk drawer and opened it, pausing to stare at its contents for a moment. He reached in and pulled a yellow book from the drawer; it was old and dusty with tattered edges, a journal of some kind. He held it up studying its cover, and then it happened — Daavic vanished.

Daavic was back in the Front Room standing a few feet from Haley. The yellow journal in his hands morphed into a small metallic kitty. He quickly threw it to the ground. Haley's Tabby cat had safely returned to her owner.

"Looking for this brother —" Damien said, holding Stravis' yellow journal out.

Jordanna, Ethan, Haley, and Gruggins were standing with him.

"I've been giving it a read," Damien continued, "very interesting, the writings of Creator Stravis. It tells of it all — his distrust of the other Creators — his friendship with the blue taletaddler — his changing of the key to the portals."

"Enough of this nonsense, he must be arrested, mother!" Daavic insisted.

"I didn't make the connection myself," Jordanna admitted. "When Ethan Fox told me of his dream — of the blue taletaddler — I didn't even consider that it might be Jasper."

"But you did, dear brother," Damien added, "you made the connection. That's why your Grimleaver buddies attacked the outpost and stole the kraken pup. You knew it would mature

273

quickly in the open ocean; it would wreak havoc, which would give you a chance to steal the journal. Fin would have no choice but to ask for a face to face, with the secret he had been keeping — Poseidon would be his only option."

"MOTHER YOU CAN'T BELIEVE THIS DRIVEL!" Daavic cried out furiously.

"Victor Qruefeldt was obsessed with the dead Creator," Jordanna added, "he always insisted that Stravis was alive. After Stravis' death, Jasper was never seen again. If Victor learned that Jasper was alive he might consider that proof of Stravis' survival as well."

"But mother —" Daavic pleaded.

"You begged for the assignment," Jordanna interrupted. "I thought it strange at the time — but talked myself into believing you were finally ready for more responsibility."

"Here's another interesting passage," Damien read from the journal:

> . . . at the feet of a grumpling lies the key, but I've made a few changes. I must protect them from themselves, I fear their thirst for power will be their worlds undoing. They've become evil, especially Zamalador, the others fear him, he has a hold over them. I've changed the lock on the portals, but they will be none the wiser, even if I must take this to an early grave.

"So you gave the forest trolls the hell pods to burn down the Silent Forest," Ethan interrupted. "Without its protection, the Grimleavers would be free to grab the grumplings — you thought they were the key."

"But that's not the first we've heard of that — grumplings and the portals," Jordanna added. "Ethan, the poem book — remember the poem . . ."

Ethan produced the book of poems from his pocket tote.

Gruggins looked down from Haley's shoulder and mumbled something under his breath.

Ethan gave Gruggins a strange glance as he handed the book over to Jordanna.

"Here it is," Jordanna read from the book:

> To find the key things must unfold,
> At a grumpling's feet the secret's told.
>
> Four portals locked away so tight,
> Unlock the door to begin the fight.

Jordanna handed the book back to Ethan.

"I could sense your frustration in the Silent Forest brother," Damien added. "When the grumplings were not there, I knew Gruggins would be your next option. Luckily I beat you to it — if you hadn't been busy leaving the dread outside the Deadwood Saloon I may not have."

"Lies . . . all lies . . . I swear to you mother!" Daavic continued pleading.

"I didn't abduct Gruggins," Damien continued, "he came along willingly. He had been expecting me. But imagine our surprise dear brother, when Gruggins began having flash backs — flash backs that could only have come from our sister, Danielle."

Daavic's eyes grew larger, he was listening carefully. His body was tensing up, his pleading stopped suddenly, and then Daavic began to cry.

"But you made one fatal mistake brother," Damien continued. "You knew that Haley and Danielle were one in the same — so you took them to the wishing well to swap their memories. Ethan would not recognize Danielle's memories, and you couldn't chance jogging Haley's — she might remember who she really is — she might remember what you did to her. But what you didn't know —"

Daavic paused to catch his breath. Jordanna was hanging on his every word. Her eyes were tearing up.

"What you didn't know was that Gruggins naps inside the well — he shared a drink with the children — he holds our sisters memories, not Ethan — memories of you helping Victor Qruefeldt kill our father."

Jordanna was looking at Daavic in disbelief as he stood before her cowering.

"What are you talking about? What wishing well?" she asked, turning towards Damien.

"A secret room in the Moongarden," Damien replied. "Daavic and I stumbled upon it long ago when we were hiding — the day we climbed the skyclimber. The well holds special powers, sharing a drink of its water swaps certain memories. Have you ever wondered mother, how I learned of Daavic's zebra prank?"

"That's why you made us drink from it," Haley interrupted, "you nearly insisted that we drink from that well."

"But you didn't know Gruggins was in the well," Damien continued. "He drank from the bucket as you lowered it, Gruggins received our sister's memories — memories that he sees differently. Interesting thing about grumplings, they have many special abilities, they can see through a cloak of deception — they see only the truth."

"What are you saying?" Jordanna cried out. "What did Gruggins see — ?"

"He saw the truth mother, it was Victor who killed my father," Damien explained. "Victor Qruefeldt was disguised as me, he used hydromorph blood — the blood of Newt Dripmore — the Grimleavers have known about the hydromorph secret for a long time."

Jordanna looked to Gruggins who gave her a confirming nod.

"How — ?" she asked, "how did Victor kill my husband?"

"He used a Heldrick Von Grim puzzle box — but there's more to tell mother," Damien replied. "Gruggins told me every detail, we discussed it for hours. There was a struggle, Ryvias grabbed the puzzle box just before he was killed and dislodged the rift key from it — the rift key that now sits on my sister's finger."

Haley held her hand out. Everyone in the room looked at the strange infinity ring on her hand. Daavic fell to his knees, he was whimpering loudly as Damien continued to tell the story.

"Danielle witnessed the whole thing. She thought she saw me struggling with Ryvias — she thought I killed him. She ran to our father's side once Victor was gone. With his dying breath he put the rift key on her finger. He made her promise to tell no one where she got it and with that decision he saved her life. Later the next morning, Danielle stumbled upon a secret meeting in the Moongarden — Daavic was talking with Victor Qruefeldt when they spotted her spying on them."

"HE MADE ME HELP HIM!" Daavic cried loudly, he was finally breaking down. "Victor said he would kill us all if I didn't help him. He said we would suffer a fate worse than death —"

"Later that night!" Damien loudly interrupted. "Daavic entered Danielle's room with the puzzle box — he was there to kill her. They were not aware of the missing rift key; the one she now wore on her finger. When Daavic used the keyless puzzle box it did not have the desired effect. Danielle vanished — they thought it had worked its magic but it didn't. It sent my sister into the future — to the boardwalk where I was watching Ethan Fox."

"But why did it send me there?" Haley asked. "Why do I only remember that my name is Haley?"

She too was now tearing up.

"There are still many pieces to the story that I have yet to figure out," Damien replied. "But I can assure you my dear, you are my long lost sister —"

"You are my daughter!" Jordanna cried, bending down to give her a hug.

"Victor lied to me! He said the puzzle box would only make her forget! He never told me it would kill her!" Daavic pleaded. "Please you must forgive me! I beg of you! He forced me to help them — !"

"Why! Why does Victor want to unlock the door to the portals?" Jordanna cut Daavic off.

Her loud commanding voice startled Daavic.

"He has always wanted them open," Daavic answered. "He thought it impossible — The Book of Creators was the key. But when he learned of the key being changed, it renewed his interest."

Ethan looked over at Gruggins who was still perched on Haley's shoulder. The phantom bubble was floating above Gruggins' head. Ethan opened up the book of poems and began studying the pages; he was deep in thought.

Jordanna repeated a passage from the poem:

Unlock the door to begin the fight.

"Well if it's a fight they want — it's a fight they'll get," she said. "We are going to find the key to the portals. We are going to unlock that door —"

"I've got it!" Ethan loudly interrupted. "I think I've found the key!"

CHAPTER TWENTY-FIVE

UNLOCKING THE PORTALS

"Funny thing about Grumplings," Ethan started, "they have many special abilities . . . isn't that what you said?"

Damien nodded in agreement. "They can even read the secret language of the Creators."

Ethan held the poem book up so Gruggins could see the cover. "Can you read the symbols Gruggins?"

"Of course — can't you?" Gruggins replied. He read:

A Moment in Eternity

Ethan opened the book showing everyone the new page that had grown out in the Study. He read the last verse of the poem:

Creator from a chosen world protect it at all costs.
A Moment in Eternity, will tell you when you're lost.

There was a pause. Then —

"This book," Ethan continued, "it's been trying to tell us things this whole time — I think it is the key. The Creator from a chosen world was Stravis. He must have snuck this book through after The Book of Creators. Jasper is a taletaddler, he could have easily been there, nobody would have seen him — he could have been there and snapped it up before anyone ever saw it."

"Of course," Jordanna agreed, "it warned us that the Silent Forest was about to burn, and then later, on Kraken Island it told us of the plight of the vamprils — that's how I knew Nicholas wasn't delirious — when he said they were there."

"And it warned Ethan and I that we were about to be eaten by creepy crawlers," Haley added.

"And listen to this," Ethan continued, flipping to another poem. "At the end of this poem it says," Ethan read:

> . . . believe not the book of gold.

"I think the book of gold is The Book of Creators. It was telling us not to believe what it says. And then there's this verse," Ethan read:

> To find the key things must unfold,
> At a grumpling's feet the secret's told.

"Sounds almost like the passage from Stravis' journal," Damien interrupted.

"Yes, the Grimleavers mistook his words for meaning that a grumpling was the key," Ethan added, "or at least a grumpling would know something. But I think it means something else entirely."

"What are you getting at, my dear?" Jordanna asked.

Ethan walked to the door to the portals and opened it up. Bright colorful beams of light shimmered off the metallic spheres creating a pattern on the floor, a trail of tiny footprints down the black carpet.

Then — he repeated:

At a grumpling's feet the secret's told.

Ethan pointed down at the pattern on the black carpet. "Gruggins, would you do the honors?"

Gruggins knew what Ethan was asking; he fluttered off Haley's shoulder and joined him at the door. He landed on the carpet and began walking the trail of footprints — his feet were a perfect match. The phantom bubble followed Gruggins as he walked the carpet towards the black marble slab at the other end. Damien moved the coffee table that stood in his path near the center of the room. When Gruggins reached the space where the table had stood, something happened — a small golden pedestal suddenly appeared on the carpet. Symbols were etched on its surface:

A Moment in Eternity

"That's why the phantom bubble was always following Gruggins, it's attracted to gold," Haley said excitedly.

"Yes — and that's why it always hovered over the coffee table when Gruggins was away," Ethan added. "And if I'm right, this should do the trick."

Ethan walked to the pedestal and placed the poem book on it. Nothing happened at first, but then the book began to glow. It then slowly melted into the pedestal as it changed shape. When the transformation was complete, a toaster sized golden pyramid had replaced the pedestal. A small hole bored down through the top of the small monument.

"Where did the book go?" Haley asked.

"I don't know . . ." Ethan replied.

A golden rod suddenly began to push up from within the hole. As it grew taller, a small saucer began to grow from the tip of the shaft. The rod continued to rise out of the pyramid; it grew to about three feet tall before it stopped. The phantom bubble slowly floated down towards the end of the staff; it gently came to rest setting itself down in the saucer — it was a perfect fit. Then, the bubble slowly began to change as well; it was solidifying into a flawless sphere of glass — a magnificent crystal.

"Look, the footprints," Ethan said as the trail of colorful light disappeared from the floor.

The light reflecting off the portals was moving; it changed direction as if the portals were somehow aiming the beams. Suddenly, laser like beams began to blast from the four spheres: one red, one green, one blue, and one yellow. They were aimed directly at the newly formed crystal ball on the end of the staff. The colored beams of light entered the baseball sized crystal at the same spot, but they emerged out the other side, split into their respective colors like a prism. Four small colored symbols were projected onto Daavic's robe as if the crystal prism was somehow decoding a signal.

"Step aside!" Damien ordered his brother, pushing Daavic out of the beams path.

The beams zipped across the room projecting much larger symbols onto the four corners of the marble slab at the end of the carpet. They grew brighter and more intense as the symbols began to etch into the black slab, and then the bright beams of light suddenly shut off.

Ethan and Haley looked at each other. They recognized the black symbols etched into the slab. They were the symbols from the Creators' crest.

The room was quiet as they stood there wondering what might happen next, but nothing happened.

"Now what — ?" Daavic's voice broke the silence.

"I think we know . . ." Haley said.

Ethan reached into his pocket to retrieve his pocket tote. He tugged it open, pulled out the four pieces of the Creators' crest, and handed them to Damien.

"Where did you get those?" Jordanna asked.

"We found the Creators' crest in the lair of the spider gecko," Haley replied. "It was stuck in the wall and covered with cloaked gold — if Gruggins wasn't stashed away in Ethan's pocket tote we would never have seen it."

Damien was standing at the black slab. He began to place the symbols from the Creators' crest into their respective corners — they were a perfect fit.

The symbols melted into the slab as if repairing the damage caused by the etching. When the last symbol was in place the slab began to sink down into the floor like a piece of ice melting on a hot stove. The slab disappeared into the floor exposing a large empty portion of wall, nothing else was there.

"The slab, it must have been put there to project the lock upon the door," Damien said.

They turned their attention back towards the front door.

"Well, what are you waiting for — give it a try, mom," Haley said, looking Jordanna in the eye.

They both began to cry.

Jordanna rushed to Haley's side and knelt down beside her; they embraced each other.

"I missed you so much," Jordanna said, "I never stopped looking for my dear Danielle. I'm not sure how it is you returned to me the way you did — after all these years — we've got a lot of catching up to do —"

"Mom —" Haley interrupted, "could we stick with Haley? I still don't remember anything — but somehow that seems more like my name to me."

"Of course, Haley," Jordanna replied.

Jordanna held out her hand and a ball appeared. She handed it to Haley.

"Go ahead Haley, what are you waiting for — I want you to be the one, give it a try."

Haley wound up and threw the ball through the front door. A second later it zipped back through — the door to the portals was still locked.

Ethan caught the ball as it bounced in front of him. He glanced back at the wall, where the black slab had been standing, and at that moment he had an epiphany.

"Haley you silly girl — you can't go out the in-door," Ethan said.

Everyone turned to see what Ethan was looking at. It was the giant mirror. It had moved itself to the empty spot where the black slab had stood — it had finally found its place. The mirror was aimed perfectly; the front door and the portals were reflected on its surface like it was the door itself.

Ethan wound up and threw the ball at the mirror.

And this time, it kept going, bouncing out onto the checkerboard plane and rolling past the portals. Ethan had discovered the secret; the portals were unlocked after all.

"We did it! We unlocked the door to the portals!" Haley announced excitedly.

But her celebration was short lived. A clapping noise began to ring out; it was coming from the basement. The door beneath the staircase swung open. A man was clapping as he climbed the stairs from the basement. It was Victor Qruefeldt, and a grimtailed dread was perched on his shoulder.

"Bravo — Bravo — well done Ethan Fox — I couldn't have done a better job myself," he said.

"I should have recognized your stench," Jordanna said, stepping in front of Haley to shield her from the Grimleavers leader.

Victor was tall with piercing red inset eyes. He wore a flowing black robe with army style boots. His face was disfigured and covered with scars. He had no hair on his bald head but bony ridges poked up from his skull in places, giving his head a brainy look. But his most noticeable disfigurement was his ears, they were enormous; they protruded up sweeping forward and coming to a point over his head like horns.

"It appears young Ethan Fox has done me a great service — been more of a help to the Grimleavers cause than this one," Victor said, pointing at Daavic; a look of disgust swept across his disfigured face.

"But master! I left the vortex in the basement as you asked! I let you into The Residence! I've done all that you've asked for all these years!" Daavic pleaded. "I've done even more! I'm loyal to you! That's why I sent the vampires after the boy! I knew he would be of use to us — !"

"You sent them — !" Ethan interrupted.

"I'm afraid, dear Daavic," Victor interrupted, "that your secret is out. You're of little use to me now. I'm sure you all remember my friend, Poe."

"CAW — CAW," the dread screeched.

"Poe, tend to Daavic's death," Victor ordered the bird.

"No! Please not that! I beg of you master!" Daavic pleaded.

He must have known what was coming, he was begging for his life.

"CAW — CAW," the dread leapt from Victor's shoulder and flapped its wings. It circled above them in the empty space where the ceiling was missing.

"PLEASE! I CAN STILL BE OF SERVICE MASTER! TAKE ME WITH YOU!" Daavic pleaded; horrified by what was to come — he looked terrified.

The dread suddenly swooped down from above diving at Daavic. It whizzed by his face leaving a small black vortex behind. It looked just like the one from the Grimleavers attack on Deadwood, but this one was much smaller and much darker.

Damien started towards his brother to help, but it was too late, there was nothing he could do.

"STAY BACK! IT'S A DEATH VORTEX!" Daavic shrieked.

A bright ray of light shot out from the center of the vortex. It moved down the length of Daavic's body as if it was scanning him. Daavic was becoming transparent. He was slowly dematerializing.

"IT BURNS — AAAAAAAAAAAHHHHHHHHH — IT BURNS!" Daavic cried out in pain.

He began to change shape like the blob in a lava lamp; his head was smooshing into an oblong shape, he was slowly coming apart — he was being sucked into the death vortex. Daavic was quickly reduced to a swirling mass of screaming pieces as the vortex sucked him in like a vacuum cleaner. The dread swooped back down at the vortex and returned to Victor's shoulder.

The vortex was gone. Daavic was gone — Daavic was dead.

Damien and Jordanna looked helpless. They had just witnessed the demise of another Ravenwood — another Caretaker that died at the hands of Victor Qruefeldt.

"You'll pay for this —" Damien started towards Victor, but Jordanna quickly grabbed his arm stopping him.

"Have you ever seen a Heldrick Von Grim puzzle box?" Victor asked, reaching into his robe.

He pulled out a shiny black cube; it was made from the same metallic material as Haley's ring.

"Very powerful weapon this tiny cube is. Heldrick was a mad genius — the best Krator had to offer —"

"He was an evil murderer!" Jordanna interrupted. "He should have been thrown into the fire pits of Hades!"

"Of course it's not nearly as useful without its rift key," Victor said, raising his arm.

Haley's infinity ring quickly unraveled and flew across the room into his waiting hand. The top of the puzzle box magically opened up. Victor dropped the rift key inside and the box quickly sealed back up.

"As much as I'd love to stick around and catch up, I've got the portals to attend to," Victor continued ever so sarcastic. "Poe — after you — my dreadful pet."

The dread leapt from Victor's shoulder and flew through the mirror. It glided over the portals and opened up a large grey vortex above them. Victor Qruefeldt was quick to follow his flying pet. He ran behind it, jumped through the out-door, and dove into the vortex. The dread swooped through after him and the vortex closed back up — Victor Qruefeldt was gone.

IN THE
BEGINNING

Everyone slept in late the next morning. Jordanna called for an afternoon meeting in the Study. Alexander, Nicholas, and Brianna gave Damien a warm reception once they had learned the truth. They were surprised by the news of Daavic's demise, that he had been helping the Grimleavers all along, that he had helped frame his brother for his father's murder.

Gruggins was a no show, but Ethan and Haley arrived shortly after the others. They could both sense that something felt different about The Residence. There was a different energy about it. Jordanna was eager to get started as soon as they arrived. She had briefed the others on the events of the previous day — there was already news from the elemental worlds.

"After the portals were opened," Jordanna explained, "the Council of Elders sent a courier — news of something that might explain why the Grimleavers were so eager to open up the portals. As it turns out, the lock on the door to the portals was put there for more than one reason. The Creators never told us of its other purpose."

"But what other purpose could it serve?" Brianna asked.

"It prevented the Grimleavers from entering the human world," Jordanna replied. "A unique mechanism was used; it scanned the Earth searching for a special marker the Creators had added to the Earth's atmosphere — it attaches itself to all un-Earthly creatures without them knowing."

"But wouldn't that include us as well?" Alexander asked.

"Evidently their mechanism could make the distinction between good and evil," Jordanna replied. "It wasn't a perfect scheme, but it worked — sure Grimleavers could enter the human world in small numbers, but only for a short time before it would find and expel them. Entering a second time would cause the offending Grimleavers to spontaneously combust."

"That explains why the vampires were so easily dissuaded from abducting Ethan," Damien said. "They seemed almost eager to leave".

"Yes and why they've never appeared to care much about the human world — their hands were tied," Alexander added.

"Which means — our job just got a lot more difficult," Jordanna said.

"But I'm still confused about one thing," Nicholas spoke. "When Damien interrupted at Caretaker Council, how did you know to trust him? He had been blamed for Ryvias' death for so long. We had hunted him for years — how did you know — ?"

"By the heart of Wormfreid," Damien interrupted.

"By the heart of Wormfreid," Jordanna said, smiling at Damien. "I used to read to Damien when he was a little boy. Daavic had no use for stories but Damien just loved the tales of Wormfreid. One night when I was tucking him into bed, we made a pact, a pact I thought he had long forgotten. We decided to make up a secret word; something he could use to tell me if things were terribly wrong, something he could say openly, and nobody else would ever know its true meaning. But Damien wasn't happy with just a word. He thought that might sound odd, so he chose a phrase. His favorite phrase from the book I read to him every night — by the heart of Wormfreid."

Jordanna wiped a tear from her cheek.

"I'm confused about something as well," Ethan spoke up.

"Well out with it — my dear," Jordanna said.

"How did Haley end up with me?" he asked. "It can't be a coincidence — I remembered a poem I've never heard before — Daavic sent vampires after me. And if grumplings are so all seeing, then why didn't Gruggins recognize Haley as Danielle in the first place?"

"Sounds like you've more than a few questions," Jordanna smiled. "I cannot begin to explain the workings of a Heldrick Von Grim puzzle box — a very dark weapon from a very dark time in our history. It was only rumored to exist at all. Somehow wearing the rift key saved Haley's life. How my husband even knew to do that is a question I've been pondering myself. How she was drawn through time and found you is another mystery, as are the other side effects the puzzle box had on my daughter."

"What side effects?" Haley asked.

"Well — your memory for one," Jordanna explained. "It appears you lost all memory of Danielle and gained a new identity that you identify with more strongly. But there is another more profound side effect, one that explains the second part of Ethan's question. You are human —"

"But how is that possible?" Damien interrupted. "Danielle was a Ravenwood! My sister was a Caretaker!"

"As I pointed out earlier, we can't begin to know the workings of the puzzle box or how this happened, we only know that it did," Jordanna replied. "Gruggins saw through the shape shifter disguise in Danielle's memories because he was seeing the truth. He did not recognize Haley as Danielle because in the truest sense she is no longer Danielle. But he was still drawn to her. I think we've all witnessed how smitten Gruggins is with Haley."

"Wow, there is still so much we don't know . . . seems like we've got our work cut out for us," Damien said.

"Does that mean you've decided to accept my proposal?" Jordanna asked.

"Yes mother — I have," Damien replied.

"Proposal — ?" Alexander's question hung in the air.

"Yes — I've asked Damien to join us — he will be taking over Daavic's role," Jordanna said. "But I expect he will have a much more active role in day to day affairs. He will become my number one, my eventual replacement."

"I'd been hoping to hear such news. A bit of congratulations are in order for master Damien," Gruggins' voice was coming from the Study table.

He'd been there all along, cloaked and napping right beside them.

"What — you didn't think I'd miss the festivities did you?"

Gruggins winked at Haley as he fluttered up onto her shoulder. "Woke up when I heard my name," he whispered into her ear.

"Gruggins, so glad you could make it," Brianna greeted. "I have a burning question that you might be able to answer."

"Well don't choke on the words, spit them out," Gruggins replied.

"Why would the grumplings leave the Silent Forest? And where would they go?" Brianna asked.

"That's two questions," Gruggins replied. "Unfortunately, I don't have a good answer to either. They were happy in the Silent Forest, or so I was told. Only a handful of other places they could go and be safe from the leprechauns."

"Kraken Island is one," Jordanna added, "but the vamprils are adamant, the grumplings are not there."

"Kraken Island —" Haley repeated, "I'm still confused about something on Kraken Island. Why would the Grimleavers abduct one of those cute little pup creatures? The ones we saw were cute. How could one of those cute little animals wreak havoc like Damien said they could?"

"Kraken Island is a special place," Jordanna explained. "It was designed by the Creators to keep the kraken pups in their infant state. Kraken pups are very cute little creatures indeed, but on Earth they grow into very nasty creatures as adults. In the open ocean they nearly double in size every day for the first week — they reach adulthood within weeks. In the teen and young adult cycle of their life, they have shape shifting ability. Imagine a white shark the size of a whale, but at full adulthood they become even more horrendous."

"Shnickyrooners and things like that," Irvin's jabbering rant quickly took center stage. "Have you ever measured the green strip of bacon lips that normally gets reserved for picture frames? You'll often find loads of toad rubbish taped between the pink envelopes of skunk odor that hangs from the fiberglass chair."

"I'm going to miss all of your keen insights," Ethan replied.

"But how did Ethan Fox know?" Irvin asked. "I was told to keep it a secret until I arrived."

"How did Ethan Fox know what — ?" Ethan asked.

"That it is time for you to leave," Jordanna replied.

"But he's not safe, you can't let him go!" Haley protested as tears began to stream from her eyes.

"Irvin will miss master Ethan as well," Irvin added.

"As will Gruggins McGhee," Gruggins hopped from Haley's shoulder to Ethan's and gave him a small hug on his neck. "I kinda enjoyed hanging out in your pocket tote — on-the-go adventurer you are. Irvin called one right."

"We can't send him back — !" Haley insisted.

"I'm sorry dear — but we must," Jordanna said. "It was Daavic that sent the vampires after Ethan Fox. The Grimleavers had no interest in him — he will be safe now."

295

"And besides that," Alexander added, "the Grimleavers have the whole human world to focus on now. They will be far too busy to bother with Ethan Fox."

"But I don't want him to leave!" Haley cried.

"It's okay Haley, I'll be all right," Ethan said, comforting her; tears were flowing from his eyes now as well.

"I will personally keep an eye on young Ethan Fox myself," Damien said, comforting his sister.

"Will I ever see any of you again?" Ethan asked.

"That's hard to say, but somehow I think so," Jordanna replied. "But you mustn't speak of your time here with anybody — not even your parents."

"Of course not, they'd think I was crazy anyway," Ethan said. "But how will I get back? What will my parents think has happened to me?"

"Irvin will escort you to the proper door, the one Gruggins used to infiltrate your pocket tote — one of the negative doors," Jordanna explained. "Your parents will not know that you were ever gone."

Ethan slowly made his way towards the out-door. The Caretakers lined up in a row so he could say his goodbyes to each of them on his way out. They were huggers, even the men. Ethan was going to miss the Caretakers and the magical world they had shown him.

Haley was the last in line. By the time Ethan reached her, he was nearly out of tears. Haley had finally regained her composure from her earlier outburst; but as Ethan approached her, she lost it again. A tear rolled down Ethan's cheek as he looked into her eyes and then they fell into each other's arms. They hugged for several minutes. Neither of them wanting that moment to end, but Ethan knew it had to.

"Hmm-hmm hmm . . ." Ethan began to hum into her ear.

It was the tune he had heard Haley humming to herself on their first night at The Residence.

"We will see each other again," he whispered to her, "this isn't the end — I can feel it."

"Me too," Haley whispered back.

"Say goodbye to Mrs. Moongarden and Azron for me," Ethan said.

They broke from their long hug and Ethan followed Irvin through the out-door. They entered The Hall of Doorways and turned right. Ethan was going home through one of the negative doors.

"The negative third door on the right," Irvin announced as they arrived. Irvin saluted to Ethan as he pulled the door open. Irvin wasn't a hugger.

"Shnickyrooners!" Ethan cheered.

Irvin gave him a wink as he stepped through the door.

Ethan saw purple and green pin-spots in the darkness. He was becoming light headed, and then it was bright — he was back on the beach. He staggered forward as he tried to overcome his dizziness. He almost lost his balance, then stumbled back and bumped into something. Ethan's eyes came into focus just in time for him to turn around and see what he had bumped into. It was Haley — she was falling down the staircase in the beach sand.

CHAPTER TWENTY-SIX

"It was me all along — I pushed Haley down the stairs," he said to himself.

As Ethan started down the beach, he began to ponder the events of the previous couple of weeks. Would he ever see Haley and the rest of his new friends again? He had a strong sense that this was only the beginning, the first chapter of a much larger story.

The Caretakers would have their hands full now. The Grimleavers were sure to begin making their presence felt in the human world — not to mention that there was still an adult kraken on the loose. Would the Grimleavers come after him again? Jordanna seemed pretty sure he would be left alone but he had his doubts. After all, he had been the one to solve the puzzle to unlocking the four portals. He was sure to be on Victor Qruefeldt's radar by now.

Then there was the poem. How could he have written it? It had to be related to the past he could not remember. His parents were keeping a secret. Surely they knew more than they were letting on — they must be protecting him from something. And how did his dad come to possess one of the portal books? Was he somehow connected to the Caretaker world?

Ethan would keep the secret as he had promised Jordanna. He would not discuss his time at The Residence with anyone, not even his parents. And finally there was Fin. His short talk with Fin Drenchler had clued him in to a few things, but it had left him with even more questions. Ethan was sure he would see them all again. Fin had practically told him as much, but he would keep Fin's secret as well. He had so far, and if Fin was right, everyone's safety depended on it.

He ran down the beach to where he had left his parents almost a week ago. George and Betsy had just finished frolicking in the surf and were walking back to the beach blanket. When Betsy noticed Ethan was gone, she scanned her eyes up and down the beach, and then she spotted him walking toward them and pointed him out to George.

"Go for a walk along the beach tiger?" George shouted.

"Yeah dad — just a short one," Ethan replied, smiling to himself.

Ethan was back with his parents. He had missed them more than they would ever know.

Two days had gone by and things were pretty quiet around The Residence since Ethan left. Jordanna and Damien were in the Study discussing strategy. There was still a kraken on the loose and the Caretakers would need to implement an expanded role to protect the humans from the Grimleaver onslaught they knew was coming. Haley entered the Study as they discussed the matter. She was wearing a half-black half-white Caretaker robe like the one her mother and brother wore.

"What makes matters worse is the Heldrick Von Grim puzzle box," Damien explained. "We've never dealt with a weapon like that. We know almost nothing about it —"

"Oh yeah, about that," Haley interrupted, plopping down onto the sofa near the fire. "I forgot to tell you before . . ."

Haley reached into her robe pocket, pulled out her infinity ring, and slipped it on her finger.

"But how did you — ?" Jordanna asked.

"When Victor Qruefeldt first arrived, you stepped in front of me to shield me from him," she replied. "I used my copycat to copy it. I was wearing the copy — Victor Qruefeldt took my copycat."

"Quick thinking sis, you have no idea how many Caretaker and human lives you've just saved!" Damien beamed at his sister, he was very proud of her.

There was a knock on the Study door. Dorkin Drumbles entered and rushed across the room.

"Headmistress Ravenwood — there has been a development in the Gallery — a most unusual painting has just completed — you must have a look at it."

Jordanna, Damien, and Haley accompanied Dorkin back to the Gallery. They had already moved the new piece to the viewing room. Dorkin wobbled over to the piece and pulled back the cover so they could study it.

It was a painting of the desert and sand dunes with deep blue eyes peeking out from beneath them. There was an indentation in the sand near an old airstrip and a flying saucer was zipping off into the sky above. A colorful flag was planted in a sand dune nearest the impression — a flag with the Creators' crest displayed on it.

"The Eyes of the Desert Sand," Jordanna said. "This looks like an artist's interpretation of the poem, nothing more. Why has this been deemed important?"

"I don't know, I had the same thought," Dorkin Drumbles replied. "Nothing here looks important to me. I wonder if the witches are finally going mad — ?"

"Didn't you tell us that sometimes it's not obvious at first, that sometimes you need to study it for a while?" Haley interrupted.

They stood in silence for several minutes studying the painting. It was quiet in the viewing room and then she saw it.

"What the — ?" Haley's voice broke the silence. "It can't be possible!"

"What! What do you see?" Jordanna pleaded.

"That symbol on the painting, the small symbol in the lower right hand corner," Haley replied. "That is a secret ID. He made it up himself — Ethan Fox painted this painting!"

AFTERWORD

The Chrysalis Chronicles is a new book series of fantasy novels that I am in the midst of writing. I have mapped out much of the series from beginning to end; *The Eyes of the Desert Sand* is the debut novel of the series. I invite you to follow me on Facebook at Edwin Wolfe or Twitter at @wormfreid or send me an e-mail at wolfe.edwin@yahoo.com.

On another note, www.ChrysalisChronicles.com is a new web site we are developing, where you can enjoy an online experience based around the Chrysalis Chronicles books. When finished, it will include news and announcements on upcoming events, as well as all sorts of other relevant information from the world within the Chrysalis.

— Edwin Wolfe, *Author*

This book

was art directed by

Eric Moeszinger. The art for the

jacket was created using Adobe Creative

Suite, Illustrator and Photoshop. The text was set in

12-point Adobe Garamond, a typeface based on the sixteenth-century

type designs of Claude Garamond, redrawn by Robert Slimback in 1989.

This book was typeset by Lori Moeszinger and printed and bound

at Malloy Incorporated in Ann Arbor, Michigan. The

Managing Editor was J. K. Spencer; the Continuity

Editor was JoAnn Egli; and production

was supervised by Aauvi House

Publishing Group.